THE
CHIEF FACTOR'S
DAUGHTER

The
CHIEF FACTOR'S
Daughter

VANESSA WINN

TouchWood
Editions

DOUGLAS COLLEGE LIBRARY

TouchWood Editions
www.touchwoodeditions.com

LIBRARY AND ARCHIVES CANADA CATALOGUING IN PUBLICATION
Winn, Vanessa, 1966–
The chief factor's daughter / Vanessa Winn.
Includes bibliographical references.
ISBN 978-1-894898-93-5

I. Title.

PS8645.I5727C55 2009   C813'.6   C2009-902905-7

Editor: Marlyn Horsdal
Cover design: Pete Kohut
Front cover image: Andrea Gingerich, istockphoto.com
Author photo: Robert Creese, robertcreese.com

BRITISH COLUMBIA
ARTS COUNCIL

Canada Council   Conseil des Arts
for the Arts   du Canada

We gratefully acknowledge the financial support for our publishing activities from the
Government of Canada through the Book Publishing Industry Development Program
(BPIDP), Canada Council for the Arts, and the province of British Columbia through the
British Columbia Arts Council and the Book Publishing Tax Credit.

Mixed Sources
Product group from well-managed
forests, controlled sources and
recycled wood or fibre
www.fsc.org   Cert no. SW-COC-000952
© 1996 Forest Stewardship Council
FSC

85%

The interior pages of this book have been printed on 100% post-consumer recycled
paper, processed chlorine free, and printed with vegetable-based inks.

1 2 3 4 5 12 11 10 09

PRINTED IN CANADA

To my family.

Chapter One

Expectation was written in every face, which
before had been placid, even stolid; for with occasional visits from Her Majesty's ships of war, the
great event of Victoria had been the advent of the
Princess Royal once a year, with the latest fashions
of the Old World and fresh supplies, human and
material, for the Honourable Company's service.
Now, with vessels arriving and leaving constantly,
with thousands pouring into the port, and 'sen-
sation' news from the Fraser daily, a new mind
seemed to have taken possession of Victoria . . .
—Richard Charles Mayne, RN

The Fraser Gold Rush breathed the air of possibility into the
village of Victoria, and while the men prospected for gold
and speculated on land, the women speculated on prospects of another
kind.

It was to the infinite regret of his daughters, then, that Mr. Work
had banished them from Fort Victoria since the spring, when the gold
miners had flooded the trading post en route to the Fraser River. The
fort's stockade, once a bastion of security, was now surrounded by a
mushrooming town of tents and ramshackle buildings teeming with
men of every description. But the Work daughters could watch the
transformation only from a discreet distance. Even riding about the
surrounding country now required a male escort, which, in a family

with five girls still at home, and only one son of age, proved a limited source of escape.

Of the five sisters, Margaret Work, having a thoughtful disposition and being inclined toward the quieter pursuits, bore the new constraints the best, but she soon tired of being sequestered at home. Hillside Farm was far enough from town to be left unspoiled by the new development, and its daily routine went on, undisturbed except by visitors. Margaret often sought diversion in books during the summer mornings, but on one particular day the stifling August heat of her room drove her downstairs. There she found her mother engaged in taxidermy.

With the restlessness of one who has been condemned to wait, Margaret stood in the sitting room, watching her mother's detached expression as her fingers deftly worked over her latest taxidermy project, a raven. The silence of the dead hung over the room. Only the distant sounds of the cook in the kitchen and, still farther away, the harvesters in the fields calling out to one another occasionally interrupted the quiet. A faint breeze stirred the chintz curtains, partly drawn to shut out the summer sun. Margaret turned toward it, letting it fan over her face. The breeze died and, with a suppressed sigh, she turned back to the prostrate raven. Her youngest sister, Suzette, leaned over the table with the fascination only a three-year-old could muster for a dead bird.

"Help Suzette hold it, while I do the feet," said her mother, not glancing up from her work.

Margaret took hold of the bird reluctantly. *The devil makes work for idle hands,* she thought with a tinge of bitterness. Its feathers were sleek and very smooth under her fingers. The eyes had already been done; they fixed Margaret with a glassy, impenetrable stare. She turned her attention back to her mother, who was expertly fitting the stiff, curled talons to their final perch. Mrs. Work had several pieces of oak branches for the purpose, and she held each up to the raven in turn before selecting one. She was carefully inserting it between the claws of the feet when they heard a commotion upstairs; excited voices reverberated down the stairway.

Mrs. Work looked up from the bird.

"I'll go," volunteered Margaret, and hurried from the room.

She found her younger sisters, Mary, Kate and Cecilia, crowded into the dormer window of her own bedroom, which had a good view of the road. The object of their attention drew forth a steady stream of hopeful conjectures from 16-year-old Kate.

"Who is it?" asked Margaret, with restraint.

"Can't you hear it, Margaret?" cried Kate.

"If you were quiet for a moment, perhaps I might," replied the elder.

"A rider!" said Kate impatiently. "Listen!"

Margaret joined her sisters at the window. As yet she could see no one, but in the pause in the chatter she plainly heard the distant beat of horse's hooves. She listened intently to discover if it would die away and the rider pass by, or if the horse would be turned down the drive to Hillside.

"A visitor at last," said Kate. "Who do you think it could be? What is taking him so long? Do you think—"

"Shhh, Kate!"

The hoofbeats seemed to grow louder. Margaret held her breath, and presently the rider came into sight.

"An officer!" shrieked Kate in Margaret's ear. "Mary, an officer!"

Mary did not quite share her younger sister's enthusiasm and stepped back a pace from the window. The three other girls crowded closer into the dormer window, vying for the best outlook.

"Who is it, who is it?" asked nine-year-old Cecilia, leaning out the casement and pressing her face against the glass of the open window.

The navy blue-uniformed rider cantered down the lane, a cloud of August dust rising behind him.

"I think it is Lieutenant Mayne," said Kate slyly to Margaret, winking conspiratorially.

Kate had a childhood memory from nine years before, of her elder sister being a favourite with Mr. Mayne, then a young midshipman stationed on the Pacific Coast on HMS *Inconstant*. Since that time, Margaret had been disappointing as a source of romantic intrigue for Kate's youthful imagination. So much so that, when Mayne returned to Victoria eight years later as the first lieutenant of HMS *Plumper*, Kate had gleefully resurrected their romance, regardless of what tenuous ground it was founded on. Such teasing, while enjoyable in an embarrassing sort of way to an infatuated girl of 15, had now become exceedingly irritating to a spinster of nearly 24.

Her lips compressed into a firm line, Margaret turned back to the window. It appeared, however, that Kate had guessed the rider's identity correctly. "Come away from the window," said Margaret, grasping her skirts with one hand and Cecilia's arm with her other. She managed to pull the reluctant girl back into the room, but once separated from the window, Cecilia bolted for the door.

Margaret hung back while Kate and Mary followed closely after Cecilia. On her own way out, she glanced in the full-length mirror, the only one of its kind in the house. Having it in her room was a privilege that went with being the oldest daughter at home. Mary poked her head back in the doorway.

"You look *fine*," she said, a reassuring smile lighting up her pretty face. The high points of Mary's brows were close to the centre of her face, from where they sloped steadily down toward her temples, giving her a perpetual look of hopeful expectation. Nodding convincingly, as if to lend emphasis to her words, she disappeared down the hallway.

Margaret sighed and smoothed a few dark stray hairs back into place. Her hair was in the style that had been *de rigueur* for most of the 1850s: parted in the middle, pulled back, and rolled under at the nape of the neck. She stared resignedly at her dusky reflection. She was the brunette of the family, her complexion as dark as her mother's. She turned from the mirror paused at her doorway to change from her moccasin slippers into more formal shoes and hurried after her sisters.

Downstairs, they were all sitting composedly in the drawing-room when the knock came. Kate jumped up, but there was no need to go to the door; it opened at once and the caller let himself in. All doors in the colony were open to the navy; soon after arriving in Victoria the officers put aside standing upon ceremony. The officer appeared in the doorway of the drawing-room. Margaret, slightly amused by playing her role of feigned surprise, rose.

"Lieutenant Mayne! Won't you come in?"

"I can't stop, thank you," he said, his tall frame filling the doorway. "I only came to tell you that, having learnt this morning that the *Plumper* is to remain in the harbour tonight, we have determined to give a ball—"

Kate leapt forward, as if to declare her readiness.

"—an impromptu hop, really," he continued with a smile. "Despite the late notice, I hope we can count on your attendance?"

Margaret looked over at her sisters, whose faces had brightened considerably, excepting young Cecilia. Margaret turned back to the naval officer.

"I think it quite likely—"

Lieutenant Mayne turned from her and looked down the hallway. Margaret heard the silken rustle of a dress on the bare wooden floorboards a moment before her mother appeared. To Margaret's dismay, she saw that Mrs. Work had a few down feathers in her hair. Margaret bit her lip in consternation. *At least she took off her apron,* she thought, and shot a furtive glance at Lieutenant Mayne's profile. He played the perfect gentleman and showed not the slightest sign of anything amiss. Suzette had followed in her mother's wake, her fair head peeking out from behind Mrs. Work's voluminous skirts. Lieutenant Mayne bowed, winking at Suzette when his head was lowered, and repeated his request. Mrs. Work, gathering the few details necessary, readily assented. "Won't you stay?"

"No thank you, ma'am. I still have a few more stops to make, and we are giving little warning as it is."

And with another bow he was gone. When the door shut behind him, the room erupted.

"A ball, a ball!" Kate cried, grabbing Mary and dancing about the room. Amid their laughter, little Suzette clapped her hands and joined in the dance. Mrs. Work shook her head and clucked her tongue. Margaret was more reserved with her delight. Most of the windows were open in the midday heat; Lieutenant Mayne, his hard-soled boots clipping down the dry path as he walked to the front gate, could no doubt hear the commotion he had caused.

"Only think," said Kate, freezing in mid-step, which sent Mary colliding into a chair, "we will at last meet the officers of the Boundary Commission! They will surely be there. They must!"

A detachment of Royal Engineers had recently arrived in the Colony of Vancouver Island, to map the boundary between British and American territories on the mainland, and they were based at Esquimalt Harbour, five miles away. The Work daughters, like all the young ladies of Victoria, had been anticipating the addition of the Boundary Commission officers to their circle with considerable excitement, and this ball would surely introduce them.

The invitation transformed Hillside; a flurry of activity filled its rooms. Gowns had to be chosen, wrapped in canvas to protect them from the dust, and sent over to the girls' married sister, Sarah Finlayson, who lived nearby at Rock Bay. For a shipboard party, the Work girls usually travelled by boat from the Finlayson homestead on Victoria's Upper Harbour to neighbouring Esquimalt Harbour, where the larger ships, such as naval vessels, lay at anchor. The gowns would go to Rock Bay in an ox cart; the girls would follow on foot and change into them at their sister's home.

Cecilia followed the older girls forlornly from room to room.

"I'll never get to go to a ball," she pouted, while little Suzette danced circles around her, waving ribbons in the air. "I'll probably die before I turn 14."

"*Mon Dieu!* Do not say such things," said Mrs. Work, a slight frown creasing her brow. "Thank the Lord for your good health."

"Be glad you live in a colony where there are so few ladies," said Mary, who, at nearly 21 years of age, had already seen quite a number of balls. "In England girls often don't come out until they are 16."

"And sometimes younger sisters do not come out at all until the elder ones are married!" laughed Kate.

"Fie!" snorted Cecilia. "We should be waiting forever for Margaret!"

Margaret, who had been picking the raven feathers out of her mother's hair, took them to the window without a word and threw them out. A few moments later, when the conversation had taken another turn, she drew Cecilia aside and reminded her, in the strongest terms she dared, that it was only two years since their brother Henry had died at 12, and that she ought to consider more carefully the effect such idle talk of dying might have on their dear mother. Suitably chastised, Cecilia refrained from further complaint, and contented herself with heavy sighs.

In a very short period of time Mrs. Work had her three grown daughters ready for the ball. There was no question of Mrs. Work herself attending. HMS *Plumper* was not a spacious vessel, and could not afford room for many chaperons; besides which Mrs. Work, who preferred to reign at home rather than rule the social scene, had the three youngest children to take care of. Mr. Work, although fond of company, would probably not go either; his rheumatism bothered him frequently of late, and kept him near the quiet comforts of his own hearth. The girls were to be escorted by their 19-year-old brother, John. It was not an office he sought, as a fur trader's son could not compete with the naval officers for the attentions of the young ladies; he could only count on a couple of dances with Agnes Douglas, the governor's daughter with whom he had a particular understanding, to break up the evening.

Mr. Work got home from attending to his business at the fort just in time to see his children off. John Work had been known throughout the Hudson's Bay Company as "the Old Gentleman" for nearly 20 years, though he was only midway through the sixth decade of his life. He bore the haggard aspect of one who had formerly cut a robust figure but had grown thin very quickly; his clothes hung on his once-sturdy frame, just as his skin hung on his hollow face, accentuated by a prominent chin and slightly hawkish nose. Except for three locks of hair at his collar, he had lost, with his slow decline in health, most of the sandy hair of his youth, and his strength had seemingly been sapped like Samson's.

His ailing frame hid, however, a lively spirit and his weary eyes held a few sparks yet. He was very fond of his children and on this occasion, as on many others, he looked genuinely pleased about the proposed entertainment for them.

"It's a pity you have allowed your face to become so tanned this summer, Catherine," he chided gently, in his weathered Scottish-Irish brogue. "A dark complexion does not do you justice."

"Perhaps, sir, if we could go into town, we could spend more time indoors, out of the sun," Kate replied, with her characteristic arched brow.

"You'll get to town when it is safe for you to do so, not before," he said sternly, but his expression did not reflect his tone of voice. "Now, away with you, before I decide the trip to Esquimalt is too dangerous for you to make."

Chapter Two

The arrival of any officials from England was welcomed as a sort of connecting link with home,
and a practical acknowledgement of the colony's
existence.

—Richard Charles Mayne, RN

*D*espite the dust that John stirred up by kicking stones along
the stump-filled road to the Finlaysons' home, Margaret was
thankful for the calm summer weather. Rough conditions made the boat
ride from Victoria's harbour to Esquimalt's treacherous, and the only
other route was the Esquimalt road, leading from the Victoria Harbour
bridge past the Songhees Indian village and on to Esquimalt Harbour.
Mr. Work had forbade travelling this road at night. Frequented by gold
miners, it had become, he told them gravely, "the scene of every kind
of vice." Only a few days before there had been talk of a riot among the
miners in town. If the weather did not allow a boat ride, then the trip
to Esquimalt Harbour would not be made.

The Finlaysons had an ample house, the first in the colony to be
built with California redwood lumber. Such prestige however, was lost
on Sarah Finlayson, whose concerns focussed on her home's domestic
duties rather than its building materials. After giving her sisters a light
tea upon their arrival, Sarah told Margaret to supervise cleanup of the
dining room and whisked Mary and Kate off to an upstairs bedroom
to dress for the ball. Over the years Sarah had developed the annoying
habit of demonstrating her disapproval of Margaret's spinsterhood by

taking every opportunity to task her with housekeeping. Sarah's eldest daughter, Mary, stayed behind to help her aunt, and they enjoyed a few peaceful moments together. Across the hallway Margaret could hear Roderick Finlayson lecturing John, the resonance of his Scottish voice overflowing the sitting room.

"Land is the way to wealth, young John, the gold rush has made certain of that. You should be pleased your father has so much of it—he's the largest landowner in Victoria! Of course, his country holdings are not worth nearly as much as city lots. Take, for instance, the lots near the fort that I purchased in the spring when the first goldseekers arrived—"

After Margaret had given her instructions for finishing the tidying to the Indian girl Sarah employed, she gestured to her niece to be quiet, and they slipped past the open doorway. She caught John's eye—he looked trapped. Helpless to intervene, she smiled quickly at him, and with her niece in tow, escaped up the stairs. Her brother-in-law's voice drifted up after them.

Tackling her hoop skirt in the makeshift dressing room, Margaret watched Kate from the corner of her eye. Her sister seemed to be in constant motion, even when she stood still; in those brief moments the animation of her face and voice increased. She was almost giddy as she solicited Sarah's opinion on this and that, largely ignoring her responses, and shooing two-year-old Annie Finlayson away. How different, Margaret thought, from her own experience at that age, those eight years before! She had been quite shy, having only been in Victoria for little more than a year, and cowed by the fort's then-schoolmistress, Mrs. Staines, the first English-born lady Margaret had ever met.

Still, Kate's excitement was to be expected. In Victoria, naval balls were the pinnacle of entertainment. The naval officers were different from the Hudson's Bay Company officers. They were more jovial, inclined to good-natured pranks and eager for dancing and singing. While well-mannered, they were witty and, although welcoming the lack of ceremony in the colony, they gave the impression they would be at ease wherever they were. The fur traders gave the opposite impression. The married officers, especially, seemed to be continually striving to set the right tone; years of isolation often left them stiff and uneasy in company. They were well-read, but lacked eloquence in speech and freedom of manner in society. The traders welcomed the strains of civilization provided by Her Majesty's ships, but it was only the bachelors who were induced to join in the jollity. The effect of a long service in the Honourable Company, on both body and spirit, was enough for Margaret to resolve never to marry into it.

"My figure was once like yours," sighed Sarah, cinching in Kate's hoop skirt. Sarah's shape gave ample evidence of the four children she had borne since her marriage eight years ago. The youngest had made his appearance just the month before, and mercifully was sleeping through the fuss his aunts had occasioned.

"Not so tight!" gasped Kate, with an airy laugh. "I can scarcely breathe! Just how many officers make up a Boundary Commission, anyway? Agnes said a dozen, so there must at least be eight."

"Fewer than that, I would expect," said Margaret, but Kate had already jumped to the next subject.

"Don't you wish you were coming, Sarah?" Kate asked, beaming in the mirror at her own petite hourglass image, accentuated by her corset and hoops as she twisted and swayed.

Sarah turned her eyes briefly heavenward, and shrugged indifferently as she turned to help Mary fasten the long row of buttons down the back of her gown, hindered by her toddler tugging on the dress's hem. Margaret suspected Sarah had no such wish. Her elder sister was shy with newcomers, and given to nerves.

At last all the hoops and gowns were on. Having dressed with greater than usual care, Margaret eyed herself critically in the mirror. She had chosen a pale grey silk for her gown; she was too old to wear white, as Kate did. Like so many of the fabrics, it had a faint bluish hue, which was supposed to counteract the yellow light of candles and oil lamps. She doubted, however, that it did anything for her own complexion. Mary and Kate joined her at the mirror, and their paler skin heightened her disappointment.

As Kate pressed forward to see her reflection, one bump from her hoops set her sisters' skirts in motion, until they were all bobbing in unison. Margaret, in an attempt to still her own gown, smoothed down the front of it, but the back swung out unbidden.

"And this is what they wear in London, this cage crinoline?" said Sarah. It was more of a statement than a question, but with enough doubt to show that it needed confirmation. The hoop skirts had arrived only a few months before and she had not yet abandoned her horsehair crinoline for the new contraption.

"You must try one, Sarah, they are so much lighter! Everyone is wearing them in England," said Kate. "And we can't catch a husband without the latest London fashions!"

Kate left her older sisters to the mirror, while Sarah helped them put the finishing touches to their attire. They were finally torn away from their reflections by a burst of laughter from Kate on the edge of the bed. Sitting on the back of the hoops had lifted the front up to her shoulders, and only her laughing face could be seen above her suspended skirt.

"That's one way to catch a husband," observed Margaret dryly.

"Remember Mama's face when we first got our hoop skirts?" snickered Kate. She attempted to mimic her mother's expression for a moment, but her mouth twitched and soon her straight face collapsed into a fresh bout of laughter.

Margaret smiled faintly at the memory. On encountering hoop skirts for the first time, their mother's expression had been typically stoic. Her eye showed wonder and disbelief but her brow proclaimed endurance. Hardly a crease had disturbed her smooth complexion, which was surprisingly unlined for a woman who had borne and raised 11 children; she had faced greater challenges before.

Sarah clucked her tongue at Kate and then turned her attention back to Mary's gown.

"You sound just like Mama when you do that," said Margaret.

"You would sound like her yourself, if you had a family of your own to take care of," answered Sarah quickly. In the mirror's reflection Mary smiled sympathetically at Margaret.

When the three were content, if not perfectly happy, with their appearance they made their way, accompanied by John and Mr. Finlayson, across the Finlaysons' terraced lawns down to the boat landing at Rock Bay, where a canoe awaited them.

"You should be just in time to rendezvous with the boats leaving the fort," Mr. Finlayson said to the company *engagés* manning the canoe.

"Aye, sir," answered the French-Canadian in charge, and they lost no time paddling down the harbour, leaving Mr. Finlayson a lone figure on the dock, rubbing his hands together as he surveyed the lawns and orchards rising gently up to his substantial home. When he was out of sight, the voyageurs struck up a chorus of "Ma Belle Rosa," much to Kate's delight.

Fort Victoria soon came into sight, with a sea of grey miners' tents stretching out from its weathered cedar palisades. As they approached, Margaret could see the other guests, dressed in their finery, boarding the boats and canoes at the company's wharf below the steep rocky bank on which the fort sat.

A little farther on, a boat pulled out from James Bay to join the convoy of small craft. A naval ship's boat was always kept in the bay close to the governor's residence, in readiness for his use, and as it neared them, Margaret recognized Governor Douglas' daughters between the sailors rowing the boat.

Kate waved gaily to Agnes and Alice Douglas; Margaret and Mary were more reserved in their greeting. Agnes and Alice had two older sisters about the same age as Margaret and Mary and both were married, which they liked to remind the Works of too often.

"Now that Alice is 14," said Margaret to Mary, with a slight pang of envy, "I suppose Mr. Douglas will allow her to attend all the functions."

"She is tall for her age—taller than Agnes already," replied Kate. "She will not look out of place at the ball."

"I hardly think her height would have affected the decision of Old Square Toes," said Margaret.

Governor Douglas was not known for liberality in raising his children, but like the other fur traders, he apparently felt that associating with officers of the Royal Navy could only benefit his daughters.

As she always was before meeting newcomers from the Old Country, Margaret was filled with anticipation, swinging from near-dread to excitement and back again. Past experience had taught her that new arrivals often judged the locals and found them wanting. Soon, however, the motion of the canoe, the slight breeze created by its movement and the rhythmic dipping of paddles in the water all combined to lull her. Leaving Victoria Harbour they had a magnificent view of the Olympic Mountains, seeming to rise straight out of the water to the south, their snowy peaks tinged pink in the evening sun. Despite their splendour, Margaret could not view them without imagining what lay beyond. The *engagés* rowed them expertly along the rocky shoreline and into Esquimalt Harbour where the naval vessels lay peacefully at anchor in the protected water.

HMS *Plumper,* a steam sloop carrying a mere 12 guns, was not a spacious man-of-war, its principal purpose being that of surveying the waters of the northwest coast. It was fortunate then, though not in the eyes of its officers, that the young ladies of Victoria were very few, numbering not more than 30. Most of these arrived *en masse* in the boats, as it was deemed safest for them to travel together.

Ascending the steep ladder lowered over the side of the ship was especially difficult in a hoop skirt, and Margaret did not like the complacent smile of the voyageur standing dutifully by the bottom step in case anyone should fall. But once the young ladies were safely on the ship's upper deck, which had been decorated with flags for the occasion, they had not long to wait before being introduced to the newly arrived Boundary Commission officers who had provoked so much anticipation.

Chapter Three

In the evening we all went to a ball given by the
officers of the *Plumper*, where we met all the
young ladies of Vancouver [Island]...Most of
the young ladies are half breeds and have quite
as many of the propensities of the savage as of the
civilized being.
—Lieutenant Charles William Wilson, RE

The last feminine foot had not yet graced the upper deck of
HMS *Plumper* when Mrs. Young, a cousin of Agnes and Alice,
approached the Douglas and Work girls, bringing with her several of
the very officers the young ladies had been so eager to meet. Margaret
knew at once, by their uniforms, they were officers of another persuasion than the navy. One wore a scarlet tunic; indeed, amid the sea of
navy blue uniforms and the more subtly coloured gowns of the ladies,
he was hard to miss.

Mrs. Young, having recently married the naval secretary to the
Boundary Commission, and being the governor's niece, usually
chaperoned at naval functions. She was not native to the country, and
had a European education, so she was considered by many, and especially
by herself, to be one of the first ladies of Victoria's society. She took
her role seriously; her countenance habitually wore a smugly complacent
smile. As she carried out the introductions with considerable dignity,
the owner of the scarlet tunic caught Margaret's attention. His warm,
intelligent eyes suggested a readiness to be amused, a readiness that

was being, at the moment, happily indulged. "Lieutenant Wilson, of the Royal Engineers, and *secretary to the Boundary Commission*," Mrs. Young pronounced with great emphasis, as his position held the importance of being the very counterpart, on land, of her husband's naval position. Lieutenant Wilson appeared to be the youngest of the Boundary Commission officers, his youthfulness allayed only by a slightly receding hairline, a moustache and sideburns. Margaret could not help but note that he did justice to his scarlet uniform.

He secured a position at the top of her dance card almost immediately after their introduction and before the governor's daughters, which did him no harm in her estimation. Mr. Young arrived to usher the officers away to the other parties of ladies waiting for introductions, and left his wife looking deflated at losing the entourage of officers she had been preening over moments before.

"Posture, Agnes," whispered Mrs. Young.

With three years of school in Germany behind her, as well as a year in London, Mrs. Young had taken it upon herself, with the approval of her uncle, to educate her cousins in the ways of the civilized world. Agnes, who was short and plump, attempted to straighten her back, but as she stood in between her taller sister and cousin, the effect of her effort was minimal. Refusing to stay put in the pecking order, Agnes strode off.

"Short steps!" Mrs. Young hissed after her, but it was too late; Agnes' hoop crinoline swung about her like a large birdcage in a fickle breeze. While Mrs. Young frowned after her cousin's hasty retreat, the other young ladies slunk off one by one in the opposite direction. Margaret was the last, but Mrs. Young was too quick.

"And Margaret, how is Mrs. Huggins? Well, I hope?"

Mrs. Young never failed to ask her this question, and Margaret, as usual, had little to offer about her sister. Letitia Huggins, regrettably, corresponded very infrequently with her sisters since she had married and joined her husband at Fort Nisqually, the Hudson's Bay Company post in Puget Sound. Letitia was closest in age to Margaret, who, except perhaps for their mother, felt her loss most keenly.

"Your family must miss her very much, although having *five* daughters still at home would be some consolation. It is nearly a year since she married, is it not?"

"A year in October," replied Margaret, thinking that Mrs. Young knew very well when Letitia had married, having attended the wedding herself. "And my family hope to have at least the two youngest at home for some time, since they are but four and nine years old."

"Yes, of course," smiled Mrs. Young. "I must say my family is very happy to have both my cousin Jane and myself remain in Victoria since our weddings in March. With *two* marriages in the Douglas family, coming so closely together as they did, it would have been quite unbearable for the family to lose us both at once, had our husbands' positions required us to move away."

"How fortunate for your family," said Margaret politely, searching for some means of escape. Relief came from several naval officers, who entreated Margaret for a place on her dance card, but with their aim achieved, they quickly moved on.

Mrs. Young leaned closer and continued in a low voice, "I do not know if my family will be so lucky to keep my sister in Victoria. She seems to be rather a favourite with the officers of the navy. But how my parents and I could bear it if she were to move to England, I cannot imagine!"

Margaret followed Mrs. Young's eyes to where her younger sister, Edith, stood basking in the attentions of the junior officers surrounding her.

"I am sure you would find the strength," said Margaret, weary of Mrs. Young's exultations. Providing timely respite, the ship's band struck up the first strains of music, and after she waited a few anxious moments, Lieutenant Wilson appeared at her side to claim his dance. With a smile that Margaret felt must rival Mrs. Young's in self-satisfaction, she excused herself from the matron, and took the young lieutenant's offered arm.

As always, a quadrille opened the dance. Margaret would have preferred a waltz. It could take half an hour to walk through the figures of a quadrille and, although supplying interesting conversation was the gentleman's obligation, she found that witty replies with a new acquaintance often evaded her.

"I can't tell you, Miss Work, how good it is to have a dance again after being at sea for so very long," Wilson began.

"It is a long voyage, sir," she agreed, even though, much to her regret, she had never experienced it herself.

"After 70 days imprisonment at sea, we quite felt like schoolboys on holiday when we finally got on shore," he continued with a laugh.

Imprisonment! The navy brought associations just the opposite to Margaret.

"We don't know what we would do without the navy," she replied. He raised his brow, with a slight smile, and she added quickly, "They are really the only defence we have, aside from the fort bastions, and *they* seem smaller somehow with hundreds of miners camped outside them."

"Well, we hope to afford you a little more protection," he replied cheerfully. After a while he continued, "What a change you must have seen here in the last few months, Miss Work! Lieutenant Mayne was only just saying that before the gold rush, the great event of the year for the fort was the arrival of the Hudson's Bay Company supply ship—the *Princess Royal,* is it?"

"Yes," agreed Margaret, a little put out by this description of life at Fort Victoria, especially considering who had uttered it. Lieutenant

Mayne! It was an unpleasant reminder of how limited he and the other officers must find Victoria.

"And then the population of Victoria doubled overnight with the first ship full of gold miners!" Wilson was saying. "Tell me, Miss Work, how did you first hear of it?"

"It was a Sunday, and we were just leaving church. Church Hill has a good view of the harbour and we could see a ship coming in, a side-wheeler, with over 200 miners aboard, as we later learned."

"What a surprise that must have been!"

"Well, there was some knowledge of gold in the country, but to what extent we never imagined." He seemed to wait expectantly for more, and after a few desperate moments she at last blurted out the question at the forefront of her mind. "Does Lieutenant Mayne think Victoria much improved by the gold rush?"

She had evidently caught him off guard.

"Not altogether, no. In economic terms, certainly. But I rather think he holds the view that such a transient population can have an unsettling influence, which of course it does." After a short pause he added brightly, "But I must say I like the excitement very much—I never felt better in my life!"

Margaret thought this a rather carefree attitude toward hundreds of unruly gold seekers, but limited her response to a smile. The conversation turned to Victoria's fine summer weather, and from there to his admiration of its scenery. Margaret thought she kept up her end of it reasonably well, all the while remembering to take careful, mincing steps to avoid having her hoop crinoline bob excessively. When the quadrille was over at last, she felt gratified to have him ask for another place on her dance card.

In the brief interlude before the next waltz her card filled quickly, but not before Lieutenant Mayne himself could engage her for the very next waltz and a later polka. He was a much-sought-after dance partner and Margaret could not help but be pleased that she had started out the evening so well. She admired him most in the summer season, when his clean-shaven face became all the more attractive, due to his weather-bronzed features; then they neared her own colouring.

Margaret could lose herself in a waltz. There was very little need for conversation in the dance, much to her delight. The constant, swirling motion carried her away, until a near collision with another couple threw her against the lieutenant. This was a common enough occurrence, the temporary dance floor on the deck of the *Plumper* being inadequate in size, but it took Margaret longer to regain her equanimity than her feet, despite Mayne's gracious inquiry to see if she had come to any harm. She chided herself inwardly; she might just as well have been the 15-year-old schoolgirl who had been smitten with Mr. Mayne those nine years before.

During his absence, Margaret had not met another officer to equal her memory of him. And when he had returned as a lieutenant last year, he surpassed her memory in all respects, except one—his openness. There was now a restraint about him and, not knowing its source, Margaret felt compelled in defence to match it. She was not, however, so fastidious as to refuse Mr. Mayne a place on her dance card. He was too popular.

The time passed swiftly for the young ladies since the gentlemen outnumbered them, nearly guaranteeing a full dance card. A supper had been put on, for which everyone was grateful after all the dancing. More importantly, when the men withdrew for cigars and port, there was also an opportunity for the ladies to discuss their partners among themselves.

"Well, Margaret, don't keep us waiting. You got to him before Mary or I could. What is he like?" pressed Kate, when Margaret joined her sisters and friends at one of the tables laid out for the supper. "The young redcoat—Lieutenant Wilson!" said Kate impatiently, in response to her sister's quizzical look.

"I don't think Mary is much interested in Royal Engineers," interrupted Agnes Douglas. "She only has eyes for Dr. Tuzo."

Dr. Henry Tuzo, a Canadian clerk with the company, had already had two dances with Mary; propriety dictated that he ought to have no more than three in an evening, which he seemed always able to acquire from Mary. This was astonishing to Margaret, considering the naval competition. Margaret saw her sister blush and smile self-consciously, but the others were waiting expectantly for Margaret's opinion of Lieutenant Wilson.

"I danced with him as well," Agnes persisted. "I found him quite charming."

"Let's hear what Margaret has to say of him," urged her sister Alice, who, despite her youth, was in the habit of prompting her sister to mind her manners.

Agnes did not wait for Margaret's response, but, with a shrug, left the table. Margaret was pleased at the others' preference for her opinion over that of her young friend, since she thought Agnes a little too accustomed, as the governor's eldest unmarried daughter, to being at the forefront of everything. Not wishing to reveal that he had captivated her, Margaret told them he was agreeable, in such vague terms that it left her listeners unsatisfied. As she spoke she had been following Agnes with her eyes; clued by her eventual silence, the others followed Margaret's gaze. Agnes had joined the Langford daughters at their table.

"The Langfords do not seem at all awkward in their hoop skirts," sighed Mary.

Margaret felt her small triumph of preference over Agnes to be a fleeting one. Agnes was really the only trader's daughter to be admitted

23

to the Langfords' closed circle; the governor's other daughters they merely tolerated.

When the Langfords, the first English family with grown daughters, had arrived in the colony in 1851, Margaret could not forget the profuse praise which had greeted the girls, from officers of the company and the navy alike. "Charming, accomplished, well-mannered and well-bred" were compliments liberally applied to describe them. At the time, Margaret had thought of Mrs. Young, then Miss Cameron, as a prime example of good manners, but the Langfords' arrival had suddenly made her seem like a false-fronted store. Through the following years, while the company officials criticized Captain Langford for his ineptitude as a farm bailiff, they encouraged their own daughters to emulate his. Margaret bore an additional envy, for the eldest Langford daughter had married a naval commander just last year.

The young ladies spent the remainder of the supper break discussing the officers of the Boundary Commission who, it turned out, numbered only seven. Margaret learned from Alice that Lieutenant Wilson was from Liverpool. She made a mental note to look it up in the atlas at home.

"What an atrociously long beard that astronomer has!" cried Kate. "Doesn't he realize how ageing a long beard can be? He looks at least 30."

Margaret laughed a little less at this than the others, since that age did not seem as far from her own as it did to her companions.

"What is his name?" asked Alice.

"Lord," replied Margaret.

"Lord, what a long beard Lord has!" giggled Kate.

Margaret and Mary, exchanging resigned looks, took this latest witticism as their cue to leave the younger girls to their amusements.

The band recommenced its music to call everyone back to the dance floor, and Lieutenant Wilson sought Margaret out for their second dance. Kate and Alice, having dawdled in the dining area, were among the last to make their way back; Margaret and Wilson could clearly see them, hurrying arm in arm toward the dance floor. In their haste they had forgotten the girth of the hoop skirts they wore, and although the space between the dining tables would otherwise easily have admitted them both, in their present attire they wedged themselves in until they were quite stuck. In their struggles to free themselves, a wayward hoop knocked over a wine glass and the resulting smash on the deck turned all eyes upon them. For a brief moment there was silence, except for a ship's steward who rushed over to clean up. The two girls, well matched in pride, eventually broke their frozen pose, backed up and proceeded singly between the tables—Alice with her head held high and looking directly ahead, pretending that nothing had occurred. Only a slight colouring of her cheeks gave her away. Kate, after initial muffled laughter, followed her in a similar manner, but with arched brows, and meeting onlookers' gazes directly, as if daring someone to comment.

Margaret felt mortified to see her dance partner's expression of amusement. However, on noticing her watching him, the lieutenant recovered his countenance immediately.

"Pardon the shortness of my memory, Miss Work, but your father is with the Hudson's Bay Company, is he not?" he inquired politely as they started their dance.

"Almost everyone you will meet here is, aside from the gold miners, of course. My father is a chief factor, and a member of the Board of Management for the company's Western Department." She wished to tell him that her father, in addition to his high company rank, had also been appointed to the Council of Vancouver Island, but did not wish to sound boastful.

"Has he been stationed at Fort Victoria long?"

"Only since '52, although the rest of our family have been here since '49. Father stayed at Fort Simpson for the summers, but he wished us to have a proper education."

To her dismay, she thought she detected a brief curl of his mouth, as she spoke the last words, before he murmured, "Quite right."

She made no further attempt at conversation. She was, in fact, relieved to have the conversation end, for she could still feel her face burning from Kate's and Alice's faux pas. This was one of the few times she felt grateful for her darker complexion. However, in case her blush was noticeable, she turned her face as much as possible from Lieutenant Wilson's, looking past his shoulder at the other dancers, although scarcely seeing them. But soon she felt as if she were being watched, and turning her head quickly to face him, she found to her surprise that he seemed to be studying her forehead intently. Of course he looked away just as quickly, and she began to think she must have been mistaken. Perhaps he had been looking past her at someone else. Nevertheless twice later in the dance she caught him looking at her in the same manner. It was most disconcerting; she felt her cheeks burn afresh and she was heartily thankful when the dance finally ended. Her hand strayed nervously to her hair to check if it was out of place, but she could find nothing amiss. There was nothing to do but try to dismiss it from her mind.

The rest of the evening proved more pleasant, nothing else of consequence occurring. It was not until they were in their bedchamber at the Finlaysons', where they were to stay the night, that Margaret had the opportunity to speak to Mary in private, and then only after listening to Kate's raptures about the evening.

Kate's spirits were even higher than on the journey out; she felt the evening a perfect success, and her crowning achievement was her three dances with Lieutenant Wilson during the latter part of the ball, more than any other lady could claim. Indeed, Margaret had to acknowledge to herself that his distinguishing her at their introduction might only have been because she was nearer to him than any other lady. After 10 minutes of revelling in her memories, amid suppressed yawns from her sisters, Kate was finally persuaded to go to their niece's bedroom, which she was to share, leaving Margaret and Mary alone.

Kate was very similar to their sister Letitia in temperament, open and warm, but without the sense that had tempered the elder. Since Letitia's marriage, Margaret had learned to better value Mary's friendship. Mary, although having warmth, shared Margaret's natural reserve; they could keep confidences with one another. Yet despite these outward similarities, there were inner differences that helped each to gain another perspective from the other. Mary was the more practical of the two; she accepted things at face value, while Margaret had a tendency to play the devil's advocate. And so they had come to depend on one another.

Margaret was disappointed then, that Mary had not yet confided her interest in Dr. Tuzo and she now tried, with indirect inquiries, to glean from her sister some idea of the seriousness of his apparent affection, as it had been a subject of speculation among their acquaintances for some time. Even when the two were not near each other, Margaret had noticed Dr. Tuzo following Mary's movements with spaniel eyes. But Mary seemed no more inclined to reveal anything on this occasion than on any other, and changed the subject with a playful smile.

"I believe Kate is rather jealous of you."

"Whatever for?"

"We all saw the way Lieutenant Wilson was looking at you while you danced together. Quite taken with you, if I'm not mistaken."

"That's far from the truth," Margaret laughed. "He looked at me most oddly, at my forehead, or my hair perhaps. It was difficult to tell."

"You deceive yourself," Mary smiled. "He looked into your eyes until you returned his gaze, and then he politely looked away, respecting your modesty."

Margaret looked at her sister in amazement, but saw that Mary was sincere. She could only wonder at this version of her uncomfortable dance with the lieutenant and began to doubt her own impression. Could Mary, who believed the best of everyone, be right? Of course, she had felt uneasy from the dance's start, due to her embarrassment over the exhibition Kate and Alice had made of themselves in their hoops, and perhaps her own judgment had been coloured by that. No answers could be obtained from her musings but she had not long to wait until she received an explanation.

Chapter Four

I went to a picnic given by a Mr. Skinner which
was very amusing though rather slow. The chief
amusement of the savage young ladies seemed to
be to eat and then scramble away into the bush
and go to sleep.
—Lieutenant Charles William Wilson, RE

The morning after the ball Margaret took down the family's
atlas from its spot in the bookcase and heaved it on to the
table in the library. It was a large, leather-bound volume, rivalling only
the family bible in its weight. She had perused the pages between its cov-
ers on many previous occasions. Once, when John had gone to school
in England, she had even tempted her mother to take a look. When
Margaret pointed out Britain in relationship to British North America
on the map of the world, Mrs. Work had been quite astounded. "Such
a small place! To govern such a large place!"

Margaret opened the atlas to the page depicting England. From
previous studies she had a vague recollection that Liverpool was on
the coast, and she eagerly searched among the cities and towns until
she located it. She ran her finger over the dot. After a few moments she
flipped to the page showing British North America. There was very little writing on it. All of the marked cities were in the east. Victoria was
not shown, only Vancouver's Island, and there was nothing to show Fort
Simpson, her home for 13 years. Under the adjacent Queen Charlotte
Islands was a small note: *Admirable location for a future penal colony.*

With that exception, the coast seemed to have offered no distinguishing features to the publishers. There were no descriptions of the vast area Margaret knew to be New Caledonia, west of the Rocky Mountains. She sighed and closed the book.

Two days after the ball aboard the *Plumper* the Works attended a picnic at the home of Mr. Skinner, an Englishman employed by the company as a farm bailiff. In the interim, Margaret had thought much about Mary's remarks on the subject of a certain officer of the Royal Engineers, and by the date of the picnic, she was quite disposed to like him. She felt sure he was to be there, since the Skinners' home, Oaklands, was situated on Esquimalt Harbour, very close to the military barracks. Mrs. Skinner's daughters had not yet reached a marriageable age, but their mother could nonetheless enjoy matchmaking for her English friends, especially the Langfords across the harbour. How could she possibly pass up the opportunity of inviting such an agreeable, eligible young man, who was nearly a neighbour?

On the morning of the picnic Margaret set off with her younger brothers and sisters, repeating the journey she had taken to the *Plumper* ball, but this time taking two of the Finlayson children along to play with the Skinners' young family. As they passed the naval dockyard in Esquimalt Harbour, the older Work sisters looked wistfully over at the empty huts on the shore.

"What a capital ride we had yesterday with Lieutenant Mayne and Sub-Lieutenant Bedwell! What a pity they could not be here today for the picnic. Why must they always be out surveying?" Kate sighed.

"It's a common misfortune of officers assigned to a survey ship," smiled Margaret.

"*You* take their loss surprisingly well," Kate replied mischievously. "I suppose the addition of the Boundary Commission will somewhat make up for the loss of the *Plumper*."

Margaret did not reply. Whether or not she agreed proved of little relevance, for when the Works arrived at Oaklands, they found themselves on the fringe of the group. The four Langford daughters, having arrived earlier, had procured the spots nearest the gentlemen, leaving the others little opportunity for conversing with them.

Immediately following the meal, the youngest children wished to ramble about the farm and Margaret dutifully joined them since, as the eldest Work present, she ultimately had the charge of her siblings and nieces. The youngsters stopped when they reached a grassy slope with a fine view of Esquimalt Harbour. Oaklands was situated on a sunny bank overlooking Constance Cove, and this slope was the Skinner children's favourite spot to lie and watch the ships coming and going. Margaret indulged in this pastime herself under the shade of a large oak, where she could easily see both the children and the harbour. She felt her chagrin at the way the picnic had turned out start to lift with the breeze, until the other young ladies joined her. The Langfords had been dispatched by Mrs. Skinner to watch over her own young children. Aflap with talk of the Boundary Commission officers, the young ladies recited and embellished their conversations in minute detail.

Mary Langford, the eldest excepting her married sister, was the only one not gushing. Margaret felt some affection for her, unlike the other Langfords, because there were rumours of unfulfilled love surrounding her. She had met the second mate of the company's barque *Tory* on the family's long voyage out to the colony and become further acquainted when he was appointed first mate on the company's coastal steamer, the *Otter*, but her father, with his awful pride, had refused to give his consent to their marriage. The story had claimed Margaret's sympathies, and Miss Langford always appeared to her in a certain light of romantic pathos. Margaret felt they were kindred spirits, and if only their budding friendship had not been interrupted by the departure of their schoolmistress,

Mrs. Staines, she felt sure they would now be closer. Their opportunities for meeting had become less frequent, and Margaret was just pondering an approach to her when her sister Suzette, growing restless, begged her to go blackberry picking. Margaret reluctantly agreed.

"We'll have to ask Mary to watch Annie first, though," she said.

Little Annie Finlayson was not so agreeable, however, and Margaret was struggling with her when Miss Langford came over and offered to look after the youngster herself. Well pleased with this token of kindness, Margaret thanked her, extricated herself from her niece and strolled down the slope with Suzette.

It was a fine day as yet, the blue sky contrasting with dark clouds on the horizon, and they wandered along the trails toward the farmhouse. Many of the berries were still red; only those in the sunniest spots had darkened to a ripe black. As they neared the garden, Suzette spied a narrow side trail going into a thicket of berry-laden brambles, the ripest ones yet. After a moment's hesitation, Margaret could not resist her sister's eager expression and picked her way gingerly into the thicket, trying not to catch her dress on the thorns, or, as she picked the berries, to stain her hands or mouth with the juice.

She had just popped a delectably ripe one into her mouth when the sound of men's voices drifted up to her. She felt suddenly like a child caught with her hand in the candy jar. She stopped chewing and listened. The voices drew closer. Turning quickly to leave the thicket, Margaret caught her dress on a thorn. The men's voices were suddenly clear and a waft of pungent tobacco smoke reached her nostrils.

"A good view from here," said one voice, and Margaret recognized it instantly as Lieutenant Wilson's.

They seemed to be directly below her, but hidden from view by the thick brambles. She struggled silently to free herself.

"I wonder how long we have to wait before *les belles sauvages* have finished their siesta," Wilson said with a chuckle. "It's rather an odd custom of the fair sex—to eat and then scramble away into the bush to sleep!"

"Perhaps it aids in the digestion," his companion suggested, laughing.

Margaret froze. The blackberry remained crushed between her teeth.

"I suppose, since most of them are half-breeds, some odd customs are to be expected. Speaking of customs, I learnt at the *Plumper* ball that two of the Misses Douglas had their heads flattened whilst they were young, although it's scarcely visible now," Wilson said.

"You don't say!"

"It was most amusing to see their attempts to appear at ease in their hoops!" Wilson said. "Although some of them danced rather well."

"Any savage can dance," replied the other.

Margaret heard a small noise behind her. In her growing agitation, she had forgotten her sister. Suzette, her face smeared purple, had evidently picked all the berries within her reach, and was trying to make her way into the thicket. Margaret put her finger to her lips in a silent warning to be quiet, and prayed for her obedience.

"Did you hear something?" said Wilson.

"Probably just a bird," replied his companion. "Look at all the blackberries! I wouldn't mind a few of those."

Margaret closed her eyes momentarily, her thudding heart threatening to escape from the confines of her chest. A small part of her wished to surprise and embarrass the men; emerging from the thicket now, though, might only serve to confirm their belief that she had been sleeping in the bush, and she feared she would be the worse off of the two parties for embarrassment. The two men, however, seemed satisfied with their pipes, and after a few more anxious moments they moved on.

Freeing herself from the thorn, Margaret left the thicket as quickly as she could, collected Suzette and headed for the farmhouse. As she ran along beside her, Suzette, her eyes wide, whispered, "Did those men see some Indians in the bushes?"

Margaret stopped to ask her what she meant, and was relieved to find that Suzette had caught very little of the conversation. Hearing something about "savages," she had assumed that there were Indians nearby. Margaret reassured her there were not. The local Songhees Indians were a peaceable people, but the gold rush had attracted greater numbers of the northern tribes to Victoria, and the settlers, fearing conflicts, had warned their children not to wander off, as they hitherto had liberty to do.

The other young ladies and children, making their way down the path to Oaklands, interrupted the sisters' conversation. Free from Suzette's questions and the dread of discovery, Margaret's anger began to vent itself. *Les belles sauvages* indeed! *Half-breeds!* How dare he! And to think that Agnes and Alice had had their heads flattened, in one of the coast's Indian customs; it was ridiculous! Margaret knew of no trader's wife who had followed this practice. Mrs. Douglas had moved far away from the land of her Indian forbears and the tradition was foreign to her mother's people. And then it dawned on her—the strange way Wilson had looked at *her* forehead at the *Plumper* ball. He'd been wondering if she, too, had had her head flattened when she was young!

The young lieutenant, of all the gentlemen, seemed to especially welcome their return when they reached the farmhouse, and Margaret fumed inwardly at his presumptions. Mrs. Skinner proposed a visit to the beach, and as they set off, Wilson singled out Margaret for conversation.

"It appears the beautiful weather won't hold out much longer, Miss Work," he said cheerfully, eyeing the horizon.

"Well, at least it lasted long enough for our walk up the bank," answered Margaret curtly, and stepped past him, leaving him puzzled and alone.

Wilson proved right about the weather; the dark clouds rolled in at an increasing pace, and sitting at the beach was cut short. To Margaret's relief the threatening storm provided her with an excuse for an early departure, and they left as soon as 12-year-old David Work, who was playing croquet in the garden, could be persuaded to end his game. A downpour came on shortly before they reached Hillside, and they arrived at the homestead drenched to the skin. Mrs. Work bustled them inside with solicitous concern, giving most of her attention to the younger children, and Margaret gratefully retreated to the solitude of her room. She welcomed Mary's entrance; it was the first opportunity Margaret had had of getting her sister alone since the picnic. As they undressed, Margaret wasted no time in relating the conversation between Lieutenant Wilson and his companion, who she suspected was one of the astronomers of the Boundary Commission.

But Mary had a generous nature, and a sweeter temper than her sister, and would not rise to Margaret's level of indignation.

"How was Lieutenant Wilson to know that Mrs. Douglas is half Cree, not Flathead, and so would not follow those customs?" she asked. "You must expect him to be green in the ways of the colony, having only been here for a fortnight."

"But even if she had Flathead blood, and was foolish enough to wish to flatten the heads of her daughters, how could Lieutenant Wilson think the governor would allow such a thing?" answered Margaret, shaking her head.

"Perhaps Lieutenant Wilson thinks Mr. Douglas was separated from his family for long periods, as you well know is often the case with traders," said Mary evenly.

"I don't care what he thinks. I'll not speak to him again. He laughed at how we appeared in our hoops! He called us savages!"

"Beautiful savages," added Mary with a smile.

"I'd rather be considered ugly and civilized," said Margaret peevishly, sinking into the one chair in the room. Then, seeing her sister chuckle in disbelief, her frown dissolved into a grin.

"By avoiding him, you deny him the chance of learning that you *are* civilized. Of course, it's too late to make him think you're ugly," teased Mary.

Soon Mary's good humour began to have its effect, and Margaret felt herself softening, although she was still incapable of completely forgiving the lieutenant.

"Half-breeds, indeed! The Company's servants, the *engagés*, are half-breeds, not the daughters of a chief factor! Mr. Wilson really has a lot to learn about the colony."

"I wonder," mused Mary, "who would have told him such a thing about Agnes and Alice?"

This had crossed Margaret's mind earlier, but in her indignation she had not considered it further. The answer suddenly suggested itself. "The Langfords! It must have been one of the Langfords. Who else would wish to turn a military officer against us?"

"Possibly," replied Mary, but without conviction.

An impatient knock at the door signalled the arrival of young Suzette.

"Come down to the dining room at once, and get something hot to drink," she ordered firmly. "Mama says so."

Her older sisters saw with amusement that she was not to be denied, and allowed themselves to be led downstairs, there to be chastised for dawdling by their mother, while they were warmed by her broth.

Just before supper that day, John rushed into Hillside's dining room, where the rest of the family was already gathered, receiving only a brief look of displeasure from Mr. Work for his tardiness. Even if his father had been inclined to a reprimand, John left him no opportunity; he was full of talk of his day's grouse shooting. Margaret tried vainly to silence him with a frown; he ought to help their father manage the farm, but as he had never been given to hard work, she was not much surprised.

John seemed, on the other hand, very pleased to see *her*. "Margaret! You're still here! I thought you'd gone and eloped on us!"

Margaret was used to his teasing, especially on this topic; she revealed no sign of being bothered.

"It was in the paper, right there under marriages: 'At Victoria Church, by Reverend Mr. Cridge, William Reid to Margaret Work,'" he recited.

She looked at him doubtfully, but could find no witty retort to defend herself.

Mr. Work stopped carving momentarily, looked up at his son and daughter and then returned his attention to the roast grouse. "It said Margaret Work, *late of Nanaimo*," he said dryly.

"I thought perhaps that was just a ruse to mislead us," John said mischievously, unwilling to let the joke go.

Margaret felt suddenly pained at his persistence, and Mr. Work, in a tone more cutting than John was accustomed to hear, said, "Of much *more* interest was the article mentioning the school prizes. I was very proud to see your name on the list, David. You are to be congratulated on your success."

David beamed; John scowled. John had been sent to England for three years to better his schooling, much to Margaret's envy, but the experience seemed to have had little effect, at least on his scholastic education. Well did Margaret remember her father's face as they had stood on the dock, watching John board his steamer for England. "He won't get a more competent teacher than Staines, if only he would attend to his studies," he had sighed, shaking his head. He had, nonetheless, sent him anyway.

John had come back from England a different person in many respects, although not necessarily in the way their father had intended. Aside from growing at least a foot in height, he looked at things differently; his eyes sometimes betrayed contempt for his home, and even, Margaret regretted to admit, for his family. This disturbed Margaret more than any of the haughty looks of the Langford girls. There was something else too—a bitterness, perhaps, that sometimes stole over his countenance. His expression often said how small and inconsequential Victoria was. Time had softened such looks, although they were not gone altogether, and from familiarity Margaret could spot them with ease in newcomers from the Old Country.

After supper, when Margaret felt she was least likely to be observed, she picked up the *Victoria Gazette* and retreated into a corner of the drawing-room with it. Reading was a favourite pastime for her; the family was accustomed, since the newspaper's inception in the spring, to see her devour it each evening. She wished to read the notice John had teased her about without anyone else watching her do it.

She studied the announcement to see how her name looked in print in the marriage column. It was the only announcement that day, the colony's lack of eligible young ladies making marriages rather rare. John wandered nearby and she quickly turned the page, her eyes flicking over the contents until she settled on a letter to the editor.

Last Sabbath was an unusually warm day. The little chapel was crowded as usual with a 'smart sprinkle' of blacks, generously mixed with whites. The Ethiopians perspired! They always do when out of place. Several white gentlemen left their seats vacant, and sought the purer atmosphere outside; others moodily endured the aromatic luxury of their positions, in no very pious frame of mind.

The writer went on to advocate segregation in the churches. Margaret did not recognize the name, but had little doubt it was one of the Americans whom the gold rush had brought in scores to Victoria;

they freely advertised their sentiments regarding race. Reverend Cridge had welcomed the black immigrants to the Church of England, as Governor Douglas had welcomed them to the colony; they had been assured that all were equal on British soil. Unfortunately for the blacks, their emigration had coincided with the gold rush, and they could not escape other Californians. Margaret reread the letter several times until, looking up, she saw John reading over her shoulder.

"You should hear what some of the Americans say about Indians," he began.

Margaret quickly closed the paper, handed it to her brother and hurried from the room. He knew very well that she was familiar with the American settlers' sentiments; her family had spent enough time at Fort Vancouver and farther south to have given her a taste of American attitudes. Indians were held to be lower than dogs, and extermination was their general approach.

She went to the back porch seeking fresh air, and saw her father walking around the garden, looking out over the fields to the forest's outline in the dusk, smoking his pipe. This was a habit from Fort Simpson, where Mr. Work would wrap himself in his cloak every evening and tour the gallery of the fort until he was assured that all was well. The pipe had worried Mrs. Work exceedingly; she had feared its glow in the dark would make him an easy target for disgruntled Indians, but it was a pleasure he had been unwilling to give up. Indian attacks were less of a worry in Victoria than in Fort Simpson, and Margaret watched her father for a long time until the nostalgia of her memories began to comfort her. But the letter to the editor became intertwined in her mind with Lieutenant Wilson's uncharitable comments about "half-breeds," and she could not shake the vague feelings of unease that had settled upon her.

Chapter Five

In fine weather, riding parties of the gentlemen
and ladies of the place were formed, and we
returned generally to a high tea, or tea-dinner,
at Mr. Douglas' or Mr. Work's, winding up the
pleasant evening with dance and song.
—Richard Charles Mayne, RN

The Works saw little of Lieutenant Wilson for the remainder of
August, which prevented Margaret from exacting her revenge of
giving him the cold shoulder. The navy also deprived her of the company
of the officers of HMS *Plumper*, as the ship was dispatched to patrol
the mouth of the Fraser River in an effort to control the flood of miners
coming into the colony. Fortunately, the month offered a few diversions.
Margaret saw her first cricket match, between the newly formed Victoria
Cricket Club and HMS *Satellite*; she could make little sense of it, but the
players' antics provided entertainment nevertheless.

Toward the end of the month, the Hudson's Bay Company steamer
Governor Douglas was launched in Victoria Harbour. Mr. Work
relaxed his restrictions on his daughters and allowed them to go, as did
Governor Douglas, for Agnes was to christen the new ship with a bottle
of champagne. As Margaret watched her basking in the limelight during
the christening ceremony, the difference between herself and Agnes, in
their roles as the oldest unmarried girls of their families, glared back
at her starkly. Agnes, at only 17, could look forward to being at the
forefront of many events such as this. When she thought of marriage,

it must be as a future certainty; she had as her reassurance John Work, Junior, waiting in the wings for her. Margaret, seven years her senior, had the uncomfortable feeling that she might have settled irrevocably into spinsterhood by the time she welcomed Agnes as her sister-in-law, if indeed John was the one she chose to marry.

In September, the slightly cooler weather encouraged more riding parties, and Margaret had the opportunity of seeing Lieutenant Wilson at several of these. The horses that Vancouver Island had to offer were obviously not of the quality he was accustomed to, and Margaret admitted begrudgingly that he had an admirable sense of humour as he attempted to stay in the saddle. The rough ground they covered would have made difficult riding even on the best of steeds, and Margaret frequently saw him cursing under his breath as he was jostled about, but he recovered his good humour almost as quickly as he regained his seat.

Margaret's reluctant admiration of his good humour was more than matched by his admiration of the equestrian skills of the young ladies, who rode astride since they had never encountered a sidesaddle. One such occasion came after the riding party was divided into groups, as frequently happened. This time Margaret and Kate were briefly separated from everyone else. The largest group, with Lieutenant Wilson, had stopped at the edge of a field where it met a small wood. They had planned to go through the copse, but a large fallen tree blocked the path a few yards in from the opening. They were debating whether to skirt round the trees, or go back in the direction they had come, when Margaret came galloping down the path from the opposite direction. Barely checking her horse, she cleared the tree, with Kate following close at her heels. Wilson and a few others had evidently not expected them to attempt it, and Margaret would not soon forget the incredulous expression on his face as his horse shied wildly to avoid hers.

"Capitally done!" called some of his party.

"Yes, very plucky," he muttered, his face all amazement.

Margaret was amused and gratified to learn later from a friend that he had been among those against attempting to jump the tree "for the sake of the ladies."

His open admiration increased over the course of the afternoon, and when Kate teasingly asked him how he liked Victoria's horses, he had the honesty to reply, with a rueful expression, "It will be some time before I ride with the ease and gracefulness you and your sisters possess." *At least there is something he thinks we do well,* thought Margaret, and she found that she was not quite capable of giving him the cold shoulder.

Being fond of a long, free run, Margaret often left the others, and later that afternoon she found herself alone on the outskirts of Beacon Hill Park. She slowed her horse to a walk, meandering through the open, park-like country that was dotted with Garry oaks and reminiscent of English scenery, or so she had been told. Approaching Dr. Tuzo's log cabin, she saw two figures ahead. They had reigned in very close so that their legs sometimes brushed when their horses shifted their feet. It was Mary and Dr. Tuzo.

Margaret saw at once how they would be perceived. It was inevitable for the imagination to leap from seeing a couple together to assuming they intended matrimony. And under what circumstances: the two of them unchaperoned, admiring his property and its pretty prospect overlooking the nearby oak meadows, as if it should soon be theirs and not his alone! As society's expectation might add fuel to a love barely kindled, dampening the risk was Margaret's only thought; no one else ought to see them.

Yet they were so completely absorbed in their conversation, their dark heads drawn close together, that something in Margaret hesitated to break up their tête-à-tête. The sounds of an approaching rider brought her hesitation to a crux; she must either join them or cut the other rider off. Mary in profile was smiling shyly into Tuzo's face, so Margaret turned her horse and set off to intercept the other rider.

Coming round an entangled mass of wild rose bushes, she met Lieutenant Wilson. "Have you seen the meadow just over that rise?" she asked with a friendly smile, pointing in the opposite direction from Mary and Dr. Tuzo. "It's a beautiful spot."

Wilson's face brightened, whether at the prospect of seeing the place or at her changed manner, she didn't know.

"I'm very glad to see you, Miss Work," he said, bringing his horse abreast of hers. "To tell you the truth, I was feeling a little lost."

"Oh, in such a small place as Victoria," she replied, "you would not be lost for long."

When they reached the meadow she had mentioned, Margaret was glad to be spared finding any particular attractions to point out by the presence of several others of their party. She noticed with some discomfort, mixed with being flattered, that the others had observed her and the lieutenant riding alone together. She could imagine them wondering whether it was by accident or design, and if the latter, by *whose* design?

That evening Margaret waited for a chance to talk to Mary alone. Mrs. Staines had taught her during her schooling at Fort Victoria that ladies did not force confidences, and she had endeavoured not to press Mary for an explanation of her attachment to Dr. Tuzo. It also went against Margaret's nature to pry. This usually reaped its own rewards because she found that her opinion, seldom volunteered, was valued more than those freely offered. But today's ride called for drastic measures.

She found her opportunity while Mary was preparing for bed, brushing her long hair, which was a shade lighter than Margaret's own and burnished with red in the candlelight. Margaret had always envied her sister's hair, especially in the summer when it lightened so much more quickly than her own.

"I saw you with Dr. Tuzo today, by his home." Although Margaret tried to make it sound offhand, it came out like an accusation.

Mary looked quickly at her sister, then back into the small mirror atop her dresser.

"You were following me?"

"No, of course not. I just happened upon you, and I left almost at once."

"You don't approve," sighed Mary.

"If it had been someone else, not me, you would no doubt be the subject of all sorts of gossip."

"I meant, you don't approve of Dr. Tuzo."

Margaret's misgiving deepened into unease. That Dr. Tuzo held Mary in particular regard was no secret, but it seemed she had underestimated the extent to which Mary returned it.

"I have nothing against Dr. Tuzo," faltered Margaret.

"As a future brother-in-law?"

"You are expecting a proposal?" Margaret's throat constricted and her voice did not come out as calmly as she intended. She sat down.

Mary shifted in her seat. "It is a possibility."

"Why did you not tell me?"

"I know how you feel about marrying into the company. I didn't wish to be dissuaded before I even knew my own mind."

Margaret seized on Mary's hesitation. "If you don't know your mind, how much better not to encourage him, Mary. There will be plenty of time, once you are sure. Give idle tongues no fodder for chatter, then you will remain beyond reproof, from yourself or anyone else."

Mary paused in her brush strokes, frowning slightly.

"I wouldn't try to jeopardize your happiness," added Margaret, feeling a little guilty for her objection. And then, groping for reconciliation, "Well, at least he's a doctor. He could always practise his profession *outside* the employ of the company."

"But he has set his hopes on becoming a trader."

"So you have discussed his plans—it has gone as far as that!" With dismay she watched Mary's face in the mirror as she continued brushing her hair. "Marrying into the company, Mary. Think of it. Posted from fort to fort in the utter wilderness, not seeing your family for years at a stretch—"

"Which could be just the case if you married a military gentleman."

"I said nothing of that."

"Mm," replied Mary, putting the brush down. "Margaret, I'm getting so *old*. I'm 21 this month! I don't want to be a spinster. In some people's eyes I probably already am."

Margaret was mortified. She persuaded her sister as best she could that she only had Mary's happiness at heart, and once Mary was reasonably convinced of that, Margaret left and went out to pace the back porch, to digest their conversation in the questionable peace of solitude.

Chapter Six

[In the 1850s] the country became like and as civilized as any respectable village in England, with the few, very few, upper ten leading—and of course the usual jealousy arose as to who was to be the leader—they were no longer satisfied to be on an equality—and so 'what we were in England or Scotland' was burnished and made the most of!!!
—Dr. John Sebastian Helmcken

The Work household's number was increased one autumn day by the arrival of a Mr. James Grahame. Margaret returned home from riding with John to find him seated with her father in the drawing-room. The supper hour often brought additions to Hillside, for with a family of nine at home, one or two more made little difference around the well-laid dining table, and Mr. and Mrs. Work had a reputation for generously opening their door to visitors.

Introductions were quickly commenced. "Ah, here is Margaret, my eldest daughter at home," was how Mr. Work described her when she entered the room. But the gentleman's position needed a longer explanation.

"Margaret," said her father, "you may remember Mr. Grahame, chief trader at Fort Vancouver. I believe you met when you were a girl, or was it Letitia? I don't recall now. He has kindly brought us a letter from your cousin John."

Margaret had seen Mr. Grahame before, and she knew from her cousin's previous letters that he had lost his wife two years ago. He bowed his head stiffly and, although he smiled, he fastened her with such an intent look as he said, "Indeed, an honour," that Margaret became vaguely uncomfortable and, turning quickly to her father, said, "All is well with my cousin, I trust?"

"I have not yet read the letter, but Mr. Grahame assures me he is well."

John McAdoo Wark was a nephew of Mr. Work's, and a clerk at Fort Vancouver. Margaret knew him to be a steadfast Irishman. Unlike his uncle, who had anglicized his name upon joining the company, John Wark had retained the original spelling of the name.

Mr. Work further explained that he had met Mr. Grahame in town a few hours earlier and had invited him home. Margaret guessed the rest: her father was anxious to extend the hospitality of his commodious home to his nephew's senior officer, and Mr. Grahame, happy to be given more comfortable lodgings than those he had procured at the fort, had readily accepted.

Mr. Work had also sent a supper invitation to the Finlaysons, both of who had spent several years at Fort Vancouver—Sarah as a young girl at school nearby and Mr. Finlayson as a clerk in the company. They were always eager for news of their old haunts. When they gathered round the table, therefore, the supper conversation not surprisingly turned to the changes wrought at Fort Vancouver since Oregon had been given up to the Americans in 1846.

The old-timers listened with gravity as Mr. Grahame related how American settlers were encroaching more and more on the fort's farm-land on the banks of the Columbia River, which the company had so painstakingly hacked out of the wilderness. "Trade with the Indians," he said, looking slowly around the table for added effect, "is dwindling."

His stories prompted much shaking of heads by Mr. and Mrs. Work, and Mr. and Mrs. Finlayson, who could remember the old fort in its glory days, but Margaret was not among that number. And while David and the younger children were riveted by his depiction, Margaret did not wish to dwell on the spread of the Americans; instead, she observed Mr. Grahame, who had escorted her into the dining room and was consequently seated to her immediate left.

Aside from their brief previous meetings, she had often heard him mentioned in her cousin's letters. Margaret or John usually read the letters first to their father, who would then relay the contents to his family later. This method had the double virtue of saving him eyestrain and his patriarchal pride in supplying news from relatives. John McAdoo Wark evidently respected Mr. Grahame, who had also been related by marriage, as their wives were sisters. Another sister, Mrs. Anderson, resided in Victoria, and they heard Mr. Grahame mentioned from that quarter as well. When his wife had died, she had left him with several children. He was of Scottish birth, as many traders were, and had the usual qualities of the trader who had spent much of his adult life in the New Country: he was civil, but in a forced way, and looked hardened for his years. Margaret thought he appeared to be in his mid-40s, but she compensated for the hard life of the trader, and his very long, already greying beard, and supposed him to be in his late 30s.

Margaret cut short her observation of Mr. Grahame when she noticed that *he* was also studying *her*, in a deliberate and very disconcerting fashion. The dinner conversation had drifted from Fort Vancouver to Victoria, all of its changes over the past few months and all its future possibilities, a favourite subject of Mr. Finlayson's. While Mr. Finlayson talked with relish of development speculation, Mr. Grahame's eyes had plenty of opportunity for wandering. His observation of Margaret did not end with supper, and over the course of the evening she frequently felt his eyes upon her. She remembered that when, before supper, Sarah had inquired after his family, he had replied that his sons were well, but that they missed their mother very much, which now gave Margaret the uneasy thought that perhaps he was looking for a replacement.

Mr. Grahame stayed at Hillside for several days. Margaret's suspicions that he was wife hunting grew, and she took care not to spend more time with him than necessary, and not to give him anything more than the civility he was entitled to as a distant relative.

With avoiding him in mind, she walked over to the Finlaysons' home on the third day of his visit, on the pretext of helping Sarah with her children. Sarah often reminded Margaret of a spinster's sisterly duties, and during this particular week Margaret felt happy to oblige.

"A sad thing, Mr. Grahame losing Susan with three sons to take care of," Sarah said over tea. Mr. Grahame's late wife had been about Sarah's age and they had known each other when Sarah attended school near Fort Vancouver. "He'll be wanting another wife," she continued more pointedly, "and with three children already he'll need a wife who is older."

Margaret began clearing the tea things off the table. As Mr. Finlayson was not yet a chief factor, he was not entitled to the services of a steward, and much of the kitchen work fell to Sarah and the indifferent Indian help she employed.

"A girl could do a lot worse than marrying James Grahame," persisted Sarah, undaunted. "He's been a chief trader for—it must be at least five years now. When the company abandons Fort Vancouver and he's transferred to another fort, he could very well be promoted to chief factor."

"No doubt at some God-forsaken outpost in the wilderness," muttered Margaret.

"Chief *factors* get the most important postings," countered Sarah.

"Like Fort Simpson," said Margaret bitterly.

"Yes, Fort Simpson! Known throughout the company as London North, with good reason! So many furs—"

"A lot of good they did Papa, in declining health in the wilds! You missed five years there, remember?"

The two sisters glared at each other across the table. When the Works had moved to Fort Simpson, Jane and Sarah had remained at the missionary school in Willamette. Letitia and Margaret, being only four and two years old, had gone with their parents, and although Margaret had longed for the return of her soon barely remembered sisters, when they finally arrived five years later, full of stories from the more populated area, she had been filled with wonder at what she had missed. Later, when the family moved to Fort Victoria and met the intimidating schoolmistress Mrs. Staines, Margaret had come to learn the advantages of a more formal education.

Sarah changed tack. "Mr. Grahame told us last evening he intends taking a year's furlough in *England*, after turning over Fort Vancouver to the Americans."

Margaret winced to hear such a shameless referral to her dream of seeing England. To hide her heightening colour, she turned away, clattering the dishes into the washbasin.

"Be careful, Margaret!" said Sarah sharply. "China does not come cheap! You forget Mr. Finlayson is still a chief trader and our means are less than Papa's. Mr. Grahame," she said after a slight pause, "is very fortunate to be within reach of such means."

Margaret stared down at the teacup in her hands. Blue and white Spode, like most of the china the company's officers used. Margaret knew all the patterns by heart; this one was British Flowers, but the china bore many chips and cracks. Margaret was tempted to say that Mr. Finlayson seemed to have enough money to buy more land, so why could he not afford more china? But she held her tongue. Although Sarah had longed for the privacy of her own home, life had not been easy for her since they had moved from the fort, with all the services it provided to officers and their families.

"Think of it, Margaret. What other chance do you suppose will come your way to go to the Old Country? It's the only way you *could* go. Dark skin, a country upbringing—you would be a curiosity on a visit, but beyond that you would never be accepted. The idea of living there can't be tolerated. You belong to the fur trade."

Sarah's pronouncement echoed in Margaret's ears with each weary step home. She had felt the brunt of her older sister's opinions before, and she knew that Sarah spoke what many others felt. Indeed, upon suspecting her preference for the naval profession, her own parents had gently endeavoured to convince her that a proposal from that quarter was unlikely. The transition from a remote colony to upper-class English society would be too difficult, they said. But while she had not believed her parents during Mr. Mayne's eight-year absence from Victoria, his return had been convincing; the restraint with which he had renewed their friendship had reduced her hopes to little more than a faint shred.

She could see that with only slight encouragement, she could very likely be Mrs. Grahame within the year, and she would avoid all the hardships of marrying a mere clerk. Traders and factors had a mystique about them that suggested wealth; even if the legendary fur trade had not produced actual abundance, they were generally treated with great respect. Marrying Grahame would be the sensible thing to do. Sarah firmly believed so; every one of her looks had told Margaret she would be foolish to pass up such an opportunity.

By the time she reached Hillside, Margaret had very nearly resolved to accept Mr. Grahame's attentions. But the instant she saw again his expression of mechanical civility, his steady and deliberate attention, something in her balked. She had the sense that when he looked at her he saw the surface only; his requirements went no further. She saw herself face to face with that expression of cold practicality for endless days at a remote outpost, with little or no other company. The thought of giving herself to such a man unnerved her. She retreated and re-examined, and after many moments of wavering and soul-searching, she came to the same conclusion she always did: that she was not so old that she must give up entirely her dream of marrying outside the company. After all, the gold rush now held out many unspoken possibilities.

Margaret tried to name her objections to Mr. Grahame in a more acceptable form, in case the necessity of explaining herself to her father arose. Telling him that the man did not love her, nor she him, would be insufficient. Mr. Work would not push her, but he might think her frivolous, which Margaret couldn't bear. A character flaw in Mr. Grahame would give Mr. Work reason to accept his daughter's lack of feeling, but the best she could do was label him immovable. Here was a man who would look impassively on tempests, whose practical respect for the facts was his driving force. Having decided that his children were in need of a mother, and he of a wife, he was setting doggedly out to get one. His steady nature must be her reason to refuse him. It was no use; Margaret felt doomed to be frivolous.

But by the end of Mr. Grahame's visit, Margaret was content to see that her lack of encouragement had reduced his attentions toward her. Mary had helped to divert him a little, but as Margaret knew her predisposed in Dr. Tuzo's favour, she did not see any danger to Mary. And with Kate much too young, in temperament if not age, for a man of 35—as Margaret had found Mr. Grahame out to be—she thought they were all quite safe.

After his departure, Margaret had to endure a few remarks from John about "missing her last chance," until he was silenced by Mr. Work who, though looking disappointed, took a less direct approach than his son and limited his remarks to a few praises of Mr. Grahame's character. Margaret sought the company of her mother, who had never fully understood the desire of the British to have their daughters married off. When her two eldest daughters, Jane and Sarah, had married nearly a decade before, Mrs. Work was relieved to see them settled but only because it meant the protection of two brothers-in-law for her other children, in case Mr. Work should suffer an early demise.

Since Jane and Sarah had married well, Mrs. Work became more reluctant to part with her younger children, even more so when she lost her son Henry at the age of 12. Mr. Work had endeavoured to convince her that they were blessed that God had taken the life of only one of their 11 children; most of their peers had not been so fortunate. Of the 13 children Mrs. Douglas had borne, only six were living. But Mrs. Work was inconsolable; not until the family feared for her own health did she begin to see reason. Nevertheless, when Letitia was married the year following Henry's death, Mrs. Work viewed her daughter's wedding in the shadow of mourning. Having lost one of her children to death, she was in no hurry to lose the others to marriage.

———·——

As summer turned into fall the tide of miners flooding Victoria began to ebb, until it turned and the miners poured out of the colony as rapidly as they had come in. They did not tarry long. The majority soon departed for warmer climes, taking their dollars with them. Accordingly, Mr. Work's restrictions on his daughters' freedoms began to ease. He enrolled Kate and Cecilia in St. Ann's Academy, following Governor Douglas' lead. The Sisters of St. Ann had opened a school shortly after their arrival from Montreal in June, but Mr. Work had been wary of allowing his daughters to pass through town to reach the school, which was situated just southeast of the fort. Now that the excitement in town had tapered off, he was eager for his children to receive what education could be had in Victoria.

Since 1854, when Reverend Staines had died and his wife had left the colony, the girls had had some informal lessons from Mrs. Cridge, the new minister's wife, but when she started bearing children, the lessons had dwindled. The Sisters of St. Ann had agreed to take students from other denominations, and Mr. Work, a Presbyterian who had long been receiving ministrations from the Church of England, was not overly fastidious. He did not object to a Catholic school, the important point being that his children grow up instilled with a fear of God.

Margaret and Mary did not attend St. Ann's; they were too old. They sampled their returning freedom one Saturday in October, when Mr. Work allowed all his daughters to go into town. Victoria's first regular police force had begun patrolling the streets, adding to Mr. Work's lenience. This new sense of security was amplified by the pride of seeing his pumpkins mentioned in the *Victoria Gazette*; the largest weighed in at a colossal 108½ pounds, his distant second a mere 68.

At last Margaret could experience for herself the changes the gold fever had wrought in Victoria, changes glimpsed only on the way to the District Church, which sat to the east of Victoria on a hill overlooking the town, or from a boat in the harbour to the west. The transformation of the familiar astounded her; in one summer Victoria had altered more than in the previous 10 years.

As they approached the town, buildings could be seen cropping up around the fort's walls where there had been mostly fields before. The tent city, which had spread out from the fort like mushrooms since the spring, was now broken up by wooden structures.

A foul odour reached Margaret's nostrils when they reached the outermost buildings and increased as they entered town. Livestock wandered about freely, which added to the pungency created by the lack of a sewer. John, upon seeing her expression of distaste, informed her, "It's nothing to what it was in the height of summer!" He seemed to be enjoying the stares of his sisters immensely.

The streets themselves were quite tolerable. It had been a dry autumn, and the dirt roads were still passable. The town offered great variety. There were the familiar: Indians selling fish, a few Kanakas venturing from their row of homes on the far side of the fort, and Black Americans Margaret recognized from church. But there were also costumes Margaret had never seen before, and indecipherable languages to go with them. John pointed down one narrow street. "Little Canton," he said, with an air of superior knowledge. She could see the Chinese men hurrying about their business and unreadable signs displayed above the cramped shops.

The miners they passed were dressed uniformly in red serge shirts and grey serge pants. A pistol and bowie knife were slung on most belts. They stared unabashedly at the party of young ladies, flanked by Mr. Work and John, making its way to the fort's gates. Margaret thought she had grown accustomed to such stares; going to church made her feel like a spectacle, since, with all the miners packing the church, the men outnumbered the women about six to one. In fact, she suspected that many of the miners attended church for the sole purpose of getting a closer view of Victoria's ladies. But now it seemed she was in their territory, and her eyes wandered frequently to the fort's bastions, rising reassuringly above the shantytown. She was relieved to temporarily escape the scrutiny when they entered the gates.

After Mr. Work had attended to his business inside the fort they repaired to Yates Street, a short section of which had recently been paved, the first of its kind in Victoria. Margaret marvelled at the macadamized pavement, so uniformly level and grey; it at once confirmed and pronounced that Victoria had become a town. Mr. Work humoured their wish to cross the road as many times as the short stretch of pavement would allow, their footsteps crunching on the crushed stone, so different from either the dust or the quagmire of mud they were accustomed to.

Mr. Work had given his daughters a limited amount of money to spend; though generous, he had a vague distrust of American goods, as many of the British did, and preferred to increase his yearly order of goods from London to reflect his growing wealth. Still, Margaret and her sisters were eager to spend their money and dragged their father and brother from shop to shop until it was gone. The new stores offered a fascinating selection to the young women who had hitherto had only the Hudson's Bay Company store to depend on. Coming out of the shop that had received their last cent, they happened to see a house being moved on rollers down the street, a procedure that John had described to them previously on many occasions and one they had longed to see for themselves. It was necessitated because city lots frequently changed hands, and buildings went up before a surveyor could lay out streets. They stood staring on the plank sidewalk until the house had rumbled past, leaving a clear view across the street to another party of onlookers staring back at them. It was the Langford daughters, accompanied by a group of naval officers and Lieutenant Wilson.

Civil bows and curtsies, some less enthusiastic than others, were exchanged between one group and the other. There seemed some confusion among the Langford party. Several of their military escort appeared to suggest crossing, but Miss Emma and Miss Sophie, with a vague turn of their heads, quickly continued on their way down their side of the street, the officers following, albeit reluctantly. Pavement or not, the street was not to be crossed by either party. While this silent exchange transpired, Mr. Work was conversing with Mr. Anderson, a retired officer of the company, and standing a little apart from his family. Margaret was glad he had not seen it.

Mr. Work began to walk down the street with Mr. Anderson in the same direction, his children behind him. To Margaret's growing discomfort, the two parties of ladies walked along either side of the street as if it were an insurmountable gulf, each pretending the other did not exist. Not wanting to acknowledge the rift, Margaret did not look over at them, but felt keenly watched regardless. To her relief, her father turned the corner at the first intersection.

"If only Papa would send us to Miss Phillips' school, instead of St. Ann's, we could better renew our acquaintance with the Langfords," sighed Kate, who, with Margaret, brought up the rear of their party. "We were much friendlier when we all went to the Staines' school."

Miss Phillips was a spinster sister of Mrs. Langford's, who ran a school adjacent to the family home, Colwood.

"They had no choice, then. What other company was there to be had? Anyway, why should you want a closer acquaintance with such upstarts?" asked Margaret, but she was already painfully aware of the answer. It irked her that, whereas the Works had two male chaperons for their four young ladies, the Langfords had nearly two officers per sister.

Margaret had suspected that Lieutenant Wilson would fall into friendship with the Langfords. They were considered one of Victoria's most respectable English families, and after all, the Langfords' home was just on the other side of Esquimalt Harbour from Wilson's barracks; they were nearly neighbours. Langford had a reputation as a generous host, although at the company's expense since his employer provided everything, and many naval officers frequented Colwood. Indeed, that they chose to go anywhere else often surprised Margaret,

57

especially when she was feeling particularly low regarding her marriage prospects. At times she thought the only reason the English family did not completely dominate society was that Langford made no secret of the contempt in which he held both the governor and the Hudson's Bay Company, and the naval officers must feel their loyalties uneasily divided when Langford began one of his tirades against either.

As autumn passed, Margaret often noticed Wilson's absence from the social events she attended, and it was not much of an imaginative leap to place him at the cosy hearth of Colwood, surrounded by the four young ladies who called it home. He was gone the last half of October to take provisions to the Boundary Commission camp up the Fraser, and when he returned the Works saw little of him. On his free Saturday afternoons, weather permitting, he seemed to prefer duck shooting to their last riding parties of the season; whether this was due to the horses or the company, Margaret could only surmise.

On those occasions when Margaret did see Lieutenant Wilson, later in the fall, she decided it was not in her best interests to shun his society. Being very agreeable, he had made himself popular about the town. Margaret suspected Kate might be forming an attachment to him, but since she saw no particular evidence of his returning it, and since Kate was in the habit of forming short-lived attachments, Margaret saw no need of apprising her of Wilson's true opinion of them.

Chapter Seven

January 1st. Was one of the wettest days we have
had, but as it is the custom here to pay all your
friends a visit on that day . . . off I went for a holiday. The first place, of course, was the Governor's
& after wishing them all there a 'Happy New
Year' went to visit the country round & finally
halted at 'Hillside,' where Mr. Work lives. I got
there about 5 & at 6 we had a large dinner party,
no stiffness or formality & we wound up with
a 'hain' dance (as an Indian would say) which
means no end of jollification. This closed just as
Sunday appeared & finished one of the pleasantest days I have spent here.
—Lieutenant Charles William Wilson, RE

The outpouring of miners through Victoria, produced by the
cold weather in the interior, slowed to a steady stream and
then a trickle. With the grey November skies came the gloomy apprehension among the residents that the miners were leaving permanently.
Some of the merchants packed up their goods and followed them back
to the warmer clime of San Francisco, and those colonists who had
invested heavily in town lots began morosely predicting a collapse. But
the Works were beyond such mercurial changes. A fortune begun in
the fur trade had been crowned by the gold rush; land had suddenly
become valuable, and the farm's harvests were in high demand. They

had the security of knowing that the rest of their days would be spent comfortably, even luxuriously, by colony standards. The miners' departure affected their spirits more than their pocketbooks, and they could spare some concern as to how the miners who remained up the Fraser for the winter, principally Canadians and Europeans, could possibly survive the harsh conditions.

The distant British government, as yet unaware of the exodus from the goldfields, had reacted to the gold rush by creating a new colony on the mainland. On the 19th of November, 1858, the vast land the locals had known as New Caledonia became the Colony of British Columbia. Margaret preferred the former name, having grown up with it in Fort Simpson, but since Queen Victoria herself had chosen the new one, it was not to be questioned.

Governor Douglas went to New Westminster to preside over the ceremonies for proclaiming the new colony, for which he was also to wear the hat of governor. The residents of the Colony of Vancouver Island, though glad of support in guarding against American encroachment, paid tribute at home mostly by commenting rather gleefully on the poor weather for the ceremony; it rained steadily all day. The birth of the new colony also gave birth to jealous rancour between the sister colonies. Donning his new responsibilities, Governor Douglas relinquished his position as head of the Hudson's Bay Company's Western Department. Three hats, it seemed, were too many, even for Mr. Douglas. The remaining Board of Managers, including Mr. Work, received the joint promotion of governing the Western Department. And so the flow of gold wound its indirect route, through position and stature even more than money, to Hillside.

By December, Margaret had given up dwelling on the miners' mass departure. Their loss held the silver lining of making the town much safer for the winter festivities. Those locals who persisted in claiming that British Columbia was a bubble that would soon burst she left to commiserate with each other. How much easier to lose oneself in the familiar round of social events that December brought! Who could resist the fir and cedar boughs trimming all the homes and business establishments in town, where the sidewalks became a perfect wall of green? Dire predictions had no place in the seasonal magic. It was unthinkable to consider, among all the Christmas cheer, that Victoria could possibly recede to the quiet backwater it had been. A bright new year beckoned on the horizon. A town had remained after the miners' withdrawal, and a town, she convinced herself, would remain.

Most of the naval ships were in Esquimalt Harbour, their out-door work done for the winter; when HMS *Plumper* returned from Nanaimo, where it had been beached for repairs to the hull, a small fleet rigged out in flags and evergreens welcomed it into the harbour. Her Majesty's officers, eager for the season's festivities, complemented the holiday mood. Balls, parties and private theatricals occupied much of the Work daughters' time and all of the younger ones' thoughts.

The culmination of the December celebrations was, in the Scottish tradition of Governor Douglas, New Year's Day. As did most of the principal families of the town, the Works held an open house, and had visitors dropping by all through the afternoon and into the evening. Dr. Tuzo was one of the first, but Margaret barely had time to observe him with Mary before many other well-wishers arrived. By mid-afternoon Margaret's usual reserve had quite worn off, from a mixture of punch and continual society, and she felt almost as carefree as any of her younger sisters. Good cheer resonated through the homestead, from her father, basking in the glow of both the fireside and the conversation with guests around it, to the youngest children, playing on the chequered Tsimshian Indian rug at their feet.

More than any previous Hogmanay holiday, the spirit of abundance seemed an almost tangible presence at the party, like an extra guest presiding over the gathering with silent generosity. Every year, the children had gifts from London, but this year the older ones had received, as a special present from Mr. Work at Christmas, a gold watch each. To think he had been saving them for nearly a full year since the last shipment of goods from London! As Margaret moved about the drawing-room, endeavouring to keep the glasses of the guests filled, she could not help but admire the way her watch glinted in the firelight.

About five o'clock Margaret was seeing two guests out when another arrived—Lieutenant Wilson. Margaret welcomed him in from the damp cold and wished him all the best of the day quite sincerely, reminding herself that it was not an evening for resentment or retaliation. In the fresh light of a new year, she could attribute his earlier careless remarks to his newness in the colony. He had since weathered enough colonial deprivations to gain a little appreciation for the residents. Margaret graciously extended her hand in friendship, and when he held it in his own, she took a small step forward and politely offered her cheek for a New Year's kiss.

His raised brow and good-humoured smile revealed momentary surprise but he gallantly leaned forward and kissed her anyway. Enveloped in the aroma of cigar smoke and rain, and so close to the merry twinkle in his eyes, Margaret felt her cheeks warming at his amusement in spite of herself. She had forgotten that this custom was not universal; she had seen other newcomers' startled expressions on previous Hogmanays. Most, however, had adopted the tradition readily enough. A French-Canadian custom, some said, as if this excused it. She remembered the first New Year's visit to the Governor's house by the Langfords. One of the Miss Langfords, elegant in the latest London fashions, had giggled with complicity to a naval officer, "We must do as the natives do!"

Not wishing to put to the test her store of good will toward him, Margaret seated Wilson by her father in a chair that one of the other guests had just vacated, and left him and her embarrassment behind. There he remained, engaged in conversation with Mr. Work and a few others, until Mrs. Work announced supper an hour later. Margaret watched from the other side of the room as he was earnestly pressed to stay for the meal by Mr. Work, in a way he could not refuse; indeed, his acceptance bore no trace of reluctance.

Neither did it go unnoticed by Margaret how Wilson's eyes lit up when he was ushered into the food-laden dining room. All types of fish, fowl, meat and pastry were displayed, among the farm's fall harvest, on the long, candlelit table. He sat down eagerly.

Margaret's pride in the family's hospitality was short-lived, however, because Mary, much to her sister's dismay, had placed Wilson near Mrs. Work's end of the table. He sat close enough to ensure conversation with her mother. To make matters worse, after seating some other guests at Mr. Work's end, where she had hoped to place Wilson, Margaret found the only seat left her was directly opposite the young lieutenant. If Wilson were to display disapproval of her family, it seemed she could not escape seeing it.

Throughout the meal, Margaret watched him covertly, especially for his reactions to her mother, for if Wilson could think Margaret and her sisters savages, what would he make of their mother, who had no formal education whatsoever? Mrs. Work did not contribute much to the general conversation, but when the topic arose of Jane, her eldest daughter, returning to Victoria with her family, Wilson inquired politely of Mrs. Work how long she had been gone. Margaret nearly held her breath as her mother replied, fearing any sign of superiority on Wilson's side, and feeling ashamed of herself for caring about what he might think.

"Nine years now since our Jane married and went to Fort Nisqually with Dr. Tolmie," her mother said. After a short pause she continued, "We are blessed she went no farther, but my prayers will be answered when she settles in Victoria."

Mrs. Work's thick accent, a mixture of French and Indian, fell heavily on her daughter's ears, but Wilson did not betray any notice of it. Margaret had not finished expelling her breath of relief when her mother continued to speak.

"But I must not complain of having a daughter across the strait, when you are so very far from home. Your family must miss you greatly."

She spoke simply, but with such warmth and sympathy that Margaret thought Wilson's eyes moistened as he thanked her for the sentiment, his voice a shade lower. Perhaps Mrs. Work noticed this as well, for she directed several dishes toward him for second servings. He refilled his plate with relish, prompting Cecilia to ask him, with a sly smile, if the Royal Engineers were never fed?

"Only hard tack biscuits and salt beef," he laughed, encouraging Cecilia to tease him some more. He bantered back with his delighted young friend, the others joined in, and he quickly seemed one of the family. He told some comical stories of his adventures since coming to the colony, and David soon looked up to him as quite an idol. Even John grudgingly allowed him a little admiration.

Another visitor arrived in the middle of supper; his apologies for intruding during the meal were quickly waved away, another chair was found and a place made for him at the table. As he sat down, he said to Wilson, "One can always count on being made to feel right at home at Hillside!" From his expression, Margaret thought Wilson was very much in agreement.

The dinner finished with plum pudding and oranges from the Sandwich Islands, a rare treat. After the meal, Wilson gave Mrs. Work his unreserved compliments and pronounced the supper sumptuous. Margaret wondered if he thought she had done it herself. The Works had a French-Canadian cook, an *engagé* of the company; as a chief factor, Mr. Work was entitled to keep a cook and a steward. They were fortunate in this, since servants were difficult to hire and keep in the colony; the too-few single women who came from Britain were usually married soon after their arrival, evidently preferring domestic servitude in their own homes to someone else's. At Hillside the ladies rarely went into the kitchen, though occasionally the younger girls entertained themselves with baking under the watchful eye of Cantal, the cook.

As they left the table Lieutenant Wilson issued his crowning compliment, "I have not had such a regular good old English supper since leaving home!"

Margaret smiled inwardly. This was praise indeed, although with a hidden sting to her father's Irish ears, but she could not miss the irony in light of his earlier comments branding them as savages. She longed to ask, *And why should it be anything else, in an English colony?*

The evening wound up with dancing; old Mr. Tod, a retired chief trader, was prevailed upon to bring out his fiddle and indulge them with a Scottish reel. The large Tsimshian rug before the hearth was rolled up, and soon stomping feet and whirling skirts filled the room, keeping time with Mr. Tod's shock of white hair bobbing up and down. He habitually took off one shoe when he played, as if his stockinged foot, unfettered by its shoe, caught the rhythm from the dancers themselves through the reverberating floorboards. At first his foot merely tapped out the rhythm, but as he warmed up the music travelled along his thin, bandy leg until it seemed to do a disembodied dance all its own. When Margaret had first seen him play, many years ago, she had feared he was in constant danger of fiddling himself right off his chair. However, he never had, and no one paid much notice now.

Hillside was one of the largest homes in the colony, but even it was not spacious enough for the merrymaking; collisions were frequent, and the party often dissolved into hilarity. Margaret thought, whenever they laughed uproariously over a heap of dancers collapsed on the floor, that they must surely be passing the point of decorum, and involuntarily glanced at Wilson for confirmation of her suspicions. Yet he seemed repeatedly to be among the offending parties and she heard him exclaim, once to herself, and twice to others, "What jolly good fun!" She finally relaxed, and the dancing went on past midnight.

"This was one of the pleasantest days I have spent here, sir," Wilson said to Mr. Work, shaking his hand vigorously as he took his leave.

"Come again, come again. You're always welcome," returned Mr. Work warmly, grasping Wilson's hand in both of his own, his Irish brogue amplified by the liquor he had consumed.

But Wilson seemed not to notice the thick accent and beamed back at him, and then at Margaret, who was standing next to her father. Margaret, a blush diffusing across her cheeks, would almost have doubted she had received such a look, if Mary, who was standing on her other side, had not nudged her.

John and David fetched the horses from the barn, the farmhands being either drunk with their New Year's libations of rum or asleep. The departing military officers lit their pipes and cigars, to ward off the chill on the long ride back to Esquimalt Harbour. Wilson and the others, clad in waterproof cloaks down to their heels, mounted their horses and began to ride off into a drizzle of rain. Wilson's mount was not one of the better ones, being small with spindly legs, and he looked quite a sight. There was much joking and calling out after the guests to "mind the mud!" and "don't lose your way!" prompting Wilson, who brought up the rear, to look back and laughingly retort, "What! On such a gallant steed as this?"

The laughter and voices of the riders lingered on after their forms were swallowed by the night, but Margaret remained in the open doorway with her father and John, who held the lantern, while the other family members drifted away inside. She knew the guests would still be able to see their hosts in the lit doorway, and several times she thought Wilson must have looked back, for she saw a pipe glowing intermittently in the darkness. She stayed there until Mrs. Work chided them to come in out of the damp. Mr. Work instructed John to leave the lantern burning in the front window, and Margaret, as she ascended the stairs, felt glad to know its light would be seen by their last departing guest.

———·———

The next day, being Sunday, gave the Work daughters an opportunity to compare their New Year's celebrations with their friends. In the mingling outside the church after the morning service, Margaret was accosted by Agnes Douglas, who insisted that they come to tea. Although pleased by the invitation, Margaret regretted the timing of it, as she had just seen Dr. Tuzo approach her father and she completely missed what transpired between the two men. She did catch Mary covertly watching the gentlemen's brief conversation.

At the Douglas home in James Bay the young ladies were soon closeted together in a tightly knit group, and while relating the previous day's festivities Kate lost no time in offering up Lieutenant Wilson as her pièce de résistance.

"Oh yes, he came here too," said Agnes offhandedly. "Ours was the first place he visited."

"He had supper with us, and stayed on till past midnight," countered Kate.

"We had a very interesting visitor in the evening, a Mr. Bushby. Have you met him?"

"Hmm," said Kate in such a way that Margaret knew she was feigning forgetfulness.

Margaret replied that they had not.

"You can't have missed him at church," said Alice. "He was in the organ loft, singing with Mr. Begbie."

"Yes, he's very musical," continued Agnes. "Do you know, Miss Pemberton invited him to tea after service today—as did I—but he had a prior engagement."

Miss Susan Pemberton, the sister of the Colonial Surveyor, had the advantage of musical training in England, which few ladies in the colony could boast of. But Bushby's musical skill interested Margaret less than whether or not Agnes would still have invited the Works for tea if Bushby had accepted her invitation.

Mary agreed that they had seen the young gentleman in church.

"He sang 'Goodbye, Sweetheart' to us last evening—what a fine voice he has!" Agnes then began to relate the particulars of the card game she had played with Bushby. Her enthusiasm for her topic made Margaret relieved that John was not near enough to hear her, as he was conversing with the men grouped around the wood stove. Her raptures were not in keeping with any mutual understanding of their future together.

"And what does Mr. Bushby do, besides sing and play cards?" interrupted Kate.

"Oh, he came here on spec, as he says. He is looking for a suitable position, an opportunity—I'm sure he will secure something. Papa says there are plenty of opportunities for young men with suitable backgrounds."

Kate finally succeeded in turning the conversation back to Lieutenant Wilson, and Margaret, not wishing to betray her interest in the subject, left the younger girls to join Mrs. Helmcken where she sat with the children. Of the Douglas daughters, Cecilia Helmcken was closest in age to Margaret, and when the Works had arrived in Victoria they had been very close friends. However, Cecilia had married the fort's doctor when she was only 17, and since then, she had grown closer to Margaret's sister Sarah. The hurt for Margaret, at the time very keen, had subsequently subsided; she understood that the common cares of domestic life and children had naturally drawn them together, and when she saw Cecilia now, all that remained of her dismay was the knowledge of how different their lives were.

Margaret and Mary, who had joined them, dutifully admired the Helmckens' children, the youngest of who, James Douglas Helmcken, sat on Cecilia's lap. Margaret had thought the Helmckens exceedingly silly in choosing this name for the infant, as the Governor and Mrs. Douglas already had a son James, and although the latter was uncle to the infant James, the two were close enough in age to grow up as cousins. Whenever one referred to "young James," therefore, his identity must be clarified. Senior and junior were no good for this purpose, as the senior proper was of course the governor himself. The little boy sat happily, unaware of the confusion he produced. Margaret's own sister, Jane Tolmie, had similarly named one of her children John Work Tolmie, but their brother John was sometimes referred to as Jack, and Margaret found it more convenient to find ridicule in someone else's family. Margaret and Mary lent sympathetic ears to Cecilia, who confided how her tiredness was growing.

"Dr. Helmcken has been so much busier since the gold rush, and his duties as the Speaker of the House are never-ending. At times it seems I hardly see him. I have sorely missed Jane and Cecilia's help since their marriages. It was very difficult to lose both my sister and my cousin in the same month," she sighed, her eyes drifting as she played idly with her son's small hand.

Margaret winced, remembering the unspoken loss behind Cecilia's faraway gaze. Last March, just two days after Jane's wedding,

Cecilia's daughter Daisy had died of croup at 18 months of age. If Margaret had been galled by Jane Douglas marrying while Daisy lay seriously ill, her indignation was nothing to what she felt when the Douglas' cousin, Miss Cecilia Cameron, had gone ahead with her wedding to Mr. Young only a week after Daisy's death. Cecilia Helmcken was still clad in her black mourning clothes.

"Of course," she said, blinking back tears, "they have their own houses to run and their own worries now, with both expecting babies, and I'm very happy to see them married well, and I still have Agnes and Alice to help."

Eyeing the younger girls gossiping, Margaret doubted whether the latter two were much consolation for the loss of an older sister and a cousin who were more sensible, however unfeeling. Cecilia Helmcken was a gentle creature and bore no malice, which only increased Margaret's resentful feelings against her friend's sister and cousin. The Work sisters both promised to help whenever their other duties permitted, and were relieved to see Cecilia's face brighten a little.

Margaret and Mary came away from the Douglas home subdued. The younger children rode in the cart with Mr. and Mrs. Work, the older ones following on foot. While John, who had found little chance for speaking to Agnes alone, attempted to extract from Kate the subjects of the girls' conversation, Margaret mentioned to Mary that she had seen Dr. Tuzo speaking with their father after the church service.

"So did I, but I didn't hear what was said. It's a heavy burden Cecilia bears."

"Yes," replied Margaret, wishing Mary had not changed the topic.

"She looks old, much older than you, and so weary and careworn—"

Before Margaret could reply, Kate joined them, evidently tired of evading John's questions, and turned the topic back to the previous evening's festivities.

They had been back at Hillside but an hour when the doctor paid a visit. Margaret, sorting washing with Suzette in the latter's room, learned of his arrival as Kate rushed by the door, poking her head briefly into the doorway to whisper loudly, "Dr. Tuzo is here!"

Margaret heard Kate descend the stairs, then return and call for Mary. Mary did not look at Margaret as she passed Suzette's doorway. Margaret had almost daily anticipated an announcement of Mary's engagement, and her only hope now was that she had made some impression on her sister when she had endeavoured to persuade her that 21 was "not so very old" and that, if she had any doubts, she had better wait. Nevertheless, she had resigned herself to the inevitable, and was quite composed when Mary returned to give her the news only a quarter of an hour later. She sent a reluctant Suzette downstairs with her washing.

What Margaret was not prepared for was the proposal's outcome: Mary had refused him.

"It was not an outright refusal. I told him that I needed more time, that I was unprepared, because it had all happened so quickly," she said lamely.

"I think you made the right decision," said Margaret quickly, as Mary stared pensively out the window at the January rain. "After all, if you decide later to accept him, what is lost but a little time?"

For the next month, Dr. Tuzo's own behaviour reinforced Margaret's argument. His attentiveness toward Mary did not diminish with her refusal; if anything, his regard increased. Margaret was relieved. Dr. Tuzo would be patient and, if Mary felt sure of him, she would have him in the end. In addition to Margaret's own satisfaction, she was pleased to note that her sister was not entirely unhappy. Mary also had some relief from struggling with the decision; she had put the question to rest, at least temporarily.

Chapter Eight

S'dy 30 Ja[nuar]y 59
. . . had a long talk with Dr. Tuzo who made me
his confidant—love affair (Mary Work a rum
'un . . .)
Wednesday 16th [February]
Last night I went to the Assembly Ball by invitation & what fun we had—most of the naval
officers were there en grande tenue—it was naturally a rather free and easy affair—for myself I was
half screwed & figged out in white tie &c I flatter myself I kept pace with the uniforms . . . You
can have no fun here at parties unless you are half
screwed.
—Arthur Thomas Bushby

*M*argaret took advantage of the winter lull in the town's
activity by paying her promised visits to Cecilia Helmcken.
On a Sunday afternoon in late January, when she and John were
returning home after one of these visits, they passed Mr. Bushby
strolling with Dr. Tuzo down Wharf Street. She already knew they
were acquainted, having been told by Lieutenant Wilson that they,
along with himself, had dined aboard the *Satellite*, but their intimacy
surprised her. Their heads drawn close together in deep discussion,
they did not see her until they were almost directly across the road
from her. Their conversation then ended abruptly; Dr. Tuzo looked

decidedly sullen. She nodded, John scowled at seeing Bushby, the other two touched their hats and both parties continued on their way; no attempt was made to cross the street, rendered a bog by the winter rains. Margaret immediately attributed Tuzo's expression to embarrassment over his delayed marital suit to her sister, and dismissed his countenance from her mind.

The next evening, after supper, Mr. Work asked Mary to join him in the library. Something in his tone caught Margaret's attention, and while her eyes unseeingly skimmed Dickens' *The Pickwick Papers* in the drawing-room, she listened for Mary to come out. She heard the door open and close, and then Mary's light footfall on the stairs. After blindly turning over another page, Margaret followed.

Mary was standing at her bedroom window; she looked over her shoulder when Margaret entered the room. Her calm face belied the flicker of panic in her eyes. "Dr. Tuzo is going to Canada on furlough."

Hudson's Bay Company officers were entitled to one year's furlough for every seven of service, but the timing of this request disquieted Margaret.

"When I saw him on Sunday he mentioned a furlough, but as a future possibility, and I was so calm I offered no inducement for him to stay. Oh Margaret, I actually told him I would be happy for the opportunity for him and he looked vexed, but still I did not try to dissuade him. I thought perhaps he was trying to provoke me and I refused to take the bait. I cannot now change my answer to his proposal after a mere month. It would be too fickle."

Margaret had to stem the increasing alarm in Mary's eyes. "Did Papa say it would be a full year?"

"No. He said he was taking a furlough to see his family."

"It may not be a whole year, then. If he were going to England, then certainly he would go for a year, but to Canada—six months would surely suffice. I'm certain he would not be parted from you for a year," she said encouragingly.

It took considerably more effort to alleviate Mary's dismay, but later, in her own room, Margaret lost some of her confidence. Was Dr. Tuzo's pride so deeply hurt that he was retreating to Quebec, the place of his birth and family home, to lick his wounds? Or did he hope his absence would make Mary realize her feelings for him? The now vividly remembered look on Tuzo's face when she had seen him with Bushby reproached her, and she wondered if Tuzo had confided his dilemma, and whether Bushby had even advised the furlough.

Two weeks later Tuzo departed for the east, and Mary's own questions regarding the gentleman's feelings remained unanswered; indeed, she felt she had no right to ask them, considering her deferral of his marriage proposal.

An Assembly Ball soon after his departure gave Margaret an excuse to try to cheer Mary up; her spirits were low, and Margaret hoped a little society would distract her. They all had new gowns, as the company's barque, the *Princess Royal*, had arrived earlier that month with goods from London. But even the prospect of wearing a new silk was inadequate to lift Mary's mood. It was all Margaret could do to persuade her sister to go.

The moment the Work sisters entered the Assembly Rooms, on the upper story of a building on Broad Street, they were set upon by gentlemen vying to get places on their dance cards. Many naval officers were present; the *Plumper* had recently returned from the Fraser, where it had been sent to assist with an uprising of gold miners at Yale.

The situation had been diffused by the diplomacy of Colonel Moody, head of the Royal Engineers at New Westminster. The ringleader, Ned McGowan, an infamous Californian criminal, got off with a fine, but the *Plumper* was much praised for her pluckiness in getting farther up the river than most of the experienced steamers did, and her officers shone in the light of their recent adventure. Everyone was full of talk of "Ned McGowan's War," as the incident was quickly dubbed. Lieutenant Mayne received his share of the glory, as he had had the pivotal role of messenger between the *Plumper* and Colonel Moody.

New faces filled the Assembly Rooms and Margaret took delight in the increasing expansion of their circle. Six months earlier, she could go to a ball and be nearly certain that she would meet only familiar faces. Now, it was almost a relief not to depend on the naval officers, much as she admired them, for society. She even ventured to grant places on her dance card to three gentlemen she barely knew.

Lieutenant Wilson had secured two dances each from Mary, Kate and Margaret, who was pleased to overhear during one of his dances with Mary, that "the Works are favourites with that redcoat—an engineer, he is, with the Boundary Commission." This proclamation came from a gentleman of no personal acquaintance to her, and to have the family recognized by a stranger gave her almost as much consequence as being named a favourite of Wilson's. The scarcity of women in the colony had emphasized the circulation of the family name in society's growing upper ranks.

The Douglas girls were not there; their sister, Jane Dallas, was expecting a baby any day and had claimed her younger sisters as companions during her confinement. Their friend Mr. Bushby was, however, dashingly present in white tie and tails, and although the officers bore most of the honours with the ladies, he managed to rarely sit out a dance. He created something of a stir during one galop late in the evening as he and Kate raced the length of the room against Sub-Lieutenant Pender, one of the *Plumper* officers, and his partner. They slid to a halt at one end of the room, only to continue the sport in the opposite direction, each stretch punctuated by squeals of laughter from the ladies. Bushby held Kate very tightly and did not immediately let go when the dance ended. Margaret headed toward them in hopes of extricating her sister from the clasp of someone she was beginning to think a very immoderate man, but Bushby released Kate when Margaret reached them.

He requested an introduction from Kate and, having got it, a place on Margaret's dance card, in which she could not oblige him. She was thankful that it was full.

"I'm afraid I have not made the acquaintance of many of Victoria's young ladies. And now," he said, consulting his own card, "if you'll excuse me, I must search out my next partner."

Margaret heard him mutter "Miss blue dress" as he wandered away. Kate leaned close and whispered with mock outrage, "He's drunk!"

Margaret stared after him. It was not the first time such an accusation had reached her ears. Only a week earlier, after a boisterous bachelors' evening of singing and laughing, Bushby and his roommate had been summoned to court by their landlord, a lawyer known for his temper, for indecent and riotous conduct, and Bushby in particular for being drunk. But Victoria had rallied to the side of the young men: the whole Bar appeared for the defendants, and the courthouse was filled with naval officers in full uniform acting as witnesses, several having taken part in the soirée. Against such support, the landlord lost heart and did not appear, and the summons was dismissed. That day the governor appointed Bushby as private secretary to Judge Begbie, Chief Justice of British Columbia.

Margaret had wondered much over this event, and where the truth lay, but of one fact she could be sure: respectable gentlemen did not get drunk. There seemed little doubt that Bushby enjoyed his liquor, and it was only a week after the Assembly Ball that Margaret and her sisters were subjected to another instance of this.

Though the winter season was winding to a close, invitations continued to flow in to Hillside. In previous years the social whirl had slowed when Her Majesty's ships resumed their outdoor work, but with Victoria's population burgeoning, their loss was less keenly felt.

Mr. Work went through the invitations carefully with Margaret. Those from new acquaintances were considered with the utmost care, and he generally had no objection to new members of the colonial government. The ranks of Victoria's civil service had swelled along with its population, and this growing segment of society was becoming more prominent in the town's upper circles.

One invitation came from Mr. Angelo, a clerk in the Customs House. Mr. Anderson, the Collector of Customs and an old associate of Mr. Work's, had introduced him to the family. An Englishman, Mr. Angelo had recently come to Victoria from the Orient and, like many of the English newcomers, had readily gained employment with the colonial administration. Margaret was gratified that she and her sisters should get an invitation from Mr. Angelo so soon after his appointment.

Margaret's feeling that this was a socially opportune dinner to attend was confirmed by the presence of the Langford daughters, accompanied by two naval officers. The officers were not favourites of Margaret's, so they could incite no jealousy in her; her only disappointment was that Lieutenant Wilson had been unable to accompany *her* party, as he had accepted an invitation to dine elsewhere that evening. Since John had not received an invitation, Mr. Finlayson escorted his sisters-in-law to Mr. Angelo's, and then departed to an engagement of his own. While Mr. Finlayson was an important person in Victoria, he did not have quite the dashing charm of a military officer. Margaret was chagrined by the exchange of coldly superior smiles between Miss Emma and Miss Sophie Langford when they saw the Work sisters enter the drawing-room alone.

Mr. Angelo had the knack of putting everyone at ease; the laughter through supper flowed as freely as the wine. The Misses Langford were seated at the opposite end of the table, leaving Margaret to bask without constraint in the conversation at her end. If the ice broke while they were dining, it had quite melted away, at least for the gentlemen, by the time they finished their port and cigars. The ladies did not thaw so rapidly to each other, but the gentlemen did not leave them unattended for long. Once they were reunited, singing and dancing were the order of the evening.

Among the party was Mr. Bushby. The Douglas girls were still unavailable, as Mrs. Dallas had just given birth to a girl, and wanted them with her. Over the course of the evening Margaret began to understand Agnes' by-now-obvious attraction to Mr. Bushby. Like Lieutenant Wilson, he had a very engaging temperament, full of spirit and enthusiasm. Both men plunged wholeheartedly into whatever circumstances presented themselves at the moment, an attribute ideally suited to Wilson's military career and, Margaret supposed, to a young adventurer who had travelled thousands of miles to a little-known colony "on spec."

She felt badly for her brother, despite his continual teasing of her. How could John compete with such a man? But she hoped Agnes' preference for Bushby might be just the dressing-down John needed, and might prompt some effort on his part, as she by no means considered him defeated; after all, Bushby would have to return Agnes' affection at least equally, if anything were to come of it. Bushby's circumstances were still uncertain, since he had only just secured a position. Socially, on the other hand, he had been welcomed with open arms by Victoria: he spent considerable time at the governor's home, he had fallen in with the naval officers, especially those from the *Satellite*, and was friends with many of the colonial officials. Lieutenant Wilson had met him and liked him; indeed, Margaret knew of no one who did not, excepting, of course, John. His musical talent, being hard to come by in the colony, was much sought after; before he had spent two months in the colony he was made honorary secretary to the newly formed Victoria Philharmonic Society.

Mr. Finlayson dropped by shortly after ten o'clock, producing a general outcry among the men.

"If your sisters-in-law leave now, sir, you will be taking away nearly half the ladies of our party! Join us for an hour!"

But Mr. Finlayson could not be induced to stay.

"Hillside is not far, sir! We shall see your sisters safely home."

"Count on it," said another.

"Absolutely," chimed in a third, with nodding assent from a fourth. "Surely they will be as safe with four of us, sir, as one of you."

Mr. Finlayson hesitated; he could not argue with the logic of numbers.

"I shall join these worthy men myself, if it would make you feel easier," declared Mr. Angelo.

Reassured, Mr. Finlayson continued on his way. This reprieve was just what Kate had hoped for and she threw herself into dancing with renewed vigour. But Mary seemed to be tiring, and Margaret began to regret not having sent her home with Mr. Finlayson. For herself she was quite happy to stay; a more intimate party was as much to her liking as the large ball at the Assembly Rooms.

After a few more dances, Margaret noticed Mr. Bushby speaking earnestly to Mary, and she was drawn closer by Mary's uncomfortable expression.

"We can't have you looking so morose," she heard Bushby exclaim to Mary, offering her some wine. "Something must be done to cheer you up."

"No, no, I'm only a little tired," was Mary's reply.

Mr. Bushby succeeded in getting Mary up for two dances, but with no great enthusiasm on her part. The hour was nearing 11, and since Margaret had overheard Mr. Bull, one of the Langfords' naval escorts, telling Miss Langford that they should leave at that hour, as he had promised Mr. Langford he would have them home for midnight, Margaret decided her party ought to leave themselves, rather than follow the Langfords out.

Margaret's announcement of their departure disappointed Kate in the extreme, but the fuss she made was not equal to Mr. Bushby's.

"Leaving so soon!" he cried, his face flushed with drink, as they were struggling into their oilskin overcoats and India rubber boots. "Well, well, we will have to send you off in style!"

And with that he broke into the song "Goodbye Sweetheart, Goodbye," boisterously accompanied at each chorus by some of the other young gentlemen. He did indeed have a beautiful voice, to be matched by no other tenor in the colony, and he put much feeling into it. He serenaded each of the Work sisters in turn, as he helped them on with their macintoshes. Margaret and Mary smiled self-consciously, but Kate laughed and played up her part of the sweetheart for all it was worth. Mr. Bushby was standing by Kate when the last note died on his lips and he capped the performance by leaning over and planting a kiss firmly on her mouth, to the cheers of his chorus and the giggles of Kate.

"We must not play favourites," laughed Mr. Bushby, and quickly bestowed the same token on Margaret and Mary. Before Margaret could collect herself, a couple of Bushby's chorus had rushed in and another had given her a clumsy kiss.

"Enough!" she cried laughingly, but it was an uneasy laugh; she was flustered and only wanted to escape. She pulled Kate away from another young man and pushed her toward the door, at the same time linking her other arm with Mary, who was quite speechless. Mr. Bushby broke into an encore as they descended the slippery porch steps. The number of promised chaperons dwindled suddenly when faced with the task at hand and only two of the gentlemen dutifully, but reluctantly, followed them out into the drizzling cold.

Mr. Angelo, who had apparently kept pace with his more indulgent guests as regards drink, called a few half-formed apologies from the door as they hurried away—he could not leave the rest of his guests, etc, etc. Margaret could hear muffled laughter from inside.

The shock of cold air intensified her perceptions, and Margaret left Mr. Angelo's party with the Rules of Etiquette from *The Ladies Handbook* ringing in her head. Surely they had violated, with Mr. Bushby's help, every rule that the authorities expounded. Such kissing! And it was not even Christmas or New Year's Day. Yet the gentlemen seemed to show no awareness of having erred. The only sign of reproof was in the icy glare of the Langford sisters, the parting shot as the Works left Mr. Angelo's otherwise-warm house.

The harsh shock of reality also revealed their escorts in another light. Perhaps it was the extra brandy they had consumed in haste to ward off the chill, but Margaret began to seriously doubt the men's ability to see them home. They wove along the sidewalk, singing as they went. When they got to the first intersection, where a single plank, stretching across the bog from corner to corner, was the sole means of human passage, the first took a few tentative steps and slipped into the mud. The second, in trying to fish him out, soon followed.

The two men tried to assist each other back onto the boardwalk, but they were so unsteady that they floundered for some minutes. In the course of their struggles their lantern was extinguished and the party was left in the dim light from neighbouring houses.

"What shall we do?" whispered Mary to Margaret, eyeing them

uncertainly. "They'll never make it across that plank, let alone all the way to Hillside."

"We can't go back to Mr. Angelo's. I couldn't possibly go back."

"Nor could I."

The gentlemen, having finally succeeded in hauling themselves out, stood before them, slick with mud and leaning heavily on each other.

"At your service," beamed one foolishly.

"Which way?" asked the other.

"You'll have to go back," said Margaret firmly. "You're sopping wet. You'll both catch your death."

"Oh, no! We couldn't possibly allow—"

A few houses down another party broke up for the evening. The light spilling from the open doorway shone on the guests as they departed down the shadowy street.

"Ah, a solution to our predicament," said one of the Works' escorts, as he lurched toward the other party, one arm held high. "One moment, please!"

"Oh, dear," said Mary.

Margaret glanced furtively in his direction; she could see people peering into the darkness, trying to make out their identities in the gloom. She turned her back to them, but knew full well this would be but a temporary postponement of their embarrassing discovery. She heard the hollow thud of someone approaching down the boardwalk.

"We've had a slight difficulty—," said the companion who had stepped forward.

"So I see," said a familiar voice cheerfully, the footsteps stopping.

"Why, it's Charles Wilson!" whispered Kate brightly.

Margaret turned to look. Their escort had put a hand on the young officer's shoulder and, leaning forward, mumbled something in his face.

"All right, man!" said Wilson, his tone altered, as he freed himself from the other man.

Out of the shadows Lieutenant Wilson approached, his staccato heels clipping evenly down the boardwalk, followed by their wavering escort. Wilson drew up short and stared at them.

"Miss Work," he said, nodding at Margaret, then to her sisters. "Miss Mary, Miss Kate."

He could not disguise his amazement. Margaret and Mary nodded back; only Kate was capable of replying.

"They've fallen in," she said, nodding toward their escorts. "We were on our way home."

"You must allow me to accompany you," he said to Margaret.

For the first time in many weeks Margaret wished him nowhere near her. She felt the urgent need for an explanation, but none suggested itself.

"Jolly good fellow!" grinned their second escort. The brandy on his breath was detectable even over the odour of the mud plastering him. Wilson's only reply was a brief look of contempt.

"We'd be much obliged," said Margaret quietly, and turned toward the intersection's plank, where Wilson carefully handed her and then Mary down, then stepped down himself and turned back for Kate. Their would-be escorts watched this feat with fascination, offering a few words of encouragement.

"I'm very much surprised at Mr. Angelo," he said, when they had safely reached the other side and glanced back at the staggering silhouettes, "sending you home with two men in—such a condition."

"We left rather quickly—"

"Those redcoats know just what to do with a petticoat!" came from the retreating figures across the street.

"—and we did not realize the—er—extent of their condition—

until we were outside," continued Margaret, but she could not look at him. She was glad he could not see her blush.

"No, of course not."

The conversation was very limited as they began the journey home. Kate, much to Margaret's relief, showed some restraint and did not expand on the circumstances. Margaret managed a few observations on the weather and other niceties, and Mary hardly spoke at all.

They passed warily the large Tsimshian encampment on the edge of the Finlayson farm. The Tsimshians and other northern tribes had been attracted in growing numbers by reports of the gold rush, and because of the hostilities between the warring tribes, now living dangerously close to one another, there was much concern on the part of Victoria's residents; no one wanted to be caught in between. Governor Douglas had taken measures to prohibit the sale of liquor to the Indians, due to its aggravated effect on them, but they managed to acquire it from an avaricious profiteer anyway, and this evening was no exception, judging by the racket coming from several quarters of the camp.

"How does Mrs. Finlayson bear up, being so close?" asked Wilson.

"Oh, Sarah mostly worries for the children. They're apt to go off exploring, like any children would, but for herself, she's familiar with the northern tribes from our Fort Simpson days," replied Margaret, glad of the opportunity to converse, and on a subject unrelated to their evening's entertainment.

"I know Mr. Finlayson is very good with the Indians," said Wilson, "but your sister must be exceptionally steady to retain her equanimity in the face of 300 Tsimshians."

Margaret smiled faintly; it was very true. While Sarah was inclined to be shy of white arrivistes, she could rise admirably to the occasion of tolerating her new neighbours, although she would prefer fewer of them.

"Do you know, at Fort Simpson we were almost abducted by raid-
ing Haidas," said Kate.

"Really!" replied Wilson with interest.

"She exaggerates," smiled Margaret, but let her tell the tale anyway.

"We—my brothers and sisters and I—used to go fishing with some
of the men and their wives. There was a stream with salmon quite a distance from the fort. One day when we returned to the fort, some Haidas
came to tell my parents that they had been watching us from close by,
without our even knowing they were there! The Haidas were ones for
taking slaves, you know. After that Papa took even greater care with us.
I suppose we would have made quite a catch. Some of us, as children,
were quite fair-haired, like Suzette. 'God's children,' the Indians used to
call us."

"But they wouldn't have dared to take us. They had the utmost
respect for Father, and the company generally," added Margaret.

There was a short pause, broken by a haunting cry from the
Indian camp.

"Still, it must have given your parents quite a scare," said Wilson
thoughtfully, looking at the Tsimshians' campfires over his shoulder.

Ten more minutes and they were at Hillside, with Lieutenant
Wilson looking excessively glad to see them home.

Chapter Nine

Nothing particular has happened this week if I
except a dinner party at Angelo's where we all got
pretty well screwed and finished up the Evening
by kissing in a furious manner the Work daughters—pretty little girl one of them . . .
— Arthur Thomas Bushby

The next morning Margaret overheard an exchange between
Mary and Kate.

"It seems Agnes isn't the only one in Mr. Bushby's favour," the
younger began.

"Favour?" was Mary's stunned reply.

"He whispered in my ear that I was great fun. Larky like the devil,
he said, but far prettier! And he held me ever so tight at the Assembly
Room ball—"

"Don't you understand, we mean nothing to him, *nothing,* or he
would never have behaved in such a fashion! Do you think he would have
treated Agnes in that way? Certainly he did not with the Langfords."

The forceful edge in her voice, rare for Mary, caught Margaret's
attention.

"He couldn't very well while they were barricaded by naval officers!
You're getting as bad as Margaret! Never let me have any fun at all,"
grumbled Kate.

In the ensuing weeks, Margaret felt increasingly uneasy over Mr.
Angelo's dinner party and the manner in which they had quit it. What

had begun as a liberty on Bushby's part worked itself up into an insult. Margaret could see little fault of her own, except perhaps in not quitting the party with Mr. Finlayson when they had the opportunity to do so. She knew there would be those, especially among the newcomers, who would point to her Indian blood and suggest she had inherited the natives' licentious vices, and she wondered if this belief had contributed to the liberty Bushby had taken with herself and her sisters.

Whether or not to tell Agnes was a difficulty, for Margaret could well imagine her response, so firmly did she admire him: she might accuse them of encouraging him, or of trying to place John in a more favourable light. Kate had already settled against informing her friend.

"If her mind is set on him, which I think it might very well be, our friendship will only suffer for it. And if he turns out to be only a passing fancy, then there is no reason that she need ever know," she said decidedly to her older sister.

Margaret, knowing the girls well matched in stubbornness, left it at that.

Lieutenant Wilson continued to pay his visits, and if he had learned anything more of the circumstances surrounding their departure from Mr. Angelo's, he revealed not the slightest whisper of it. Margaret gradually began to feel more optimistic, although she avoided town, sticking to the safer country rounds instead.

One early March morning Mrs. Work, Margaret and Suzette set off on horseback for the Ross and McNeill farms, leaving Mary at Sarah's to help for the day. The government had lately taken measures to protect the residents of outlying areas by confiscating the muskets of the visiting northern Indians, but Mrs. Work, still wary, carried her horse pistol under her cloak and remained ever watchful. The rest of the children were at school, except John, who remained at Hillside, purportedly "keeping an eye on things" while Mr. Work attended to his duties at the fort.

The forest between Hillside and the town was being pushed back in both directions, but some areas were still heavily timbered, and the ladies were relieved to emerge into the more open meadows. On the outskirts of town, the fields dwindled to small parcels in the gardens of the outermost dwellings; even these disappeared in the heart of town, where the ramshackle buildings stood shoulder-to-clumsy-shoulder as if leaning on each other for support.

After passing the town, the muddy road turned eastward, bordering the Douglas farm, Fairfield. It was a beautiful spring day, the grass luxuriantly green from the frequent rains, the Easter and chocolate lilies showing themselves in the fields and the trees and shrubs budding. At the first fork, they took the south road, which dwindled to a trail in the Pemberton estate. By the time they reached the Ross farm it was little more than a path. Mrs. Ross' 100-acre farm, while small compared to Hillside's 600 acres, was beautifully situated overlooking a large bay. Isabella Ross was the widow of the late Chief Trader Charles Ross, who had supervised the building of Fort Victoria in 1844 for a few short months until his death. While the company had provided for the Ross family, theirs was by no means an easy existence; the Ross home, like all others in the colony, was not old, yet it belied its youth. Signs of want were everywhere, from the dilapidated state of the weather-beaten house with its leaning porch to the complete lack of improvements or ornamentation inside and out. Unlike Hillside, with its neat borders of shamrocks, joined later in the season by daisies edging the front path, the only flowers to grace the Ross home were wild ones in its overgrown front garden. The cultivated garden was limited to the vegetable plot in the back.

Inside, Margaret glanced uneasily at the virtually bare walls and floorboards, an ageing deerskin by the hearth being the sole covering. They followed Mrs. Ross into the kitchen, where she made tea. Mrs.

Work had brought jams and jellies and used articles of clothing, still in very good repair but out of fashion, to pass on to Mrs. Ross and her daughters. Margaret always felt uncomfortable about this, for Mrs. Ross was not of the labouring class, which most often received Mrs. Work's charity; she was their equal, at least she would have been had her husband lived. Their misfortune cast another shadow on Mr. Work's recurring bouts of the ague.

Although the clothing was given kindly and received with appreciation, Margaret was relieved when that part of the visit was over. The two mothers then settled into a chat, of which Mrs. Ross was evidently glad. She was from Lac La Pluie in Canada West, far removed from any of her own family; the move to the west coast had not been easy for her. She had struggled on her own to provide for her nine children, almost all of who, fortunately, were now grown and more independent. Mrs. Ross had very dark hair; her father was a Spaniard, her mother Ojibway. She seldom spoke of her mother's family, nor had Margaret ever heard her speak her own tongue. Her broken English was interspersed with French and Chinook, the local trading language. Unlike Mrs. Work, who had a full round face, Mrs. Ross' cheeks were hollow and her nearly black eyes stared out from deep sockets. Margaret watched the thin woman hold her teacup; her bony, sinewy hands reminded her of her mother's taxidermy birds, with their curled claws forever clutching their last perch.

Not wanting to stare, Margaret looked out the back window. One of Mrs. Ross' sons was there, gazing insolently back at her. The Ross boys were reputed to be wild and dissolute, often getting into trouble in the town's saloons. After a lingering look, the young man went away, but soon returned, stacking wood on the back porch. *How rude!* thought Margaret, *not even coming in to pay his respects to Mama!* Even in the cool spring air, Margaret could see he was sweating. *It's the drink,* she concluded.

Two of the daughters joined them and Margaret made conversation as best she could. The children of the two families had never been close. At the Staineses' school the Ross children, who had come from an isolated interior fort, were far behind in their education—Mr. Ross, apparently, having exerted himself very little for their scholastic benefit. Apart from school, they were needed to help on the farm, and socializing had been minimal.

Mrs. Work turned to the youngest Ross daughter, who was 17. "You'll be looking forward to the ball next week, Flora."

Flora hesitated.

"Everyone is going, Margaret tells me," continued Mrs. Work.

Margaret smiled awkwardly; she had not mentioned the upcoming ball, being given by the officers of the Boundary Commission, the *Plumper* and the *Satellite* combined.

"We have no hoop skirts, so we would be out of place," said Flora quietly, gazing at her lap where her fingers smoothed and re-smoothed the folds of her dress.

"But you shall not stay away for the sake of a hoop skirt! Margaret, we have enough, surely?"

"Of course," said Margaret quickly, though she was by no means certain they did; there were four eligible Ross daughters.

"I did not mean—you give us enough already—" stammered Flora.

"You can return them after the ball, if you like, but you must go," insisted Mrs. Work.

It was settled in a few minutes, Mrs. Work's calm insistence winning out over Flora's demurring reluctance. Mrs. Ross was all smiles, as were her daughters, although theirs were mixed with embarrassment. Margaret was gracious, but underneath she was perplexed as to how they would manage. Four extra hoop skirts! The Works had only had two shipments of hoops from London, and had ordered only the minimum required, half-expecting that such an odd, awkward contraption would soon fall out of vogue. It was too late now to order more from San Francisco.

All through their next visit, with the McNeills, and on the return journey, Margaret pondered the difficulty. At home she took stock of their hoops, and came up one set short for the Rosses, even when she included a damaged set Kate had bent all out of shape during a particularly exuberant game with Cecilia and David. Several others were damaged beyond John's ability to repair them, and it was unthinkable to have an *engagé* work on an undergarment.

She discussed the problem at length with Mary, and they agreed that they should each give up two of the four hoops that belonged in their own skirts, to make the needed extra set. The skirts lacking in hoops could be filled out with extra crinoline, of which they had an abundance. They were determined to have the Ross daughters look as presentable as possible so they would get the complete sets. Kate would have the hoops that were bent, despite her youthful indignation at having to wear the consequences of her actions.

Like their mother, Margaret and Mary were proficient with their needles, but it took several trials to find out how best to minimize the loss of the hoops from their skirts. In the end the two remaining hoops had to be placed toward the top of the skirt, the rest of the fabric dangling rather steeply. Even with the extra petticoats and their beautiful new gowns overtop, they did not look quite right, but then the hoops never had, to Margaret. She reluctantly parcelled up the best of the hoop skirts to send to the Rosses, reminding herself repeatedly how little enjoyment Flora and her sisters got of the kind that the ball promised to provide.

Chapter Ten

...two of the Men-of-War, the *Satellite* &
Plumper, with ourselves, determined to join
together & give a grand ball to the ladies of
Vancouver Island...The ladies were nicely
dressed & some of them danced very well,
though they would look much better if they
would only learn to wear their crinoline properly. It is most lamentable to see the objects they
make of themselves, some of the hoops being
quite oval, whilst others had only one hoop rather
high up, the remainder of the dress hanging down
perpendicularly.
—Lieutenant Charles William Wilson, RE

*A*s the ball approached, Margaret began to feel less apprehension about meeting with disapproval there, altered hoop skirts
notwithstanding. In early March, Mr. Bushby had left for the mainland
with Mr. Begbie, on the judge's first court circuit of British Columbia.
With Bushby removed from the picture, Margaret and Mary could be
relieved of awkwardness with him. Kate on the other hand, although
as game for a ball as ever, seemed disappointed he could not attend; in
fact, despite the efforts of her sisters to persuade her of the frailty of
reputations, she seemed not to have felt the transgression of Bushby's
exuberant kisses.

Lieutenant Wilson, who had been appointed to the ball committee, visited them a couple of days before the big event, and his enthusiasm for the endeavour added to its appeal. He extracted their promise that they would be there; there was no turning back. Going to such a grand affair as Wilson promised would throw the Works fully back into society. If Bushby had talked, they would surely learn of it there.

As Lieutenant Wilson had informed them, the ball was held in the fort's marketplace, the largest building the committee could find for the occasion. It was not exactly suited for a ball, and Margaret doubted whether even Wilson could work the miracles he had hinted at. But what a surprise greeted them on their arrival, for not one inch of the interior was visible, the walls and ceiling being covered with ships' flags. Above their heads hung several large chandeliers, and on the wall, sconces; each light was encircled by bayonets, ramrods and evergreens, so that the light reflecting off the glinting metal created a dazzling display.

They stood blinking in the blaze of light, a shock after the dimly lit street. Lieutenant Wilson caught sight of them and rushed over, grinning widely at their expressions of wonder.

"However did you do it?" murmured Margaret, trying to take it all in at once. "All these flags—"

"Oh, 30 or 40 sailors made quick work of it," he laughed. "What do you think of the lights?"

"They're stunning. I've never seen anything to compare to it!"

She immediately regretted this last remark, never wishing to emphasize how little she had seen of the world. Wilson, however, looked so pleased that she soon forgot it.

"A regular fairy palace, if I do say so myself, as befits the elegance of the fair ladies it was erected for," he said, taking a step back to admire them more fully and making a gallant bow. Margaret detected a flicker of something pass over his face when he saw their skirts, but his recovery was so quick that she could not be certain.

"Won't you do me the honour of the first dance?" he asked Margaret, and then engaged Mary and Kate for two later ones.

He excused himself to greet other guests, and when he no longer fully occupied her attention, Margaret could see that others had noticed Wilson single them out. To her delight, the Langfords were among those closest to them, and Margaret caught them staring. When her eyes met those of Miss Emma Langford, the latter acknowledged Margaret with an unmistakably insincere smile and a faint nod of the head. But it was the expression in her narrowed eyes that gave her away the most. *She's jealous*! thought Margaret, and if Miss Emma's smile had been completely warm and sincere, it could scarcely have pleased her more.

She felt more eyes following them during her dance with Wilson; as he was formally dressed in his scarlet tunic he was easy to trace in the crowd. Her spirits soared despite the restrained nature of the quadrille, and her elation lasted well after the dance, tempered only by the fear of a reprisal from Mr. Angelo's dinner party. She felt more at ease on this point, however, when, on nearly bumping into one of Bushby's cohorts from that evening, he blushed, mumbled "Pardon me, I'm terribly sorry," and almost ran away. This was not the face, Margaret decided, of one who was gloating. Indeed, she seemed to evoke a similar response from some of the others involved; they scurried off after a brief but courteous greeting. Mr. Angelo himself was studiously polite, inquiring nervously after the health of herself and her family. Margaret was relieved; they seemed, in one way or another, quite deferential, and in return, she managed to be coolly civil.

Margaret's last dance before the break was with Mr. Bull, the master of HMS *Plumper*, and one of the Langfords' escorts from Mr. Angelo's party. The dance had hardly finished when Miss Emma Langford approached them. Margaret thought it must surely be on account of the naval officer, but to her surprise, after passing a few pleasantries with Mr. Bull, Miss Emma begged the officer to excuse the two ladies, as she was "determined to learn Miss Work's secrets as to how she dressed her hair so elegantly." Mr. Bull, although looking disappointed, bowed politely and retreated. Miss Emma linked arms with Margaret and the two took a turn about the room together. Margaret thought she received at least as many glances walking this way as she had previously dancing with Lieutenant Wilson.

"My sister Mary helped me with my hair," offered Margaret.

"Oh yes, of course. And what an exquisite gown you are wearing, quite gorgeous. It is a shame though," she said, lowering her voice, "that your hoops have not lasted. That dress would be shown to its true advantage with a full set of hoops. They do have a tendency to contort when not worn properly, you know."

Margaret stopped and stared at Miss Emma, who smiled serenely back at her.

"You and your sisters, for I could not help noticing they were in a similar difficulty, would have been quite welcome to some of our hoops. We have many extras. What a shame you did not ask."

"I would not presume to ask for anything from someone whose father is grossly overdrawn at the company store," Margaret shot back.

Captain Langford's debt with the company was widely known, but little talked of publicly, and never to his family. It was Emma Langford's turn to stare.

"If you'll excuse me, I'm expected at supper," said Margaret, turning toward Lieutenant Wilson, who approached from behind Miss Emma.

"There you are, Miss Work! I have got seats for Miss Mary, Kate, and yourself. We wondered where you had got to! Would you care to join us, Miss Emma?" he asked the latter politely.

She stammered out something in the negative. Wilson seemed little concerned.

"Well then, shall we?" Lieutenant Wilson asked Margaret, offering her his arm.

Margaret accepted and walked away with a strange mixture of pride and fear; she was quite astounded that she had dared to stand up to a Langford. The retort had come out before she had time to think, yet, reflecting on Miss Emma's thinly veiled jibes, she could not regret having said it. And oh, the perfect timing of Wilson's arrival! It was delicious. The whole exchange was marred only by Miss Emma's criticism of her attire, but this surely was aggravated by jealousy and spite. *A man,* thought Margaret, *would hardly notice such a thing as a missing hoop.*

Later in the evening, she spotted Lieutenant Wilson, standing just beyond her sister. He was apart from the mingling bustle, contentedly observing the surroundings which he had been so instrumental in creating. Suddenly the crowd parted and Margaret had a clear view of him looking directly at Mary's skirts with a frown, as if they were the only blight on an otherwise perfect scene. All the attentions he later paid Margaret and her sisters did not quite make up for this unspoken criticism. Margaret longed to explain the circumstances to him, but as she could not do so without shaming the Ross family, she resisted the temptation. To add to her irritation, when she finally had an opportunity to speak to Flora Ross she discovered that one of her sisters had been unable to attend, as she had caught a cold.

All this, for nothing! thought Margaret, and then relented a little, for after all, Flora and her sisters could not know what inconvenience the Works had gone to for their sakes.

Urging herself to generosity, she said, "You look so well, Flora. Why don't you keep the hoop skirt?"

"Oh no. A ball like this one, with everyone invited, doesn't happen very often, and they would be no good to us at the farm. We couldn't possibly work in them! No, you've been too kind already."

Margaret felt thoroughly ashamed, all her former grievances appearing very petty, and she devoted much of the remaining evening to including the Ross daughters in as many of the best circles as she could.

Lieutenant Mayne and Sub-Lieutenant Pender joined the Works for tea the following day, and just as they were leaving, Mr. Work returned home from some business at the fort. He looked grave and did not press the officers to stay, as was his usual custom. As soon as they departed, he summoned Kate brusquely into his library.

Margaret and Mary exchanged looks of surprise; their father, although full of high expectations, was not easily displeased with the family. After a short period Kate returned from the library, and told Margaret and Mary that their father would now see them. She retired upstairs with no indication of what the matter was, toying with their suspense.

Mr. Work lost no time in relating the affair to Margaret and Mary.

"Having met Governor Douglas at the fort, I was apprised of a circumstance surrounding last evening's ball which was most unpleasant to hear."

Pausing, he looked searchingly at his daughters. Margaret and Mary looked wonderingly at each other; Mr. Work, appearing satisfied, continued. "It seems that the Mother Superior of St. Ann's Academy expressly forbade the attendance at the ball of Kate, and others of a similar age, such as Miss Agnes and Miss Alice Douglas. Yesterday the good Sister dispatched a messenger to Mr. Douglas and myself, relaying her belief that the girls were too young to take part in such pursuits, and informing me that their attendance at the ball would result in their expulsion from the school. But it seems the girls intercepted the messenger and, promising to deliver the messages themselves, deposited them in a hedge."

In surprise, Margaret almost laughed at their audacity; knowing she should not increased the urge. She dared not look over at Mary, as she knew that with only one twitch of Mary's mouth she would lose control of her own.

"A short interview with the Mother Superior confirmed all that Governor Douglas related to me," continued Mr. Work. "You were not aware of any of this?"

The sisters shook their heads emphatically.

"I thought not. Catherine has taken it upon herself to decide what is best for her, instead of trusting the good judgment of her parents. I have confined her to Hillside for the remainder of the month, where she will endeavour to be worthy of the society she seeks. I will once again be relying on the two of you to supervise the lessons of the younger girls, until I make other arrangements. *If* I can find somewhere that will take them. Rather a wild one, that girl. Tut, tut, my daughters," he sighed, and dismissed them.

Margaret and Mary were hardly inside Mary's room when Kate appeared in the doorway.

"No doubt you know," she said as she walked in. "A whole month, stuck at Hillside! What bad luck! Just as the weather's sure to clear up for some riding parties!"

Kate continued, enumerating all the events she was likely to miss, and how unlucky it was. As she paced up and down the room, however, she began to make the best of her transgression, and soon turned her thoughts to more pleasant subjects.

"Well, I daresay the ball was worth it. There probably won't be another like it until next winter! I wonder where we'll go to school? Thank goodness to be rid of the sisters, with all their starch. Why we ever went there in the first place, I'll never know. We're not even Catholic! Going to St. Ann's just made people think of us as more Irish."

"We *are* Irish," said Margaret.

"Not *that* kind of Irish," said Kate.

The humour that Margaret had found in her sister's waylaying the Mother Superior's messenger was soon overcome by her worries about the consequences of Kate's expulsion. "Rather a wild one" echoed through her head, and she imagined it spoken by many a voice other than her father's.

"What will people say?" she asked Mary, when Kate had finally left them alone.

"People?"

"The Langfords, for a start. Kate *expelled,* and coming so soon after what they witnessed at Mr. Angelo's party! It's too much."

Mary could not offer her usual words of reassurance. Lost in her own thoughts, she picked an article of clothing out of her sewing basket instead.

Mr. Work responded quickly to Kate's insurrection and managed to get her and Cecilia into Miss Phillips' school at Colwood before the month was up, an act which, had it been calculated to do so, could not have given the girls greater happiness. He had very little choice in the matter. Despite its miraculous growth, Victoria's educational institutions, especially for girls of the upper echelons, were far outnumbered by its hotels, shops and saloons.

Miss Phillips, a spinster sister of Mrs. Langford's, had joined the family in Victoria a few years after their arrival and had opened a school for young ladies on their farm, Colwood. When she learned that Agnes and Alice were also to go, Kate was in heaven. Attending Miss Phillips's school would put them in close contact with the Langford daughters, who could only benefit their instruction; there were no better examples of young English ladies to be had in Victoria. Margaret was left in the unenviable position of knowing that she might have to rely on her 16-year-old sister to increase her own education. Mr. Work kept plenty of books for the family to read, mostly religious volumes, but there her studies at home must end, for everything she could learn from her family she believed she already understood.

Chapter Eleven

Bank of British North America. The Branch of
this Bank has taken premises for the conduct of
business. The Directors in this town are Messrs.
Wood, Watson, and Jackson.
　　　　　　—*Victoria Colonist*, May 23, 1859

*T*he gold miners indeed came pouring back into the colony with
the warmer spring weather, much to the joy of Mr. Finlayson
and other land speculators, although not quite in the astounding
numbers of the previous year. Victoria's young ladies received the news
with mixed feelings, as it meant the town had once again become more
dangerous.

By the second week of April HMS *Plumper* had left Victoria for
the Fraser, to join the *Satellite* in controlling the new influx of gold
prospectors, and the Works' social life became noticeably quieter. After
the debacle at Mr. Angelo's dinner party, Margaret decided that newcomers, even British ones, were not to be immediately trusted, and was
more judicious in accepting invitations.

Being sequestered in the country made getting into town all the
more desirable, and the month of April gave the Work daughters an
excuse for going there. In a gesture of perhaps acceptance, or at least
resignation, toward the city growing up around its fort, the Hudson's
Bay Company announced that it would tear down its palisades. The
company's public position was that the walls were being brought down
for the *ladies* of Victoria, who had got into the habit, as the narrow

wickets became unsuitable for their expanding dresses, of asking the porter to open the great main gate to let them in to shop at the company store. As one of these ladies, Margaret was overjoyed at the news and begged Mr. Work that she and Mary might see the sight. Less wary of the gold miners than the previous year, Mr. Work consented, but only if he accompanied them himself.

When they arrived at the fort, they saw that the company *engagés* had made a start on dismantling the east wall. A gaping hole greeted them, the torn-up cedar stakes piled in a heap. Margaret felt her enthusiasm wane; a slight tugging of the heartstrings prevented her from relishing the sight as she had expected. She looked nervously over at Mr. Work, fearing he must be feeling much worse than she did.

"Now the fort will truly be a part of the town, instead of an obstacle in the middle of it," she said bravely, but somehow it came out rather flat.

"Quite right, Margaret," replied Mr. Work, turning toward her and patting her arm. To Margaret's surprise, his countenance was remarkably bright. "Nothing stands in the way of civilization—it's what we've wanted all along. I just never dreamed that I'd have the good fortune to see it *here* of all places, and in my lifetime."

And to her astonishment, he took her on one arm and Mary on the other, and cheerfully followed the example of the towns-people who were already passing through the widening hole in the old fort's stockade.

After Mr. Work's business and an afternoon of shopping and mar-velling over all the new brick buildings steadily replacing their wooden predecessors around the fort, the three returned to Hillside. Kate had come home from Colwood in time to greet them. She managed to contain herself in her father's company, but once he was safely removed to his library, she broke into raves about Miss Phillips' school.

101

DOUGLAS COLLEGE LIBRARY

It was evidently, and not surprisingly, of a less academic nature than the school of the Sisters of St. Ann. Miss Phillips concentrated more on languages and social graces than on religious studies. That day she had been teaching the girls the finer points of the polka and quadrille, much to Kate's delight.

"Though she was such a bore about posture, never letting up for a minute," she sighed. "I'd show you, if you like, but you might find her pointers rather tedious..."

Kate needed only a little prompting, which Mary readily gave. But after her fifth "Do try to hold your head up, Margaret!" and "Shoulders back, Mary!" Kate altogether lost the attention of her elder sisters. Margaret and Mary sat down.

"And what else did you learn from Miss Phillips?" asked Margaret.

"Nothing of much significance," said Kate, peevishly, "but Emma told us a good joke: what is the difference between a young maid and an old maid?"

Their silence seemed encouragement enough to give the answer.

"A young maid is careless and happy, an old maid hairless and cappy!"

Margaret got up and walked to the window.

"Of course," said Kate, her youthful triumph over her sisters fading from her voice, "we did not let Miss Phillips hear it. It was not meant to be cruel."

The rest of April passed, with occasional outings to break the older sisters' routine, and with sessions of learning what they could from Kate's education at Colwood while still retaining the dignity of their seniority. Although she pressed her advantage as far as she could, Kate soon learned that Margaret and Mary would only take so much criticism from her, and moderated her method of instruction accordingly. Mr. Work added an incentive to respecting her elders by placing Kate's religious studies, which he felt lacking at Miss Phillips' school, temporarily in the hands of Margaret.

May 24th promised a change of pace. Queen Victoria's birthday was a gala event in her namesake town; festivities were planned for Beacon Hill, which the governor had lately declared an official park. The weather was the only uncertainty threatening to dampen the celebration, but this year Mother Nature bowed graciously in deference to Her Majesty and produced a gloriously sunny day.

That same day Lieutenant Wilson was due to leave for the mainland to join the Royal Engineers working on the boundary. With the prospect of an entire summer and fall without him, Margaret began to have an inkling as to how Mary was feeling during Dr. Tuzo's absence. She was determined, however, not to let Lieutenant Wilson's absence spoil the day for her.

All of the Work family attended the festivities. As the younger children were to go, Mrs. Work broke her usual avoidance of such public events. Her presence was not a comfort to Margaret, who was keenly aware of the stares Mrs. Work drew from strangers; she could not help but feel that her mother's presence did not advance the social position of her children, but in fact had an effect just the reverse.

The family proceeded to the finish line of the racetrack that encircled Beacon Hill. The riders held little draw for Margaret; there were a few naval officers among them, but as they were the type who generally preferred racing to society, they generated no interest in the young ladies. The town's 300-pound butcher was a favourite contender, but his unfortunate horse excited stronger feelings in Margaret than he did. Since Mary shared these sympathies, it was not difficult for Margaret to persuade her to take the opportunity of separating from the rest of the family and strolling up the south side of the hill to admire the view across the strait.

On the hilltop they seemed met by two oceans: a sea of blue camas rippled down the slope at their feet until it dropped off in a bluff, where the real ocean continued until it met the Olympic Mountains looming on the horizon. The view seemed to have lost its appeal for Mary, who, Margaret observed, was looking to the east more often than to the magnificent Olympic range to the south.

"There's probably still snow on the ground in Quebec," said Margaret at last.

"On May 24th, that would be rare, even for Canada," smiled Mary faintly. And then, in a more serious tone, "It's no use, Margaret. I think of him every hour of the day. I cannot shake the feeling I've made a dreadful mistake."

"Dr. Tuzo will come back, Mary. He must. Within the year he must come back. He'll get over his wounded pride, you'll see. And when he sees you again . . . he'll be powerless against your charms," she said, squeezing her sister's hand.

"Do you really think so?"

"Who could withstand them?"

The pained hope in Mary's eyes gave Margaret a stab of remorse. While pleased to see her sister a little reassured, she herself found less comfort in her own words. Margaret had become uncomfortably aware of how little, at the time, she had comprehended the risks of advising Mary to delay Tuzo; she had evidently greatly underestimated her sister's attachment to him.

"And you, Margaret. Might I enquire—" Mary hesitated.

Margaret had been contemplating the mountains in the distance and looked at her sister in surprise.

"Yes?"

"Your feelings toward Mr. Wilson. It is only my concern that makes me ask—if you—do you—"

"No, Mary," Margaret half-smiled. "I think I may safely say I am not in love with Mr. Wilson. I admit it has been a long while since I found anyone nearly so agreeable, but as to love—no."

"It is only that I did not wish you to suffer another disappointment, like your first."

"That was many years ago now. They were the feelings of a girl of 15."

"Nonetheless, keenly felt."

"Yes, at the time, although I would not admit it to Kate. Keenly felt, and a lesson well-heeded."

"I'm so glad. I couldn't bear to see you unhappy."

Mary gave her an affectionate hug, and for a moment Margaret was overcome with guilt. That her sister, while struggling with her own feelings, should have room in her heart to be concerned for another—another so undeserving! *Perhaps it is a good sign,* thought Margaret as she blinked into the horizon; *perhaps I have overestimated her unhappiness.*

As they descended the hill, the two sisters walked by a party of gentlemen whom Margaret did not recognize. One in particular caught her eye by the manner in which he regarded *her* as he politely touched his hat. Mary elbowed her side when they had passed.

"Do you know him?" laughed Margaret, when they were out of earshot.

"No, but I wager it will only be a matter of time before we do, especially if *his* wishes are brought to bear."

"You know nothing of his wishes," smiled Margaret.

"I know what I saw," said Mary mildly.

Later on, when Margaret and Mary had rejoined their family for the picnic after the races, Margaret caught the stranger covertly observing her on several occasions. She made some general inquiries among her close acquaintances as to his identity, but could get no answer. Her friends did, however, supply her with confirmation of her own unspoken opinion, by claiming him to possess the air of a gentleman.

At one point she found herself among a party close to him, separated by only a few people. He was speaking to Mr. Anderson, one of her father's associates. Margaret tried her best not to look over at them, but was irresistibly drawn when she heard her name coming from Mr. Anderson amid the din of the general conversation. She glanced over just in time to receive the impression that they had just been looking her way. So, the gentleman had apparently inquired after her identity. What else could explain it? This was gratifying knowledge, except that he now had her at a disadvantage: he was still unknown to her.

But Margaret had no time for more detecting. The group she stood with, whose conversation she had little attended, suddenly broke up, and Mr. Anderson stepped forward to introduce her.

Mr. Jackson, as the stranger turned out to be, was one of the directors of the Bank of British North America, which had officially opened for business in Victoria only the day before. His age was difficult to judge; he certainly had the air of an older person, although his youthful face belied greying hair. It was his expressive eyes, perhaps, which bore a slightly jaded expression. Margaret thought his angular features had a natural charm, especially in contrast to Mr. Anderson, whose physical hardships were focussed in a scar he bore on one cheek, a mark that the Indians had celebrated by giving him the name "S'gatch Poose." While he now filled the position of Collector of Customs in Victoria, his office had not changed the rough character of his face. By comparison, Mr. Jackson's hardships, Margaret decided, were all of the internal variety.

Mr. Jackson regarded her frankly, although not in an unfriendly way. And yet, something in his manner seemed a little restrained. Their meeting was too short for Margaret to be satisfied with the meaning of his looks. There was something penetrating about them that made her wonder if he was attempting to trace the Indian characteristics in her face, as did so many of the newcomers to Victoria, once apprised of the makeup of its female population.

Over the next few weeks, Margaret was no more able to determine the nature of Mr. Jackson's interest in her. She was sure only that he was indeed scrutinizing her, but whether she was an object of admiration or of curiosity she could not decide. His character was guarded; she had only her own impressions and those of others to build on. And Mr. Jackson, being judicious with his words, began to gather about himself a reputation. His occupation alone was enough to generate interest; the addition of good manners and an attractive appearance maintained it. Banking sat at the top of the trades, and admitted him to the upper levels of society. As a banker he was reputed to be exacting, but complaints arose from the ladies that he carried this over to society. For some he was merely hard to please. Those with a more fanciful imagination whispered of an unrequited love left behind in England. "He came out to the New World to forget her," they said. "But she may as well have followed him; he can't find her equal, no more here than at Home." Margaret was duly captivated.

On several occasions she came across him during the favourite early-summer pastime of Saturday riding parties; he apparently had an interest in the land, as he was apt to stray from the more frequented areas. On one occasion a large group had left Hillside to view the progress of the Tolmies' new farm to the north, and on the return trip had separated into smaller groups. Margaret had wandered ahead of hers and, emerging from the woods, she came upon a large clearing. Finding herself quite alone, she indulged in a gallop. It was a guilty pleasure; she knew she ought not to be alone, but she was loath to pass up the opportunity, and thinking the rest of her party not far behind, she was confident of being soon reunited. Midway across the meadow she had the uncanny sense of being watched. It was a feeling she was acutely tuned into; since her earliest childhood her parents had warned her of the stealth of Indians, and now the gold rush's allure to Californian criminals and other miscreants had only heightened the sense of near danger. She showed no sign of alarm, but drew her horse slowly in, and circled until she spotted her observer. He was mounted and stood under a few trees on a slight rise above the clearing. When she had approached close enough to see that it was Mr. Jackson, her instant relief very quickly turned into amusement.

"Are you lost, sir?" she asked, smiling.

"The trail seems to have eluded me," he said with little concern, "but as they all lead to the fort, once I find it again I shall not be lost."

"Some newcomers have found," said Margaret, "that the trails also lead *away* from the fort, depending on which direction you go."

"Since I have had the good fortune to meet you, I hope I need not be much troubled by that," he replied with a half-smile.

Margaret turned her horse homeward, and looking back over her shoulder to see why he did not immediately follow, found Mr. Jackson looking after her with great surprise.

"Are you quite certain of the route?"

"Quite," she laughed.

"Are you accustomed to riding alone?" he asked when his horse came abreast of hers. His tone held a note of disapproval, and she felt her amusement begin to wane.

"I was separated from my party," she shrugged.

"Which does not concern a young lady like yourself?"

"We have not been separated long," she said. "Besides, I have this." She parted the shawl pinned around her waist to reveal the horse pistol strapped to her side. A small section of her calf, above her boot and below her bunched skirt, was also revealed. She saw his eye settle there momentarily and she instantly felt like the most wanton exhibitionist imaginable. She quickly released the shawl and, to cover her embarrassment, said, "My mother insists upon my carrying it, at least she has since the gold rush."

"A wise precaution, I suppose, but better never to be found alone," he frowned.

"Advice which I see you heed," she said pointedly.

He gave her a look that said their differences must surely be obvious. Margaret's colour deepened. At that point the trail narrowed as it entered the woods, making riding side by side impossible, and Mr. Jackson urged his horse out in front. They rode in silence for a few moments until he pulled up short where the trail ascended a steep bank.

"It's a bit rough going," he said over his shoulder.

"It's the way I came," she replied.

When they reached the top, he acknowledged, "You ride very well."

"Thank you."

"Sidesaddles would be impractical on terrain like this."

"Yes." She wondered if he suspected she had never used one.

Within a few minutes they neared another clearing, where they heard other riders.

"I knew they could not be far!" said Margaret, feeling vindicated.

"There she is!" cried Kate as they emerged from the trees. "And she's found a stray wanderling on her way!"

Margaret dared only glance in his direction, to see his sidelong look of irritation.

Chapter Twelve

. . . it is only when I abandon the hope and wish
of laying my bones in old Scotland that I will ever
think of uniting myself in the most sacred of ties
with a female of this country.
—Dr. William Fraser Tolmie

*I*n July, Victoria's new Government Buildings, under construction
for many months, were completed. As the family of a member
of the Vancouver Island Council, the Works' attendance at the opening
ceremony was compulsory. Kept from political involvement by virtue of
her sex, Margaret's role, along with that of her sisters, was to see and be
seen. Only Mrs. Work was excused from putting in an appearance.

The new buildings were located on the banks of James Bay, conveniently close to the governor's residence. Margaret had not seen the
buildings up close for several weeks, and unquestionably she had never
seen anything to equal them, except in the pages of her history books.
They were, of course, constructed of wood, but faced with brick and
timber, which lent them an air of permanence, unlike much of the false-
fronted town across the harbour. The large central building was flanked
on either side by two smaller buildings set farther back, so that fire
could not spread from one to the other. No trees had been left standing
to mar their view across the bay to the town, or to dwarf them.

Their grandeur held limited appeal for a four-year-old, and Suzette,
within minutes of their arrival, grew bored and wandered off. Margaret,
who had been entrusted with her care, went in search of her.

"Hurry, or you'll miss the governor's arrival!" called 10-year-old Cecilia after her.

Margaret scanned the assembly. It was strange to see so many unfamiliar faces, and she searched long enough to feel a stab of alarm before spotting Suzette's straw bonnet. Ladies did not run, so Margaret walked as quickly as decorum allowed. The crowd thickened and she lost sight of Suzette for a panic-filled moment, but at last caught a glimpse of her, dodging in and out of the milling throng. Margaret ran.

"You silly goose!" she panted, collaring Suzette.

"Listen!" said Suzette. "The governor is arriving!"

The fanfare of Governor Douglas' arrival caused the crowd to surge forward, fencing them off. Between the roadway and themselves, there seemed an impenetrable wall of people.

Margaret cursed inwardly. She was perspiring, and although wearing hoops instead of layered petticoats, she still felt stifled by her silk dress in the midsummer heat.

"We should be in the front. We'll never make it back in time," she said crossly, patting her brow with a handkerchief. It gave little relief.

"I can't see," whined Suzette.

"And whose fault is that?"

Suzette winced. Relenting, Margaret picked her up, balancing her awkwardly on one hip, tilting her hoop skirt askew. At least the cage allowed some air under her skirt.

"Where will Papa's office be?"

"The Council is in that building, next to the centre one," pointed Margaret, wishing someone would recognize their familial connections and make way for them.

Looking again at the buildings, she began to take in the comments of the bystanders, and was surprised and disappointed to find them mostly unfavourable, although she had read some unflattering descriptions in Victoria's two newspapers. "Something between a Dutch toy and a Chinese pagoda," the *British Colonist* had said, but since the editor, a Canadian with the invented name of Amor de Cosmos, was known to despise the governor, she had discounted his opinion. The *Gazette* had styled the buildings "Elizabethan." But here among the public, the general cry seemed to be "How *very* un-English!" De Cosmos' depiction of crossbred styles was much repeated through the crowd and bandied about with variations, including a "Swiss cottage."

"The pomposity of Douglas," sneered a bystander loudly in a nasal Yankee twang, "calling the street Birdcage Walk, as if Government House were Buckingham Palace and he the king! For *I* have been to London myself and that is the very name of the road from the palace to Parliament—pah!"

Margaret turned slightly toward the speaker in time to see him punctuate this boast, in typical Yankee fashion, by spitting on the ground, as if to show his aversion to British soil. Catching her eye, he stared defiantly back at her, slowly chewing his tobacco. She quickly averted her face; her bonnet shielded her from his view. She did not know him, but she knew the type: not a miner but a Californian speculator of some sort, in his fine dark suit and broad-toed boots, lately arrived in the colony, but quick to find fault in its government. There were many like him. Did he know who she was, she wondered? Or had he overheard Suzette's question regarding their father?

"But it's an apt description," said a fellow onlooker. "The buildings look like ornamental birdcages!"

"And the King Canary has nearly all the members singing his own tune!" scoffed the first man with a loud guffaw and another brown tobacco spit. Laughter echoed through the group.

Margaret had read diatribes against the "family-company compact," as it was termed in the press, but never had she heard criticism made, as it were, almost to her face. She felt certain that he had meant it for her ears. Already uncomfortably warm, she felt the heat become more oppressive with her blush. "I have to put you down now," she whispered to Suzette.

Margaret turned away from the loud American, but found to her dismay that the crowd had thickened behind her as well, hemming them in, and she could not see a friendly face among it. Suzette had caught the tone of the exchange, if not the content, and looked up at her sister apprehensively, her delicate brows knit together. Determined to protect her, Margaret headed toward where the crowd seemed thinnest and stepped forward. A narrow passage opened for her, forcing her to brush past the men. Many were miners, a wall of red flannel shirts and grey serge trousers, with pistols slung from their belts. She caught the eye of one of them, leering at her. Margaret swallowed uncomfortably and pressed on, eyes downcast, clutching Suzette's hand. The crowd closed in; they were jostled and Margaret feared Suzette might be crushed. Her heart beat a panicked tattoo inside the closed cage her corset had become. *Oh, why did I lace it so tight,* was her one coherent thought as she struggled for breath.

"Miss Work, if you'll allow me," a familiar voice behind her said, and Margaret turned to see Mr. Jackson at her elbow, his mouth set in a hard line.

"I believe I could find you a much better vantage point," he said, scooping up Suzette with one arm and offering Margaret the other.

Speechless, she took it gratefully. To her surprise, the knot of men loosened, and they made their way past.

"Are you all right?"

"Yes," faltered Margaret, but she couldn't summon certainty into her breathless voice. To her embarrassment she felt dizzy and was obliged to lean on his arm.

Mr. Jackson manoeuvred them through the assembly and around the outskirts of it, to the side of the Colonial Offices building. They faced the back of the military guard and the governor as he addressed the gathering from a distance, but to Margaret the blissful shade afforded by the building was far more welcome than a long-winded speech by Governor Douglas.

"You'll get a better view from my shoulders, young lady," said Mr. Jackson.

Suzette hesitated but a moment; the novelty of the suggestion evidently outweighing what little remained of her shyness, she nodded her assent and allowed herself to be hoisted up.

"The view is much better from up here, Margaret!" quipped Suzette, her fears of mere moments before forgotten.

Margaret had released the gentleman's arm so he could lift her sister, but once Suzette was settled on his shoulders, Mr. Jackson again offered it to Margaret. Before she could decline, he insisted, "You look as if you could use it." Taking it with some relief, she felt doubly obliged to him for his earlier rescue and his continuing assistance, and could only wait for her equanimity to return in order to express it. She became acutely aware of his forearm as she rested against his side. The decorum that suggested pulling back was melting away with her anxiety, leaving her with a delicious feeling of freedom. *I must be light-headed,* she thought giddily. She had plenty of time to compose herself, as Suzette gave a running commentary from her perch. She questioned everything she saw and heard, from the ceremonial military guard to the governor's carriage ("He didn't have far to come!" she laughed), and Mr. Jackson answered as best he could, glancing occasionally at Margaret.

At length the speeches ended, the guard marched off, and Mr. Jackson lifted Suzette down. "There's Papa!" she said, bolting toward him.

Margaret awoke from her reverie with "Thank you" on her lips, but

Jackson interrupted tersely. "You ought to be more careful, especially of the miners. They are principally made up of the scouring out of California jails! I was quite taken aback to find you among them."

"It was not my intention," said Margaret, startled. "Suzette ran off and I went in search of her."

"Have you no brother?"

In his accusing look, she saw her reputation hanging precariously in the balance; her name was under greater threat than her safety had been.

"He was not right at hand, and in such a crowd as this, I did not want to lose my sister," said Margaret, growing defensively indignant and feeling her colour rising again.

"Well, no harm done, this time," he relented. In his softened tone, she heard he had spared her reputation again. "I'll escort you back to your family."

Having accomplished their safe return, he did not stay. Mr. Work was deep in conversation with Dr. Helmcken, and with a merely polite nod to John, Mr. Jackson quit them immediately. Watching his quickly departing figure, Margaret felt slighted; she wondered if he did not wish to seem on close footing with the Works.

The family, however, heard much about Mr. Jackson from Suzette. "He parted the crowd like the Red Sea!"

"Don't let Reverend Cridge hear you say that," smiled Mary. "You'll get a lecture on blasphemy."

"I must find the opportunity to thank him," said Mr. Work. "I'd like to become better acquainted with Mr. Jackson."

Margaret refrained from pointing out that Mr. Jackson had not taken the opportunity to become better acquainted with *him*.

———

Another event in July had a more personal impact on the Work family as a whole: the move to Victoria of the eldest daughter, Jane, and her family. Slowly shifting operations north of the border, the company was transferring Dr. Tolmie, Jane's husband, from Fort Nisqually in Washington Territory to Fort Victoria, much to the joy of the family, and Mrs. Work in particular. The only regret the latter had to disturb her happiness was that Jane's departure from Fort Nisqually left Letitia there "all alone," and her siblings heard "poor Letitia" mentioned with great frequency while they prepared to welcome the Tolmies into their home.

The previous year Dr. Tolmie had purchased 1,100 acres of land adjacent to Hillside. Mr. Work had overseen the initial stages of establishing a farm for his son-in-law, but the doctor had wished to supervise the construction of his manor house himself. While it was being built, the Tolmies were to stay at Hillside.

The arrival of the steamer *Eliza Anderson* from Puget Sound was much anticipated by the family, and news of its approach reached the Works in time for them to lay on a late dinner. Once the Tolmies were safely arrived at Hillside, the reunion was marred for Margaret only by seeing that they had brought with them an additional guest: Mr. Grahame.

"What a lucky coincidence that Mr. Grahame took passage on the same ship as us, Mama," said Jane. "Now you shall have all his news from Fort Vancouver, as well as ours from Nisqually."

It did not take Margaret long to discern that Mr. Grahame still had no wife, and she did not think the coincidence so very lucky.

The Finlaysons joined them after dinner, and Margaret had the added discomfort of seeing Sarah watching her closely whenever Mr. Grahame spoke to her. Margaret noticed Sarah in close conversation with Jane, who looked from Margaret to Mr. Grahame and back again, leaving Margaret with the dreadful thought she might now have *two* matchmaking sisters in town.

Jane was in her early 30s. Margaret had once overheard a colonist, upon returning from San Francisco, say that while an English woman could be said to be in her prime at 30, an American woman was grown quite old by that time. Margaret had been unsure which group she fit into. She thought it rather unfair, for if the Americans had to contend with anything like the hardships that the colonies offered, it was little wonder that they grew old more quickly than a pampered English lady. Jane, while showing a face as unlined as her mother's, had a figure so thickened by nine years of child-bearing that she quite equalled her mother in girth. She had not, however, lost her grace. Margaret watched her as she moved about the drawing-room and longed to join her, but Mr. Grahame's presence on that side of the room prevented her.

Instead, she sat with the group around Dr. Tolmie, who was in the midst of telling stories about American pioneers. Dr. Tolmie was a devout Scot, inclined to be too serious in Margaret's opinion. She had always marvelled that the physical trait of his high forehead perfectly matched his inclination to high-mindedness, but given an encouraging audience, as he had now, he displayed a sense of humour too little seen.

"I won't soon forget the McAllisters," he chuckled. "How they would boast of their hardships to the new settlers! 'We were so poor when we arrived,' they would say, 'that we had to live in a hollow tree and were only kept from starving by the charity of the Indians!' And all the while, at the time they were speaking of, I knew them to be selling shingles to the company for ten dollars per thousand. He was credited with 130,000 of them!"

Margaret was disappointed to see Mr. Grahame join the group. He had stories of his own to tell about the American settlers around Fort

Vancouver, and soon he and Dr. Tolmie were exchanging tales that grew taller by the minute about the folly and brashness of the Yankees, much to the enjoyment of their listeners. Margaret made a small concession in granting Mr. Grahame a sense of humour, although she felt him lacking in subtlety. Many of those gathered round were children, who came and went as their ability to sit still allowed. When Mr. Grahame's and Dr. Tolmie's repertoire of stories began to dwindle, Margaret would have retreated were it not for one small nephew asleep in her lap, the youngest of the Tolmies' six boys.

Dr. Tolmie got up to stretch his legs and left the room with Mr. Work. Mr. Grahame sat down beside Margaret.

"He's warmed up to you very quickly," Mr. Grahame said to her in a low voice, stroking his long beard. He leaned closer to admire the sleeping child.

"We always wished to see more of Jane's boys. Although," Margaret replied, eyeing two of them tussling on the rug, "in a week's time we may regret it!"

"Oh, I cannot believe you will regret it, not seriously," he replied earnestly. "The children certainly seem to like the attention—especially from you."

His voice as he spoke this last was a little gruff and his look showed he expected a reply. Margaret supposed he was waiting for a response such as "I am as fond of the children as they are of me," but she could not quite bring herself to fulfil his expectations. Instead she replied, "I've noticed no preference for me. On the contrary, they seem more taken with Mary! She is quite wonderful with boys."

Margaret blushed with surprise at herself, ashamed that she had made such a bare-faced recommendation of Mary to spare herself from Mr. Grahame's attentions. The gentleman seemed quite unaware of Margaret's embarrassment, as he was intently studying Mary, who was settling a dispute between young William Tolmie and Suzette. Suzette had been insisting that her nephew, who was a year older, address her as Aunt Suzette; the older child adamantly refused. Mary had intercepted just as the argument teetered on the brink of fisticuffs.

Mr. Grahame turned back to Margaret.

"Perhaps I should lend some assistance to your sister. Boys can be rather troublesome at times."

Margaret's relief at being rid of Mr. Grahame was temporary; Jane sat down beside her and resumed where the gentleman had left off.

"You have the knack," she said, beaming at her sleeping son cradled in Margaret's arms.

"Oh, Jane! You're not going to start too, are you?" sighed Margaret.

"Start what?" Jane asked, innocently enough.

Margaret searched her eldest sister's face briefly. Jane had their mother's look of imperturbable serenity; there was no sign of scheming, only a slight, amused surprise.

"Sarah's been very heavy-handed with hints lately. Once Letitia was married, she turned her attention to *me*, and has hardly let up for a minute. She thinks I ought to have a brood of my own by now."

"Pray, do not marry on my account—I've been very much looking forward to help from you and Mary," smiled Jane. "At Nisqually, Letitia was soon too busy with her own little one to give me any assistance."

"I suppose Sarah thinks she can manage with only one of us," replied Margaret. "And there's always Kate. I sometimes think Sarah's embarrassed to have two unmarried sisters over 20 in the family."

"She might think differently now she has to share you," said Jane, patting her sister's arm affectionately. "And, I seem to recall, Sarah was past 20 herself, when she married."

"Only *just*, as she so frequently reminds me."

"Well, at any rate, I was 23, and it certainly did me no harm to wait, although, at the time, I thought William would never make up his mind to ask me," said Jane.

"I'm 24 now, Jane."

A blink of her eyes was the only sign of Jane's surprise.

"Time does fly by. I thought you were just 23. But no matter, there are still plenty of years ahead. Mr. Grahame has no competitors?"

After a slight pause, Margaret replied, "No, none that I expect to amount to anything." Jane was beginning to look sympathetic, which Margaret could not bear. "Well, Mr. Grahame is in no danger of breaking his heart, whatever Sarah may have said to the contrary," she quickly said. Remembering her recommendation of their sister's maternal qualities moments earlier, she added with a self-conscious smile, "He seems just as taken with Mary, as with me."

"With Mary!"

Frowning slightly, Jane regarded Mary and Mr. Grahame, who were still in conversation together.

"Sarah's told you, then, about Dr. Tuzo?" asked Margaret.

Jane hesitated, and then replied, "A little. But why don't you tell me yourself? It will be the next best thing to hearing it from Mary, and I know you will be more generous with the details."

Smiling, Margaret complied. She related as much as she thought she could without betraying Mary's confidences. Jane, after all, was entitled to her due as a sister. Mary's predicament, just like her marriage proposal, belonged to them all. And with Jane Margaret always slipped easily back into familiarity, their time apart melting away as it does between two of similar minds.

Whether or not Mr. Grahame showed more interest in Margaret or Mary, or which of the two young ladies discouraged him more, were questions soon little considered by the ladies themselves. Mr. Grahame, after a stay of a few frustrating days, left on the Nanaimo packet for the

Cowichan Valley, where he and other land speculators were looking to purchase property. This only served to fuel Sarah's conjecture on the gentleman's plans for his future, and she made many a remark to Margaret about Mr. Grahame settling down in the Cowichan Valley in 10 year's time or so, and how conveniently close to Victoria it was. Margaret saw little convenience in the distance, which she felt rather far, but in a few weeks even Sarah desisted in remarking upon it, and Margaret was left to her own speculations.

Chapter Thirteen

My father also taught me boxing. I remember he
secured the services of a boy who was two years
older than I, and how that fellow used to ham-
mer me I will never forget; but I had to stand
up and take it, because I had the utmost respect
for what my father could do to me in the event
of my failing to obey orders ... He was a great
student and reader and possessed a good library.
He led a clean life and was a strict disciplinar-
ian with his growing family. He was a profound
student of religion ...

— Dr. Simon Fraser Tolmie,
son of Dr. William Fraser Tolmie

Dr. Tolmie soon lived up to Margaret's memories of him and
proved to be an exacting parent. One of his favourite mottos
was "an hour in the morning is worth two at night"; thus he had his
eldest sons up at five o'clock in the morning to go over their lessons for
the day, before they went off to school with David.

Although Mr. Work did not grace these early studies with his own
presence, he believed they might benefit his children. Those above
school age enjoyed exemption, but Kate, Cecilia, David and Suzette
complained bitterly to their elder siblings. Kate could not always drag
herself out of bed, so Margaret or Mary put in an occasional appearance
to appease the vigilance of Dr. Tolmie. When Margaret shepherded

Cecilia and Suzette downstairs, she always met with the same response from her brother-in-law.

"Are we all here?" he would ask, a frown creasing his high forehead.

"Yes," said Margaret firmly, believing that Kate ought to be allowed a little leeway as she was very nearly grown.

Dr. Tolmie would eye her doubtfully, but held his tongue; he would not overstep Mr. Work's authority, but gave the distinct impression that things would be different if *he* were the head of this household.

Margaret could not agree with the doctor's motto as she regarded the children staring blearily across the table at each other. But they were quiet, and attentive in a sort of stunned way, and so were perhaps easier to instruct. It seemed to Margaret to go against all natural feeling to get out of bed before the sun had so much as streaked the summer sky, and she wondered if the Tolmies' new home could possibly be habitable by winter.

Much of the Tolmies' belongings remained boxed-up in crates, but Dr. Tolmie, unable to do without his books, had requested some space from Mr. Work. Looking forward to new reading material, Mr. Work had readily made room in his library for some of his son-in-law's volumes. To the elder's disappointment, Dr. Tolmie chose to fill half of his allotted space with catalogues of the botany specimens he had assembled from his adopted homeland.

To Margaret, however, they were a novelty, unlike his other unpacked books, which were mostly religious volumes, and one early morning, tired of listening to his lesson on the Collects, she asked if she might look through some of the catalogues. Pleased to have anyone take an interest in his latest acquisitions, even a young lady of uncertain scientific education, Dr. Tolmie permitted her idle perusal of the treasured catalogues, limiting himself to one warning: "Take great care." The pages were filled with pressed flowers and leaves of infinite variety, accompanied by sketches and neatly labelled in Latin. More fascinating, in a morbid way, were his insect boards. Butterflies, moths and other insects were pinned carefully to the boards, flattened out to their full extent.

She took his magnifying glass and held it up to one butterfly's iridescent wing. It must have been recently added to the collection; its colour had not faded, but beckoned with such lustrous brilliance that Margaret put her finger out to touch it.

"It will not last if it's handled," Dr. Tolmie broke in curtly.

Margaret looked up to see her siblings' and nephews' eyes, briefly illuminated with a flash of interest, upon her, along with the doctor's stern gaze. Suzette, who had never known her sister to be in trouble, was wide-eyed. Margaret withdrew her hand.

About a week after Mr. Grahame's departure, Mr. Bushby returned to Victoria from the mainland, where he had been on his second tour of duty with Judge Begbie. Margaret could now see him with tolerable composure. He treated the Work daughters as friends of his particular friend, Agnes Douglas. That Agnes was a favourite was now in no doubt: when he was in town, Bushby was firmly entrenched in the Douglas home. The only question Margaret's observation of the two could not settle was the seriousness of the young man's attachment. It would not be the first time a young gentleman would seem a permanent fixture in a home until a return to the Old Country abruptly ended all discourse.

John had apparently adopted this as the most probable outcome for, although he was angry and resentful at Agnes' cooling demeanour toward him, the arrogance of youth carried the day and he seemed to believe he would win her back in the end. And he had not been totally forgotten by Agnes. While Bushby was away she still received John's attentions, but with less enthusiasm than she had hitherto shown.

Margaret hoped she saw a sign in John's favour the Sunday after Mr. Bushby's return. The Works had been invited to the Douglas residence for tea following church. Mr. Bushby evidently had another engagement, and Margaret watched Agnes walking with John several yards ahead. Agnes' expression was very warm, her countenance animated as she talked. Margaret could not see John's face; he kept it fixed on the ground before him. *This is no way to encourage her,* thought Margaret. *Do not avoid her eye!* A moment later, Margaret got her wish. John turned to Agnes, but his face, far from being endearing, had a black, angry scowl. He spoke a few sharp words to Agnes and then struck off toward the Helmcken house, which the party was passing.

Kate fell in beside Agnes; they spoke briefly, and then Agnes hurried on ahead to her home. Young Martha Douglas claimed Margaret's attention with a posy of daisies, and by the time Margaret caught up to Kate, Mary had reached her first.

"What do you think?" whispered Mary, her eyes wide. "Agnes has broken off with John!"

John did not appear for tea, not surprisingly to Margaret, but much to the consternation of Mr. Work, who knew nothing of the rupture. Agnes was unavailable for comment; she had taken to her room with a headache.

Mr. Bushby, it soon became clear in the following weeks, had not asked Agnes for her hand, although the young lady appeared to expect it at any time. When the subject was hinted at, she grew evasive, blushed, simpered and smiled.

This unfortunate turn of events for John was followed by one of a graver nature for everyone. Before July was up, the threat of American annexation, stirred by the gold rush, was brought sharply into focus, not by gold, but by the death of a pig. The simmering dispute over the British–American boundary through Haro Strait erupted with the shooting of a stray company pig on San Juan Island by an American settler, and Mr. Dallas was sent in the company's ship *Beaver* to investigate. The American officer in charge, General Harney, claiming Dallas came on an English man-o-war to arrest an American citizen, landed a detachment of men on the pretext of protecting American settlers. Despite the seeming insignificance of one pig, its death stoked the fires of nationalism, and the threat of war loomed darkly on the summer's bright horizon.

The Pig War on San Juan Island became the talk of the town. Accurate details were difficult to obtain. Each issue of the *Colonist* and the *Gazette* produced more questions than answers. Mr. Work's arrival home each evening was eagerly awaited, in hopes that he would bring more news from Governor Douglas. The strain in her father's eyes caused Margaret infinitely more worry than any of the developments he could relate.

In mid-August while searching the paper, Margaret read the surprising news that Mr. Angelo, host of their memorable winter dinner party, had been convicted of falsifying accounts in the Customs House. Margaret felt herself doubly duped by him: she and Mary already knew him to be of less than sterling character in his private life, and now he was exposed as a fraud in public life. It was an important lesson in not assuming that the English newcomers, by virtue of their birth and education, were of a superior cut than themselves, but Margaret could not revel in her budding feelings of equality. All seemed overshadowed by the imminent threat of American annexation and, even closer to home, by the gloom John's mood cast over Hillside.

Against the backdrop of political conflict, Margaret watched John go through his own private war. His pride struggled with his attachment to Agnes, and in spite of all his digs over her spinsterhood, any vengeful feeling Margaret had quickly dispersed. John quickly rebuked, however, every gesture of sympathy from Margaret or any other of his sisters. Margaret wished he would not spurn Mary's attempts, especially, to console him, as Mary badly needed a distraction from her own quiet despondency.

Margaret had little opportunity to speak with Agnes alone over the next few weeks. Her visits to Hillside ceased, and whenever Margaret paid a visit to the Douglas household, either Mr. Bushby was present, or Agnes made herself scarce. When she could procure an escort to take her, Margaret visited Cecilia Helmcken, in hopes of learning more, or even getting a private moment with Agnes, and one afternoon toward the end of August she finally got it.

Margaret was sitting in the Helmckens' small sitting room, reading the children a story while Cecilia supervised her Indian help, Dick, with dinner preparations in the kitchen. Several of Dick's family members had arrived on the kitchen doorstep that day, wanting to use Cecilia's pots and pans; Margaret could hear Cecilia's wearied tones among the others, all speaking Chinook, the trading language.

Footsteps were heard on the front walk outside the sitting room, and one of the children leapt to the window, crying out "Aunt Agnes!" just before a rapid knock came on the door. The door was flung open and she entered the room. The glow on her cheeks was more than what a short walk from the Douglas home could give her; animation filled her face and her eyes sparkled.

"Where is your mama?" she cried, picking up one of the children and giving her an affectionate hug. "I have such news!"

"The Pig War has been settled?" suggested Margaret eagerly.

"Oh no, nothing like that," laughed Agnes. "Something altogether different."

Her expression was so cheerful that Margaret looked at her very keenly. Agnes checked herself, appearing to recollect the current political excitement they were all anxious over. In between putting off the children's excited queries over her news, she pieced together the following for Margaret's benefit: "Would that I had news of that! It is all very worrying—we could all sleep much better if it were all settled—Papa would like it settled, you know. If he had his way," she lowered her voice here, "I think he would have sent all our men-o-war and taken the island—Mr. Young agrees they would have made quick work of the American warships—but although Papa is Vice-Admiral, Mr. Young says the captains wanted direct orders from the Admiralty—and now it is dragging out horribly."

Cecilia emerged from the kitchen, saving Margaret from forming a reply to such a deluge.

"Oh, Cecilia, do sit down, I've such news!" said Agnes, clutching her sister's arm, and then, for suspense, waited until her sister complied. "Arthur asked Papa for my hand!"

Before Cecilia could respond, she continued, "And what do you think? Papa has postponed him! He said we were both so young— well, naturally I thought of you. I thought you would have a laugh at that, seeing as you were married at 17, and I'm 18 now! But times have changed! And Papa said Mr. Bushby's salary was so small, how could we get by on it? Well, Arthur said afterwards to me, 'Why the devil doesn't he make it larger?'" Agnes giggled. "If it makes Papa happy we will wait of course. He insisted that Arthur pay 'no particular attention' to me in the meantime! That is the funniest thing—what a lark! But, wait we must."

She paused long enough to catch her breath, and for her sister to offer a few hesitant words of delight, and when they had been warmly received, Agnes turned tentatively to Margaret.

"I hope you can wish me well in my married life, Margaret. And—that John may be able to, eventually. We were merely childhood sweethearts, you know. It was only a matter of time before one of us found a true love. I'm certain he will find *his* soon."

Her look was hopeful, but Margaret could only give her own good wishes; she offered no reassurance of John's good will. She knew Agnes to be a lighthearted, unaffected girl, certainly without malice, and perhaps she even believed her account of John's feelings.

Only slightly subdued, Agnes contented herself with extracting promises of secrecy from her nieces and nephew.

"It is not a public engagement, you know—Grandpapa wants us to wait. He thinks us too young—fancy that! So you must keep it secret," she admonished with another giggle.

Margaret smiled wryly. Agnes had deftly ensured its publicity.

"I must go and tell Jane. It will take her mind off this San Juan pig difficulty. I don't call it a war to *her*, you know," she said, looking at Margaret. "In her condition, having had a baby, she finds it all very distressing. I do hope it is settled soon—I think I should like to spend my honeymoon there. Such a lovely spot."

Margaret stood with the children as they waved goodbye to their aunt at the door. Cecilia did not get up; she was tired, but watched Agnes walk down the path from her seat at the window. When Margaret shut the door Cecilia exchanged a wearied look with her friend, sighed and said, "Thank heavens Papa has postponed her."

Chapter Fourteen

September 3rd. Left Westminster for Victoria...
& got once more among civilized people. Directly
I landed I started off to spend the evening with
the Works & thank them for all their kindness;
you can imagine how astonished they were to
see me open the door & walk in. They got up an
impromptu hop immediately...
—Lieutenant Charles William Wilson, RE

The first Saturday in September, Suzette claimed a promise from her father to take her into town, in celebration of her starting school that month and her upcoming birthday. Margaret and Mary, who were to accompany them, found occasion to appreciate the advantages of a nearly five-year-old's tenacity and charm. Suzette's earnest entreaties to "name a day!" had procured this trip from their father much more quickly than their own mild-mannered supplications could ever have done.

The early September sunshine showed no inkling of its demise into autumn, and the Work ladies were quite content to wait for their father on the boardwalk outside the stuffy Post Office, where he attended to the business of sending off letters to family in the Old Country whom his daughters had never met. Suzette's eyes were round with wonder as she watched the goings-on in the street. Men of every colour and nationality passed by, many tipping their hats to them, and the Wells Fargo Express wagon rattled down the deeply rutted street, the mud that created such a quagmire in the winter having dried to a hard-baked, cracked finish. If mud was the bane of Victoria's winters, dust was its summer counterpart. A coating of it settled on them in the wake of the wagon, the thin film crowning their heads graduating to a thicker layer on their lower skirts. It filled their nostrils; they coughed and sneezed along with all the other inhabitants of the street. But Suzette would not be tempted into the shelter of the Post Office. The attractions of the street were too great.

Several acquaintances stopped to greet them; the last to do so before Mr. Work emerged was Mr. Jackson. Suzette had not seen him since the day she had perched atop his shoulders at the opening ceremony of the Government Buildings, but having fond memories of the event she was eager to renew the acquaintance.

After cordially returning her "How do you do," Mr. Jackson addressed himself to her sister. "Are you quite alone, Miss Work?"

"Of course not!" piped up Suzette. "She is with Mary and me."

"Our father is in the Post Office," replied Margaret.

"No doubt he did not intend for you to wait long. He must be detained and would wish you to return inside."

"Oh no!" said Suzette.

"Then permit me to walk with you until he is finished."

"Papa will worry if he cannot see us when he comes out," said Mary.

Mr. Jackson began to look impatient. "We will turn around at the end of the block."

Suzette, in happy acquiescence, pulled Mary forward by the hand. Mr. Jackson followed, offering Margaret his arm. She took it with mixed feelings.

"It does not do," he said in a lowered voice, "for young ladies to stand about on the street."

"It was only a few minutes," replied Margaret defensively.

"Long enough."

They stopped, at Suzette's request, to look in the window of a nearby bakery. Mr. Work joined them just in time to hear his youngest daughter say confidently to Mr. Jackson, while holding fast to his sleeve, "My mama and papa would be delighted if you would have supper with us this evening."

This threw the party into a brief moment of confusion. Margaret and Mary, embarrassed and a little amused, looked to their father and each other while Mr. Jackson hesitated politely and Suzette waited expectantly for his reply.

"Most delighted, indeed," said Mr. Work reassuringly.

Mr. Jackson accepted and in another moment was gone.

The flutter of feelings that possessed Margaret at the idea of his coming to dinner rather startled her. She began to admonish Suzette for giving the invitation, but Mr. Work interrupted her.

"No, no, I can honour Suzette's invitations, providing she remains as judicious in the giving of them as she demonstrated just now! I have been meaning to ask Mr. Jackson to dinner, and have only wanted the opportunity. Besides, I must not balk at getting acquainted with those I purport to represent."

Mr. Work, though lacking confidence in Victoria's elected government, took his appointed position as Vancouver Island Council member seriously.

All the way home Margaret silently berated herself for her agitation over the upcoming dinner. Guests were frequent at Hillside; she was rarely thrown into a quandary by the prospect of them. *It must be on account of John that I am anxious*, she justified. Since hearing of Bushby's proposal to Agnes, John's mood had only blackened, and he could barely rouse himself to common courtesy, even for company.

And then there was her mother. Mr. Jackson had only met her

briefly; he had not yet had the occasion for a closer acquaintance. She dreaded that he might respond to her warmth with cold civility or, perhaps worse, that he might fawn over her. There were those, in the past, who had ridiculously romanticized her Indian blood. They invariably held the view that Mrs. Work was the daughter of an Indian princess, and treated her with a mixture of reverence and scientific fascination, as if they had come across a species of rare plant in the wild. Mrs. Work's mother was indeed the daughter of a chief, but this was not to be wondered at, since most traders who took native wives married into powerful families, thus strengthening their safety and their trading ties, and ensuring future profits.

Whatever her feelings, Margaret managed to bear the prospect of Mr. Jackson's company with fortitude. The supper hour arrived at last and, after spending longer than usual at her dressing table, Margaret descended to the drawing-room. Her agitation proved unnecessary, for when Mr. Jackson arrived he was soon drawn into conversation with Dr. Tolmie. Finding they had a shared interest in public education, they remained conversing on that subject for a half-hour. By this time Margaret, although much calmer, found she suffered from hurt pride, for there was nothing in Mr. Jackson's behaviour during his tête-à-tête with the doctor, save one glance in her direction, to suggest he thought of anything but colonial politics.

Formality was short-lived at Hillside. The geniality and warmth of its hosts, combined with a full house and the antics of young children, ensured a lack of ceremony. And there among them all sat Mr. Jackson with perfect ease, reclining slightly in his chair, while debating the issues of public education with a very decided air. *So comfortable in his own skin,* Margaret thought enviously. Gone was his formality, but none of his natural dignity. He had made the colony his own, while holding himself above it.

Dr. Tolmie was at length wanted by his wife; Mr. Jackson advanced in Margaret's direction, but stopped in front of John.

"Another bountiful harvest this year, Work? Hillside enjoys some renown in town. The land has rich soil, it would seem. I've half a mind to try my own hand at it."

"I've learnt that townsfolk often have little idea of the toil that goes into farming. Haven't got the backbone for it."

Margaret blushed for John, whose increasing dissipation had caused their family enough concern for Mr. Work to reprimand him. Even more than his words, she was taken aback by the hostility in his tone. She waited uneasily to hear Mr. Jackson's reply.

"Without a doubt, but I may yet give it a try." He raised his eyebrows as he spoke, but showed no anger or resentment at John's words. He caught her eye just then, and she quickly turned away, embarrassed by both John's behaviour and having Mr. Jackson see her witness it. Before she could make good her escape, Mr. Jackson was at her side. Now that he was there, Margaret wished him elsewhere. She prepared to defend her brother and looked him squarely in the eye.

"I trust, Miss Work," he smiled, looking over to where Suzette played on the chequered hearth-side rug, "that your youngest sister has not led you astray again since we met at the Government Buildings."

This was such a departure from the topic she had expected—a disapproving comment on John's abruptness—that she only replied, "No, sir."

"I see you have fully recovered from your brush with the 'outscourings of Californian jails'—as I think I termed the miners on that occasion."

"Indeed," she half-smiled, "that was more than a month ago. I think I may have recovered by now."

"It seems I may have judged prematurely. Although some of the miners fit the description I assigned them, there are those among them who are educated, well-bred young men. The gold rush attracts from every rung of society, and appearances in the colony are more deceptive than elsewhere."

Margaret took this as an apology to herself, for his brusqueness to her on that occasion, as much as to the miners. She wavered over the forwardness of saying "I forgive you," but was saved a reply by the front door suddenly swinging open, which produced an instant pause in the conversation of the drawing-room's occupants. She turned to see who would walk in.

They had not expected to see him until winter, but there in the doorway stood Lieutenant Wilson. His physical appearance surprised as much as the timing of it. He wore the red serge shirt of a miner, knee britches and a corduroy coat. Margaret was most startled by the change in his face. His features had become weather-bronzed—indeed, darker than Margaret's own. Evidently he had spent as much time in the summer sun as Margaret spent avoiding it. She thought it looked very well on him.

He seemed greatly pleased to see the astonishment his sudden presence had produced. David and Suzette were immediately at his side. Mr. Work stepped forward to give him a hearty handshake and turned to introduce him to Dr. Tolmie and Mr. Jackson. The girls hung back a little, smiling and giggling at his forgotten manners, which seemed to baffle Wilson until one of the Tolmie boys enlightened him, by exclaiming loudly, "You've still got your hat on indoors!" much to the amusement of the whole party.

"You must excuse me," he laughed, doffing the offending article, "and my dress, but when I landed in Victoria I had to start off at once to see you all."

He was welcomed and made a general fuss of. Within minutes Kate and Cecilia clamoured for a dance; old Mr. Tod, who had also been invited at Margaret's suggestion, was urged to bring out his fiddle, and with very little prompting he complied. As a Scot, Mr. Tod favoured reels; there were no complaints, except a little grumbling from John. Margaret had enough opportunity before supper to appreciate the reel's partner-swapping and to find that Mr. Jackson danced well.

When they were called to the dining table Lieutenant Wilson escorted Margaret in; Mr. Jackson offered his arm to Mary and sat a little farther off. Margaret saw his expression of surprise at the liberties Wilson was taking as he began to pass the numerous dishes round the table.

Wilson said warmly, while dishing out roast grouse, "I can't tell you how good it is to be back among civilized people. It is quite like coming home! Indeed, my western home is what I call Hillside, Mrs. Work."

"And you are very welcome in it, Charles," she replied, beaming.

Margaret revelled in having Mr. Jackson hear such praise, and from the mouth of an officer of the Royal Engineers.

"Och! You speak as if you had been out in the wilds!" said Mr. Tod, shaking his white head and wagging a gnarled finger at Wilson. "I'll tell you what it is to be removed from the haunts of civilized men. When I was posted to Island Lake, at about your young age, I fired a round from the fort's cannon to celebrate the victory at Waterloo, when the news reached me there—in 1818!"

"Only three years late!" smiled Mr. Work. "I thought it was four."

"Nay, nay, 'twas three, and that was plenty!" cried Mr. Tod, eyes twinkling.

Kate, who sat opposite Margaret and Lieutenant Wilson, rolled her eyes heavenward. It was an oft-repeated story. Margaret looked down at her plate until she could suppress the laugh that tugged at the corners of her mouth. She looked up to find Mr. Jackson watching her; a shadow of a smile passed over his face before he turned back to Mr. Tod.

"And where is Island Lake, sir?" he asked.

"Somewhere near the North Pole," laughed David, and snickers broke out among the younger folk.

"Might as well have been!" said Mr. Tod wryly, "for the frequency I saw anyone but my men and the Indians!"

"How long were you there?" asked Mr. Jackson.

"Only a decade or so," replied Mr. Tod.

"To endure such privations," said Mr. Jackson, "bears testimony to a very firm mind."

"Aye, only the firmest could endure the privations of *this* country," the old gentleman answered quietly.

This introduced a sober note among the family, who knew of Mr. Tod's personal experience with mental infirmity. He had once brought a Welsh wife out to the Indian Country, only to have to take her back to the Old Country, and leave her there in an asylum. There was an uncomfortable pause, during which Mr. Jackson looked puzzled.

"While we only penetrated the very edge of the wilderness," said Wilson at last, "I must say how deeply we are indebted to you, Miss Margaret, and your sisters, for the gauze bags you made to put over our heads. The mosquitoes were dreadful! Many an evening we sat puffing on our pipes through the bags in an effort to keep them further at bay, blessing you, and holding sentiments rather the opposite for them."

"We were glad to be of service," she smiled back. She could almost feel Mr. Jackson keenly watching this exchange; she dared not look over. "We are happy to see you haven't been drained completely dry. We heard such reports!"

"As well you might! The 'squitoes swarmed about in myriads. Once the mules and horses were driven into such a frenzy by the wretched things that they stampeded through our camp at night, and right over my tent pegs, nearly bringing my domicile to the ground! Such howling from its inmate you've never heard the likes of!"

Everyone was eager for news from the mainland, and the activities in the other colony occupied most of the dinnertime conversation. Lieutenant Wilson was a lively storyteller, and even if his audience had not given him their rapt attention, his enthusiasm for his subject would have secured it.

"My riding has much improved from last year," he said, smiling at Margaret and Kate. "Only a few days ago I was riding from Darrah's camp down to Lord's camp in Chilliwack, and had to ride for half a mile through a dreadful fire. I had to jump one log which had just fallen, much against the horse's inclination as it was burning away at a great rate."

He went on to describe with great admiration the Mexican muleteers and packers, and the manner in which they broke in a horse.

"I never saw such a display of horsemanship," he said. "You could not perceive that José had moved an inch in his saddle and I am morally certain that the best English jockey would not have sat the horse a quarter of an hour. My horse was broken in the same manner at the beginning of this summer, but having been running on the prairie certainly did not look as if he had been. When he was brought out for my viewing José wanted '*el señor* Wilson' to mount, but the *señor* declined the honour of having his neck broken on a Sunday, and waited until the following day to try his steed."

The table toasted the survival of *el señor* Wilson.

"It was not done without a few bumps and bruises," Wilson smiled ruefully, and catching Margaret's eye, "I am sure there are others who could have more gracefully avoided breaking their necks."

After dinner Mr. Tod was again asked to get out his fiddle, and they danced until Sunday commenced. Mr. Jackson did not stay so late and Margaret learned, to her surprise, that the pleasure of seeing Wilson again did not quite outweigh the disappointment of Mr. Jackson's early departure.

Chapter Fifteen

[The naval officers] were welcome everywhere
and behaved themselves like what they were—
gentlemen. No harm came from them to the
ladies, but in process of time, the [local] boys
were spoiled, because the youngsters associated
much with them, and thus the officers having nothing to do apparently, these youngsters
thought this a fine thing, and so neglected or did
not take to work.

—Dr. John Sebastian Helmcken

During the summer Mr. Jackson rented a pew seat in the Victoria
District Church several rows back from the Works. Margaret
had noted on several occasions that he had a good position for viewing,
if so inclined, her customary seat, at the opposite end of the family pew
from her parents. The younger children sat in the middle, broken up by
Mary and Kate.

On the Sunday morning following Mr. Jackson's dinner at Hillside,
Margaret did not see him enter the church. After the family had been
sitting for a few minutes she stole a glance back. There he was; he caught
her glance and returned it with a courteous, though not particularly
friendly, nod. She quickly nodded back and faced forward.

Throughout the sermon she could not do Reverend Cridge justice. Her mind wandered to the previous evening and their guests.
She could not make Mr. Jackson out. He had been polite to her

mother, not in the cool way she had dreaded, but Margaret had been left with the uncomfortable impression that he had been taking note of each and every one of her mother's mannerisms. Toward herself, she thought there had been some warmth, and yet, just as she was about to return it, he had withdrawn it. She wondered much over Mr. Jackson's restraint with John, and whether it resulted from good manners or from sympathy, for he had very probably heard of Agnes Douglas jilting him.

John sat beside her now on the aisle seat, shifting about resentfully. The church's reverent atmosphere could not lift the perpetual scowl he had worn for the last four days. Agnes sat two rows ahead, in the front Douglas pew. John's scowl deepened into a grimace with the hymns, when Mr. Bushby's tenor, mingling with Mr. Begbie's bass, soared out from the organ loft above all other voices and seemed to vanquish the very cobwebs from the rafters. Margaret said a silent prayer of thanks that the singing duo was due to leave for the mainland in the next week for another court circuit.

There seemed no respite from the cloud John's mood threw over them at Hillside. A similar temper prevailed at the Finlayson home, where Margaret reluctantly turned her step later that week. The circumstances of gloom were of a very different nature, but the effect was the same. During the dry summer weather a chain gang toiled under the morbid task of moving corpses from the fort's abandoned graveyard to the newer churchyard opposite the District Church. Among the remains was one of the Finlaysons' daughters, and Sarah could hardly bear the thought of her little Catherine being disturbed. A wound that had scarcely begun to heal was being dug up with her daughter. Margaret had done her best to suggest gently that Catherine could not be at peace with a bustling town growing up on top of the fort's old graveyard, and how much better a resting place was the serenity of Church Hill, but Sarah was alternately sharp or morose in response. "You tell that to me when you have a child lying cold in the ground," she had snapped the first time Margaret had tried to soothe her.

Later attempts had met with only woeful silence. Margaret had grown weary of her complete inability to give solace, and it was only with great effort on this particular day that she had sent Mary to Cecilia Helmcken's and taken on the duty of attending Sarah herself.

"I was expecting Mary," was the terse greeting Sarah gave when Margaret arrived at the Finlayson house.

"I sent her to see Cecilia Helmcken. I thought the walk would do her good," Margaret replied with forbearance.

She followed Sarah into the dining room and helped her lift the cases of silverware onto the table. It was polishing day.

"She'll get a surprise if she goes into town," said Sarah offhandedly after a few minutes of silence. "Dr. Tuzo has come back."

"Come back! Dr. Tuzo! When?"

"Last night. And that's all Mr. Finlayson could tell me. You needn't badger me for more."

Margaret could hardly contain herself. Overjoyed, she began polishing the silver with great relish. Dr. Tuzo had returned early, long before his year's furlough was up; it was more than she had hoped for. He must have missed Mary terribly, she thought. And now Mary would be restored to happiness. At last, here was some good news for the family. Margaret would not allow herself to be disturbed by thinking of Mary's inevitable departure from Hillside in the near future. *Mary will reside in Victoria at least for the time being, and I will have to be content with that,* she thought firmly, proud of her generosity of spirit.

There was a spring in her step on the walk home; visions of the happy expression that the news would spread across Mary's worn face urged her on. When she reached Hillside, she bounded up the staircase like a school-girl and burst into the room she temporarily shared with Mary without a thought to knocking. She came to an abrupt halt a few steps in, and for a moment, all she could do was stare in confusion at her sister. Mary sat in the corner, her face stricken. It was with great effort that Margaret willed herself to cross the room and kneel down beside the chair.

"What happened?"

"Henry—"

"Sarah told me he has returned. You have seen him?"

Mary nodded. Margaret waited painfully for her to continue.

"He brought back his—" Overcome, she put her hand to her mouth, as if she would hold in all her grief.

Margaret had a terrible sinking feeling, as if her heart were falling slowly into the depths of her abdomen. A dreadful suspicion arose in its place, in the form of an old fear. It was not unknown for fur traders to take a furlough to a more civilized part of the world and come back with a more civilized wife.

"He brought back his sister," said Mary at last, having subdued her feelings enough to speak.

"His sister!" interrupted Margaret, with welcome relief. "But why—"

With a brief motion of her head and hand, Mary waved away the thread of Margaret's returning hope.

"I met her. Emma Langford introduced us at the fort. His sister, Mrs. Alston, told a group of us that he is engaged to be married."

"Oh no, oh no, Mary, it can't be—"

"It's quite true. She told us all about it. She could speak of nothing else."

Her voice was hollow. Margaret continued to shake her head slightly in silent denial; she could barely endure to look at her sister.

"But—I can't believe it," she said helplessly.

"His sister is overjoyed for him. It seems his betrothed is a childhood friend of theirs—"

Mary's voice caught and she ceased speaking. Margaret felt wretched because she knew, whatever her own feelings were, Mary's were far worse. She took Mary's hand and her sister started to cry. She remained sitting very still though, as if by not acknowledging her tears she could will them away.

"You said you saw him?"

"Briefly. When he came to collect his sister. He looked at me as if he scarcely knew me."

"How could he? Marry another? When he felt for you what he did—"

"How can I know what he felt for me?" asked Mary. "If he truly loved me, he could not have replaced me, and so quickly—in a matter of months. One does not forget so easily, one does not."

Her voice trailed off to a whisper. Margaret's throat felt insufferably tight and it was some minutes before she could reply.

"The way he would look at you, with such tenderness—I never dreamt he could do such a thing."

"Looks have ever deceived," said Mary numbly.

Margaret cringed inwardly. "Oh no, Mary, you mustn't believe that. He did care for you, I'm certain of it."

"Yes," she said, wiping away another tear. "But not enough to stop him from marrying another."

Margaret stayed silently by Mary's side until her sister's tears were spent and she asked for solitude. Margaret went out into the garden and paced back and forth between the oak trees. Gradually the jumble of her thoughts, punctuated here and there with *what have I done?* took on a rhythm that began to match her pacing, until she began whispering to herself, over and over, "I will never meddle again, I will not meddle . . ."

It was inconceivable to Margaret that Dr. Tuzo had simply found someone he preferred to Mary. She waited with alternating impatience and dread to see him herself. This happened on Sunday at church. He hardly looked at Mary at all, but when he did, his eyes had lost completely the solicitous spaniel look he had worn around her before his furlough. Instead, they were flat and cold.

The following Sunday was little different. The only thing of note in Dr. Tuzo's behaviour to Mary was the lack of it—he was studiously avoiding her. During the week, they saw him in town, coming toward them down the street; he turned the next corner before they met. There was no acknowledgment of Mary, or of what she had once been to him, except when absolutely required by social necessity. Margaret was appalled; Mary was crushed.

His avoidance had the one benefit of suggesting the strength of his former feelings toward Mary, but she was difficult to persuade. She struggled daily to reach some understanding of his inconstancy. Her own mistakes she knew too well.

"If only I had revealed more of what I felt! But I wished so to be certain, to give my feelings without reservation. If I had given him more reason to hope . . . At least I would have the comfort now, of knowing he was fully aware of what I felt for him."

Margaret found it was much better, for Mary's sake and her own, to focus on Dr. Tuzo's weakness, rather than his hurt pride and her part in persuading Mary to refuse him. Margaret deplored his inability to withstand the discomfort of Mary's uncertainty, leaving her sister, now sure of her own feelings, to suffer the real affliction. It would be his fatal flaw, she decided with righteous indignation.

It was not sisterly compassion alone that fuelled her verdict, for she felt that he had committed a crime against his own feelings. She did not doubt that he had denied his love for Mary by engaging the affections of another. And she knew not exactly how, but she hoped that he would be punished for it. Margaret, being a firm believer that love should overcome any obstacles in its path, felt that his buried feelings might wreak their own retribution. Mary would haunt Tuzo for the rest of his life.

To Mary she tempered the vehemence of these thoughts. She allowed that perhaps Dr. Tuzo mistook Mary's indecision for feelings of a shallow nature, since she would question them.

"But you were right to question them, Mary. Feelings ought to be questioned before embarking on such an important step as marriage. Dr. Tuzo seems to have done very little of that himself."

Unable to revive Mary's typical cheerful outlook, Margaret attempted to assume it for her, but she found herself unequal to the task. The only good she could see coming from Mary's unhappiness was that John was distracted from his own. But his condemnation of Dr. Tuzo's character was so complete that Mary, after hearing it, was left all the more wretched for feeling an attachment to such a man.

One evening, after a particularly low day with Mary, Margaret was leaving their shared room, when she found John waiting in the shadows of the hallway.

"How is she?"

"I hope she will be better tomorrow, for getting some rest. I think it would be best if you didn't see her now."

"You must be feeling rather pleased with yourself, for the way things have turned out," he smiled.

"What do you mean?"

"Now you have company, for the long days of spinsterhood ahead."

"I never wanted to hurt Mary," whispered Margaret, pushing past him.

John grabbed her arm, and the candle she held fell to the wooden floorboards. He quickly ground out the flame under his heel.

"It's a bit late now for regret, isn't it? Tuzo's found himself a white wife. The days he'd be satisfied with a trader's daughter are long gone." His face, half-masked in darkness, seemed contorted with bitterness. "Why so surprised? *You* would not have a trader's son, would you? There were several interested, weren't there, *in your younger days*?"

His voice had twisted into a sneer with these last words. Margaret winced. John let go of her arm and she hurried down the hall.

Chapter Sixteen

I am aware that my family, being natives of this
country, would not be fit for society, but that
gives me little concern . . . they are mine and I am
bound to provide for them.

—John Work, Senior

The next morning Margaret again met John in the hallway;
he paused in midstep as if to say something, then changed
his mind and brushed past her. Perhaps it was her red-rimmed eyes
that held him back. She had lain awake far into the night, thinking
over John's judgment of Dr. Tuzo's marital preferences, but in the end
had dismissed his idea as unlikely. There was something cosmopolitan
about Dr. Tuzo, with his English mother, father of French descent,
Caribbean birth and Canadian upbringing, which surely put him
beyond prejudice.

Mary also noticed Margaret's tear-swollen face and exerted herself
to some semblance of cheerfulness.

"I don't know what I would do without you," said Mary, pausing
from her needlework to squeeze Margaret's hand.

This was too much to bear; Margaret crumpled over her lap and wept.

Through her tears, Margaret could see the red pinprick puncture
marks in her sister's fingers, where Mary had inadvertently stabbed herself in her distracted efforts to lose herself in activity. "Mary, how can
you ever forgive me?" cried Margaret when she could find her voice.

"Forgive you? Whatever for?"

"For persuading you to delay Dr. Tuzo!"

Mary surprised her sister with the glimpse of a smile.

"Margaret, you are not to blame. You must not think I don't value your counsel highly, which I do, but your advice only added weight to Papa's."

"Papa advised against accepting him?" Margaret echoed, dumbfounded, wiping away a tear. "But why?"

"Papa has been very worried about Letitia, knowing that she was to lose the support of the Tolmies when they left Nisqually, with Mr. Huggins still only a clerk, and no hint of promotion. And you know all the trouble they've had there—the threat of an Indian war with the Americans. He did not want to see me in a similar situation, so with Dr. Tuzo's future uncertain, he thought it best to wait. I could not, in good conscience, ignore the advice of a father who has, for so long, had our well-being closest to his heart."

"No, of course not," said Margaret without conviction, adding sheepishly, "I've been very silly."

"If I had known you blamed yourself, I would have told you much sooner," replied Mary. "I was too blind to notice anyone suffered but myself."

"Oh no, I won't have you feeling badly for me," Margaret said emphatically. "I want you to know I have made a solemn promise to myself not to meddle in the future."

"Well, I forgive you wholeheartedly," said Mary with a faint smile, which was, however, soon eclipsed by a sigh. They sat in silence for some minutes, and then Mary resumed, "Papa had some further objections to Dr. Tuzo that I could not quite agree with. Of course, it makes no difference now, but I should like to hear your opinion of them."

Margaret said she would gladly oblige.

"He said he was a little troubled by Dr. Tuzo's background, that alone it would pose no difficulty, but coupled as it is with his rank of clerk and uncertain future, he was uneasy."

"His background! Which part? Surely Papa could not object to Dr. Tuzo being Canadian!" said Margaret.

"He did not say quite that. He only mentioned the roundabout route the Tuzo family took before settling in Canada, and referred to the English being apt to question Governor Douglas' ties to the West Indies—"

"But Dr. Tuzo's parents are both known, well spoken of. His mother, although a governess, was *English* no less!"

"Yes, but Papa said his father's family had been in the West Indies for some generations, and although there was no wrong in that, he said it was merely the *association*. His colouring is rather dark," she conceded. "Papa said there was an air of mystery attached to Dr. Tuzo that someone coming straight from the Old Country would not have. Tuzo, he said, would not *assure* acceptability. He said that times were changing swiftly here, and the British will set the standard, and that we ought to be careful."

Margaret could form no immediate reply to this speech. "I confess I am very much surprised," she said at last.

"Then I am glad," said Mary, "that we agree."

———

Hillside was thrown into further turmoil later that week when John declared his intention of going to the goldfields to make his fortune. It was a private announcement, made during an evening interview with Mr. Work, but the whole family soon learnt of it when John stormed out of his father's library and then from the house. The ladies, who were sitting in the drawing-room, heard rather than saw all this, and Mrs. Work hurried to the library to investigate. She returned, evidently disturbed, but would not relate the particulars until the younger children were in bed. Later in the evening, when this had been accomplished, she drew Margaret, Mary and Kate close around the drawing-room fire.

"John wants to go the goldfields," Mrs. Work said quietly, with dismay. Her daughters' eyes grew wide.

"Of course, your father refused him the capital he needs. The goldfields! *Mon Dieu*! Heaven help him if he gets there."

"He still intends on going?" asked Margaret.

"He claims he will, but he spoke with anger and haste. He has little money of his own. Oh, but why is he not content with his father's fortune? Why must he have his own?"

"For Agnes' sake," said Mary, after a brief pause.

Margaret slowly nodded her agreement. "But to spite her, or to win her back?"

"My poor boy," sighed Mrs. Work.

"Mama, he will be back soon," said Margaret, rousing herself. "When he has cooled down. And, as you said, he has little money. He knows how inflated the prices are up the Fraser; he would be foolish to go. I doubt he will even take passage to New Westminster. He'll come to his senses."

"I hope so, and soon," sighed Mrs. Work. "Your father is most displeased."

After many more minutes of reassuring their mother the girls went up to bed, stopping at the library to wish their father good night. If he had been angry he showed no sign of it; to Margaret he looked merely weary. He looked a little surprised when they came in, as if he were far away and their entrance made him recollect where he was.

"Ah, Margaret," he said, looking up with watery blue eyes. "Yes, good night. Good night Mary, Kate dear."

They each kissed him in turn.

"Do you need help with your writing tonight, Papa?" asked Margaret, after her sisters had left. "You look tired."

"No, no, my dear, I'm just finishing up now. You go on to bed."

It appeared he had hardly started, but she went.

The following morning, although John's empty spot at morning prayers seemed to speak loudly, he was not mentioned until the family sat down at the breakfast table. Suzette looked longingly over at his empty chair and burst into tears.

"But when will he come back?" she cried.

"Probably sooner, rather than later," said Mr. Work kindly. "There, there, eat up. Whatever will Miss Phillips think if we send you to school hungry?"

Mary's low spirits finally took their toll. The day after John's departure, when she was prevailed upon to walk to town with Mr. Work in the smoky, late September air, she took cold and came down with a cough. The Tolmies quickly vacated Hillside and went to stay with the Finlaysons; with an infant and young children, they could not take risks with contagion. Young Henry Work had died of rapid consumption, and any illness at Hillside brought this painful memory to the fore, especially a cough. Mary's rattled Mrs. Work exceedingly, in a way that nothing else could.

As yet, Margaret did not think Mary in any danger; nor did Dr. Tolmie, who attended her, believing himself impervious to infection by virtue of his profession. But neither of them could impress this belief on Mrs. Work. Margaret regretted the loss of Jane Tolmie from Hillside. If her mother could only see Jane's calm expression, like a daguerreotype of her own, then Margaret felt sure she would resume her customary serene outlook, as if the image could govern the original. Margaret and Kate soothed their mother as best they could on their own.

Two days went by, and John was sighted in Victoria. It appeared he hoped to raise enough capital for the goldfields by gambling. Mrs. Work begged Margaret to write a letter to him. She dictated her earnest supplications for him to come home, and Margaret added a few of her own, although what they were worth to John she knew not. She tried to convince him that Mary's illness, combined with his absence, had affected their mother greatly, and hoped for the best.

Mr. Finlayson managed to deliver the letter to a cohort of John's, with the result that John returned to Hillside just before supper that evening, apparently having gambled away what little money he had. All he had to show for his adventure were dark circles under his bloodshot eyes. He let his inquiries into Mary's condition suggest his explanation for his quick return. Supper was awkward, but under the distress of Mary's illness Mr. Work offered no reproof to his son, and an uneasy truce held through the meal.

For a few days Mary's cough worsened, and she seemed to be on the brink of at least influenza, if not something graver. She ached and grew feverish. Mrs. Work, for a time consoled by John's return, became anxious again and took to stealing into her daughters' room at night to check on Mary. Several times Margaret, who, despite the empty rooms left by the Tolmies, had refused to leave the one she had shared with Mary during their stay, awoke to see her mother bending over her sister's bed, straightening the bedcovers or patting her brow with a cloth.

On one particularly restless night, Mary's fitful coughing kept both of them awake until late. Margaret reapplied the Turlington's Balsam Dr. Tolmie had given her, and at last it seemed to have some effect; Mary quietened and Margaret dozed off. She awoke some time later, thinking she had heard something. The room was lit by candle-light, and she looked over to see her mother kneeling at Mary's bed in a devotional attitude, her hands clasped and her head bent in prayer, speaking so lowly that Margaret could hear only snatches.

For one horrid moment Margaret feared that Mary was dead, but she was relieved almost instantly by Mary stirring.

"Mama?" she asked weakly. "What are you doing?"

Startled, Mrs. Work looked up and hastily wiped away a tear. "Keeping watch," came the quiet answer.

"You should not be on the floor," said Mary, with a little more strength in her voice. "It's drafty."

Mrs. Work took her daughter's hand and squeezed it.

"Really, Mama. I would sleep much easier if I knew *you* were getting rest yourself," insisted Mary.

"I am here if Mary needs anything," Margaret reassured her.

Mrs. Work sighed, got up stiffly, kissed both her daughters and left the room.

Mary seemed a little better in the morning: her fever had abated and she bore a more cheerful, if pale, expression. Each subsequent day she gradually improved until Dr. Tolmie declared her in the clear.

To Margaret it appeared as if Mary got better out of a sense of duty to her family, especially to her mother. Whenever Mrs. Work was near, Mary smiled more and fretted less. She ate, although Margaret could see the food had no taste for her and brought no satisfaction; she forced it down. When the weather was fine she would take a stroll in the garden with Margaret or her mother, but she eyed the autumn foliage with a listless eye. And yet her air was a decided one, her step purposeful. She plodded toward recovery.

After her illness Mary's need for discussing her disappointment grew less; she drifted in and out of conversation with Margaret. On one occasion she said, "I have one consolation. The worst is over. I have nothing worse to suffer. His wedding will only be the culmination of this present grief."

Margaret hugged her sister, but could not articulate agreement. *This* was not the worst. She had seen suffering beyond Mary's, deep as it was. The worst was their mother's all-consuming grief when their brother Henry had died, Sarah's loss of her young daughter Catherine, Cecilia Helmcken waking one morning to find her first-born dead in his cradle, only to have to bear the anguish again a few years later with her daughter Daisy. But Mary would now be spared such a loss, at least for the near future. And *this* was Margaret's only consolation in having helped to ruin Mary's happiness.

Something like a calm settled upon Hillside after Mary's illness, at least as near a calm as a household of nine could attain. Mary seldom left Hillside, except to go to the Finlaysons' occasionally. Her first church service was regarded with much apprehension; she could not escape seeing *him* there, but neither could she escape going. When her health allowed, therefore, she went.

Mary behaved irreproachably throughout the service; she did not once look in Dr. Tuzo's direction. Margaret hoped fervently that she could avoid him after the service, but when that time came and the congregation milled outside in the crisp October air, she saw him look over several times, then excuse himself from his companions. It was no use—he came over to the Works' circle, and, after shaking hands with Mr. Work, he spoke to Mary. She had turned away in confusion when he approached; Margaret tried to engage her in conversation, but there he was at Mary's shoulder, and Margaret's rather one-sided dialogue had to cease.

"I was very sorry to hear you were unwell, Miss Work," he said to Mary, after nodding to Margaret.

Miss Work! How awful to hear the civility of mere acquaintances pass over his lips, thought Margaret. She saw Mary flinch slightly when he spoke them.

"I trust you are much improved?"

"Yes, very much, thank you." Mary's voice, though quiet, was steady; her face, a wooden mask.

The pause that followed, although short, weighed heavily upon them all.

"A pleasant morning," said Dr. Tuzo and then, after eyeing the cloudy sky, "at least it is not raining."

Mary looked up uncomprehendingly at the sky.

"Rather grey, though," said Margaret, dryly. If she managed to keep her contempt out of her voice, she very much doubted she succeeded with her eye.

Dr. Tuzo shifted from one foot to the other and looked over in his sister's direction.

"If you will excuse me, I should rejoin my sister. You have met, I believe?" he asked, as if just recollecting his manners.

"Yes," answered Mary, in a barely audible voice. "I have had the pleasure."

Margaret neglected to say she had *not* had the pleasure.

"Well, good day," said Dr. Tuzo, touching his hat. And then it was over.

Margaret silently but vehemently cursed his retreating back, notwithstanding the sacred soil she stood upon.

Mary fought back tears all the way home. Margaret talked.

"Mr. Dundas is a very good speaker," she said of the new Anglican clergyman who had recently been sent out from England to fortify the growing colony. "Just think, when the new church is built—if the rumours are true—it will be a much shorter walk for us! Everyone says a new church ought to go in the north end of town. We will not have to walk through so much mud to get there. And an iron church, sent from England! I should very much like to see it built."

Such a solid structure, even a prefabricated one, would not go up overnight and Mary, in succeeding weeks, had to accept the idea of attending many more services at the old District Church before escaping to the sanctuary of the new one. Dr. Tuzo's residence was much closer to the District Church; he would undoubtedly keep on worshipping at the older edifice.

On subsequent Sundays Dr. Tuzo made no further attempt to speak to Mary, but neither did he studiously avoid her as he had previously. When chance threw her in his path, he inquired into her health and then a simple "good day" seemed to suffice. Margaret knew not which was more mortifying to her sister.

Chapter Seventeen

It would ill become me to pass over without a word that society in which I have spent four as happy years as any of my life, from which I have always met with the greatest kindness, and in which it will give me real pleasure again to mix if fate should send me to Victoria. That my opinion is shared by most of the members of my profession, any impartial witness of the social proceedings of the last five years will allow; and if most of the ladies of Victoria have not joined that profession, matrimonially at least, it has been from no want of invitation on the part of its members.

—Richard Charles Mayne, RN

The fall that began so dismally for the family at Hillside culminated with a funeral. Late in November came the shocking news of the death of Mrs. Cameron, the governor's sister, after a short illness. She had been well-liked, even by those who criticized her brother and her husband, the Chief Justice of Vancouver Island. A jolly woman, she had never displayed the formidable gravity of Governor Douglas. The Camerons' home, Belmont, was situated at the mouth of Esquimalt Harbour, and was frequented by naval officers, Mrs. Cameron being a favourite with them. Not surprisingly then, they insisted on giving her a naval funeral.

The morning of the funeral was fittingly dreary; even naval pomp could not dispel the gloom, except perhaps for the young children, dressed in their white mourning clothes and blissfully ignorant. The fur-trading families had a prominent place. The Douglases, Helmckens, Works, Finlaysons and Tolmies surrounded the grave and poor, young Edith Cameron, sobbing in her father's arms. It was strange to see Mr. Cameron's expression; its chief characteristic of benign complacence had been entirely wiped away, leaving desolate emptiness. Cecilia Young, standing on her stepfather's other side, looked almost as distraught as her sister, holding her handkerchief to her face and leaning heavily on her husband, who was attired in his full naval dress.

Those who objected to the government and Hudson's Bay Company stood well back; Mr. Langford, especially, had made no secret of his contempt of Mr. Cameron, whom he had declared a "person of obscure origin." *He must know*, Margaret thought, *that as sincere as his sympathy for the family might be, it would seem false indeed to make a display of it after denouncing Mr. Cameron so publicly.*

Seeing the navy and the company people all gathered together in close proximity, with hardly any intrusion of newcomers, reminded Margaret of yesteryears and evoked a bittersweet nostalgia, intensified by the knowledge that those former times were slipping irretrievably away. Reminding her of this, Mr. Bushby stood among the Douglas clan and next to Agnes. He had returned from the mainland just a few weeks previously.

Eight sailors bore the casket to the edge of the grave, which was full of water from the November rains, and lowered it over the side. Reverend Cridge read. Agnes wept openly and Bushby put a comforting arm around her; she leaned into his shoulder. Margaret glanced sideways at John. His face was as clouded as the dark reflection in the water of the grave.

When Reverend Cridge had finished, Edith, Mr. Cameron, Mrs. Young and Mr. Douglas each dutifully threw a handful of soil onto the coffin. Spelde, the gravedigger, then came forward, but as fast as he could shovel earth into the grave, the casket would tip, defying burial and staying buoyant in the murky water. Edith's sobs took on greater fervour.

"Come away, come away," Mr. Young urged, but Edith was reluctant to leave the damp cold of her mother's last resting place and, even as she was led away, kept looking back. The other mourners waited respectfully for her to pass before they followed, but their attention was called back to the grave by harsh words from the churchwarden to Spelde. His response to the warden's "Do something, man!" was to jump into the grave to keep the casket down with his own weight, while his assistant began madly shovelling. The mourners had seen it before, but looked on for a moment with fresh horror, then began turning away.

Margaret hated winter funerals. She could not help but think of the chilling, dirty water seeping into the coffin, and Mrs. Cameron, a lady once known universally for her warmth, lying in it. She tried to think instead of heaven, but was foiled by the dull grey November skies hiding paradise so completely from the mortal eye.

Leaving the churchyard they passed the Langfords. Mr. Langford looked grim but not a dry eye remained among the ladies. Margaret felt thankful that her own family was not so set apart from any other that they would not at least have the relief of expressing their sympathy openly to the bereaved.

Mrs. Cameron's death set a sombre tone in Victoria. The naval ships were by this time all in Esquimalt Harbour for the winter and several members of the Boundary Commission, including Lieutenant Wilson, had returned from the mainland, but despite the reunion the usual Christmas festivities were respectfully curtailed.

Nevertheless, entertainment survived courtesy of the 1860 New Year election for Vancouver Island's second parliament. Civic life must go on, and Chief Justice Cameron must endure the ordeal along with the other colonial administrators. In politics, mourning could, without remonstrance, give way to public excitement. Dr. Tolmie was to run for Victoria District, so there was no question as to where Mr. Work would cast his vote. The household became engrossed with the antics of the candidates for Victoria Town. For the Work family, the town candidates' greatest promises were those left unspoken: they assured a lively election. Of the four running, three were especially diverting.

Mr. Cary, the colony's first Attorney General, was the town's incumbent candidate. By all accounts a brilliant lawyer, his mental sharpness was matched by an acerbic tongue. His fury often found its mark in Chief Justice Cameron, whom Cary had been known to call "an ignorant pig-headed old fool, who knew nothing about the Law and who he felt degraded to appear before." This did not endear Cary to the Works, whose sympathies remained with Mr. Cameron, especially since the recent loss of his wife. Mr. Work allowed that Mr. Cameron had no legal training, but said it had little affected his capacity as judge.

The Work family took some enjoyment from Cary's tirades against his opponents, particularly Amor De Cosmos, the *British Colonist* newspaper editor, who was held even lower in their regard. Although Canadian by birth, he was championed by the Americans and, even more unforgivably, by the antigovernment faction as well. His "family-company compact" moniker for the colonial administration had become a rallying cry for the agitators. Mr. Work, as a chief factor with the company, felt De Cosmos too biased to fully encompass a "love for the universe," as the newspaperman's self-chosen name professed.

Lieutenant Wilson amused the Works on his frequent winter visits by recounting the debates of Cary and De Cosmos at the Victoria

Theatre. The ladies could not go themselves, but they eagerly drank up whatever they could later hear of them. The drama the candidates worked themselves up into, as related by Wilson, seemed quite equal to any of the theatrical performances Margaret had seen there. "De Cosmos," he said, "swaggered across the stage and boasted of travelling through California with a revolver in each boot! With what cheering and hissing ad lib from the respective parties you can well imagine. And, if this was not enough, to top it all off he was inebriated!"

Margaret was hard pressed to imagine which could be funnier: seeing Mr. De Cosmos' bombastic performance for herself or watching Wilson and her brother impersonate him. She was glad that Lieutenant Wilson had resumed his visits to Hillside; he dispelled a little of the gloom that had settled on the place with the dampness of winter. What the fires did for the corners of the rooms, he did for their spirits. Even Mary smiled a little more when he was there, and not in the forced, reassuring way that saddened Margaret, but smiles of real, albeit fleeting, amusement. As for Wilson, if he wondered over Mary's melancholy spirits, he said nothing of it to Margaret; perhaps he thought she had taken Mrs. Cameron's demise particularly hard.

The other candidate of special interest was Captain Edward Edwards Langford, bailiff of Colwood Farm, and another would-be reformer whose attacks on the government were all too familiar. He was running for office, for the second time, with complete disregard for the qualification, since he could not fulfil the property requirement; Colwood was owned, after all, by the Puget Sound Agricultural Company, a subsidiary of the company. Whether or not he could succeed was a question of some debate. His family's rising social success, as his five English-born-and-bred daughters reached marriageable age, was matched only by his growing financial debt to the company. To the sensibilities of the six ladies at Hillside, of far worse offence was his dreadful snobbery; he had refused to consent to one of his daughters marrying into the company, despite his own present employment with it.

On Boxing Day, Captain Langford's address to the electors went up all over town. There were no surprises. After briefly proposing an inquiry on taxation, a more liberal land policy, wider franchise and reduced expenses in the courts, he launched into a diatribe about the government and the judiciary. One item was particularly galling; he declared the council members to have been fur-traders long "withdrawn from the busy haunts of civilized men," which made them incapable of "impartial and practical" legislation. Margaret was relieved to find that her father was not singled out; that misfortune went to Donald Fraser, who had replaced old John Tod on the council the year before.

Like Cary, Langford often targeted Vancouver Island's judiciary. Though his address was distributed one month to the day after Mrs. Cameron's death, Langford did not spare Chief Justice Cameron in it, except to use a little more subtlety than hitherto had been his custom. This time his attack was cloaked in a quote from one of Governor Douglas' own dispatches to the British Colonial Secretary, regarding calling the first Assembly in 1856:

> It is, I confess, not without a feeling of dismay that I contemplate the nature and amount of labour and responsibility which will be imposed upon me, in the process of carrying out the instructions conveyed in your despatch. Possessing a very slender knowledge of legislation, without legal advice or intelligent assistance of any kind, I approach the subject with diffidence.

The narrow window of opportunity created by the Langford ladies' sympathy for Edith Cameron in her mourning was slammed shut by Mr.

Langford's address. The young ladies had made a point of calling on Edith soon after her mother's passing and had kindly offered to fetch anything she needed from town, as they were among her closest neighbours. But how could the women ignore the hostilities between their fathers, when they were posted all over town?

Lieutenant Mayne came to tea at Hillside on New Year's Eve, to partake in the Hogmanay celebration, and Margaret was glad to have some respite from the election talk. Although she would have liked to hear his unreserved opinion on the subject, Lieutenant Mayne held to the tradition that politics did not mix with young ladies, and limited himself accordingly. One of their earliest visitors, he was surrounded by the family as they sat around the fire in the drawing-room.

"One of my fellow officers has some good news," he said, soon after settling comfortably into his chair.

All eyes were instantly upon him.

"Oh, aye?" asked Mr. Work.

"Mr. Bull has recently become engaged to be married to Miss Emma Langford."

"It must be very recent indeed!" cried Kate. "She said nothing about it at school before Christmas."

"I believe Christmas was the very day," smiled the lieutenant.

Regardless of how unpleasant the news of a younger woman marrying was to Margaret, she felt very keenly for Mary, for whom marriage engagements now had particularly distressing associations. Mary showed a very composed countenance, however, and Margaret supported her by doing the same.

"You must pass on our congratulations to Mr. Bull," said Mr. Work.

Margaret nodded, and hoped she sounded sincere when she asked, "When is the happy occasion to be?"

"Very shortly, early February, I believe, before we take the *Plumper* to San Francisco for refit. Mr. Bull has asked Captain Richards to stand up for him."

I very much doubt we will be invited, thought Margaret suddenly. There was a time, only two short years ago, when a wedding would have brought the whole community together in celebration. But since Victoria's population had swelled with the gold fever, the cracks in its society had deepened into rifts. Previously, invitations were unnecessary; everyone came to a wedding. Now, even a family such as the Works could be overlooked.

"Poor Mrs. Langford," sighed Mrs. Work. "She will miss her Emma when the ship goes back to England. Two daughters, now, married to the navy!"

Two daughters! thought Margaret.

"It is a good thing for Mr. Bull," smiled Mr. Mayne, "that Mrs. Langford does not have quite the same sentiments on the subject as you, Mrs. Work, or perhaps she would not have given her blessing!"

He seemed happily unaware of Margaret's chief thought: Mrs. Work would probably never be called on to give her blessing to a naval marriage. Mrs. Work, perhaps struck by the same idea, appeared pleased.

"When do you expect your ship to return to England?"

"That remains in the hands of the Admiralty," said the lieutenant, spreading his hands out, as if the workings of that great institution were like the mysteries of the Almighty—incomprehensible to mere mortals. "Perhaps Miss Emma may yet enjoy a few more years here with her family."

"She will have her sister Louisa waiting in England when she goes," said Mary. "That will make leaving Victoria easier for her."

Margaret swallowed. At times she wished Mary not quite so generous in nature. Subdued, Margaret looked down into her lap, and when she lifted her eyes again, she noticed Kate watching her. It took a moment to understand the expression on her younger sister's face, but then she realized with dismay that it was pity, and she excused herself and left the room.

Chapter Eighteen

> January 2nd. This evening kept as New Year's
> day, I went to a large dinner at my old friends, the
> Works. There were about 30 at dinner, nearly all
> of the family & a regular good old English one it
> was, such a display of fish, flesh, fowl and pastry
> as is seldom seen. We danced away till 12 & then
> all hands sat down to a sumptuous supper & then
> set to work dancing again until a very late hour.
> —Lieutenant Charles William Wilson, RE

A few days later, the Works ushered in 1860 with another celebration. With the Tolmies, Finlaysons and friends, the party
numbered about 30. Among the last to arrive at Hillside, Lieutenant
Wilson came through the door mud-splattered from his long ride from
Esquimalt, but beaming at the family's warm New Year's welcome. They
helped him off with his dripping cloak to find him holding a rolled
placard in his hand.

He unrolled the sodden-edged poster as though offering plum pudding. "I took it off the wall at the Hotel de France. Someone," he said,
"posted them all over town before dawn." Drawing him closer to the fire,
the family gathered around to hear him read.

> To the Electors of Victoria.
> Gentlemen,
> Some injudicious person, assuming my name, has put forward

in answer to your requisition, a long winded and spiteful address, containing many things which I, of course, should not like to have repeated, among other things, His Excellency's complaint that he was without any intelligent assistance, when I was at his elbow; a statement that I required a full discussion of the whole subject of Taxation, before I could form any opinion in reference to it; and other matters showing a shallowness of comprehension and an envious disposition, which I really ought to be ashamed of.

The easiest way for you, gentlemen, to judge of my merits, is to make a short statement of what I am, and what I have done.

I came here about eight years ago, the hired servant of the Puget Sound Company, for the wages of about Six Dollars a week, and my board and lodging; the privileges of board and lodging were also extended to my wife and family, in consideration of the Company's having the benefit of their labour on the Farm of which I was to have the charge.

I was brought out here at the expense of the Company: I was placed on the Farm I now occupy, bought by the Company, stocked by the Company, improved by labour supplied by the Company entirely. In fact, I have not been put to penny expense since my arrival in the Colony. The boots I wear, and the mutton I and my family and guests eat, have been wholly supplied at the expense of the Company; and I flatter myself that the Colonial reputation for hospitality, as displayed by me at the expense of the Company, has not been allowed to fall into disrepute. I have given large entertainments, kept riding horses, and other means of amusement for myself and my guests: in fact I may say, that I and they, have eaten, driven, and ridden the Company for several years, and a very useful animal it has proved, though its ears, gentlemen, are rather long.

All this time I was and am the Farm-Bailiff of the Puget Sound Company, at wages of 60 pounds, ($300,) per annum, and board, a position I value much too highly to vacate until I shall be kicked out of it. I have refused to render any account, any intelligible account, of my stewardship: in fact I had kept no accounts, that I, or anybody else, could make head or tail of. When requested to give satisfactory explanations, I told my owners pretty squarely, that they should have no satisfaction except that usual among gentlemen; and as I know nobody would call me out and pistol me, I commenced a system of abuse with which you are doubtless tolerably well acquainted; at the same time currying popularity with my farm servants, by letting them eat and drink, play or work, just as they liked, which I could do cheap, as the Company pays for all.

I am sorry to say, however, gentlemen, that although pretty jolly just now, I have not been careful enough to keep a qualification for myself for the House of Assembly, although I have run my owners many thousands of pounds in debt. However, I hope to bully them out of their property entirely—"improve" them out of their land. How I propose to do this, seeing that all the land, capital, stock, and labour, has been provided by them, is a secret. In the meantime, if I should not be fortunate enough to nail a qualification before the Election, I shall do as I did before, hand in a protest against the grinding, despotic tyranny, which requires a qualification at all, notwithstanding Runnymead and Rule Britannia: The House, I doubt not, will allow me to sit, and I shall be too happy to serve you as I have served my present employers. I have the honour to be, gentlemen,

Your most obedient
E. E. Longford

The family exchanged wide-eyed looks of wonder and mirth at this unexpected, belated gift to the community. Mr. Work, Dr. Tolmie and Mr. Finlayson, as senior officers of the company, were well acquainted with Mr. Langford's extravagance; the bailiff's excesses particularly affronted Dr. Tolmie, who was inspired by thrift and held the unenviable position of manager of the company's farms. Highly principled, Tolmie attempted a grave expression under his furrowed brow while listening to the slanderous squib, but the corners of his mouth danced a jig. Although the company had not escaped scot-free, Langford was exposed to the worst ridicule in the unhappiness of their prolonged relationship.

"And what was the reaction in town?" inquired Mr. Work, his Irish brogue more lyrical than usual.

"Mr. Begbie was at the hotel earlier, and attested to the truth of Mr. Langford's contract with the company, much to the astonishment of the crowd."

The family spent the next hour discussing who had written the hoax. The author could not be the dignified governor himself; he didn't possess enough humour. Chief Justice Cameron was far too deep in grief to do such a thing. The misspelling of Langford's name, a possible precaution against slander, suggested legal knowledge. They bandied about Attorney General Cary's name; he had recently demonstrated a sense of being above the law when arrested for furious riding on the James Bay Bridge.

Kate teasingly suggested Wilson himself, since he had shown such amusement in producing the placard, but this he denied so emphatically that the idea was soon dropped.

"I have enough respect for the gentleman, although not necessarily his political beliefs or his manner in expressing them, that I would not so much as consider having a hand in it," he said firmly. "However, since it was posted so liberally about the town, I thought it only a matter of time before you saw it somewhere, and I might as well bring it myself."

The dinner was as sumptuous a one as ever graced the table at Hillside, and dancing followed until the stroke of twelve o'clock, when they all sat down again to supper. Yet more dancing went on until they greeted the early morning hours. Throughout, Margaret felt a kind of secret, guilty pleasure that Mr. Langford should be made the source of such a public joke. And what a blight on Emma Langford's matrimonial plans! It felt as if justice had been done.

———————

A few days after the New Year was welcomed in, the Right Reverend George Hills, first Bishop of British Columbia, arrived from England. The next Sunday was anticipated with no little curiosity; everyone wished to hear him speak. That the Mother Country had deemed the new colony worthy of its own diocese was gratifying; yet Reverend Cridge was well-liked and it was difficult not to view the bishop as a usurper, especially when he stepped up to Reverend Cridge's pulpit in Reverend Cridge's church.

Bishop Hills appeared very refined, with a gentlemanly bearing. His long, elegant fingers rested lightly on the church's massive leather-bound bible. He introduced a prayer to His Excellency the Governor, as was the Canadian custom. *Agnes will be pleased with another distinction*, thought Margaret dryly, then chided herself for feeling spiteful in church toward the younger girl. The bishop spoke earnestly of leaving his parish of Yarmouth, which evidently struck a homesick chord with some members of the congregation, as many an eye glistened with remembrance, particularly among the navy.

The choir in the organ loft sang exceptionally well for the occasion, although Mr. Bushby's tenor was a little subdued. His voice did not take flight as readily as before, and he appeared to Margaret, sneaking a glance over her shoulder, a little glum. Perhaps the bishop's sermon had affected him, she mused, or possibly it was only that the other choir members had improved, causing Bushby to lose a little of his shine.

Leaving the church, Margaret saw Mr. Jackson among the group of men surrounding the bishop. Sundays were one of the few opportunities she had for seeing him of late, and she did not like to miss the chance of speaking to him, if only to exchange a few words. She had formed the habit of sticking close to Jane's family after the service, since Mr. Jackson rarely let a Sunday go by without exchanging a few words with Dr. Tolmie and, subsequently, herself. But today he seemed fixed by the bishop's side and Margaret turned reluctantly away from the church as her family set off for the walk home. Lieutenant Wilson had joined them, however, to walk as far as the Esquimalt Bridge, and that was some consolation.

When they were a quarter mile from the church, Mr. Finlayson asked Mr. Work for his opinion of Bishop Hills.

"The bishop," said Mr. Work slowly, "it would appear, is rather High Church."

Margaret listened intently. Reverend Cridge was a Low Church man.

"The chaplain seems to have welcomed him openly," said Mr. Finlayson.

"Yes," said Mr. Work thoughtfully.

"What is 'High Church,' Papa?" asked Suzette.

"It means a bishop is high up in the church," said David condescendingly, from the lofty position of his 13 years.

"Very true," smiled Mr. Work, "but the term rather signifies that Bishop Hills believes in his own authority, and in ritual and ceremony."

Suzette stuck her tongue out at David and nothing more was said on the subject, to Margaret's regret. She wondered how the bishop and Mr. Cridge would get on together.

"Mr. Begbie certainly sang in fine form this morning," said Mr. Work.

"As well he might," muttered John.

Mr. Work looked inquiringly at his son.

"Mr. Begbie," smiled John sardonically, pausing for effect, "is said to be the author of Mr. Langford's election placard."

"Mr. Begbie!" said Margaret and Kate in unison.

"Said by whom?" asked Mr. Work.

"Most everybody," shrugged John, putting his hands in his pockets.

"Tut, tut," replied the senior noncommittally, but his eyes held a twinkle.

"Have *you* heard this?" Kate quietly asked Lieutenant Wilson, a moment later.

"One hears rumours," he shrugged with a smile.

John fell a little back from his father, who resumed his conversation with Mr. Finlayson.

"One hears," John said, "that Charles Good, the governor's private secretary, was Begbie's accomplice."

Margaret regarded her brother doubtfully. His face seemed a peculiar mixture of envy and disdain. Mr. Good had his eye on Alice Douglas and so had the governor's interests at heart; love and youth could easily incriminate him. But dignified, stately Judge Begbie, who never held court without the full robes of an English judge! This was another thing altogether.

"Is it so?" Kate, eyes wide, asked Wilson.

"Speculation," he laughed.

"Little help you are," laughed Kate, giving his arm a playful push.

"Mr. Begbie!" said Margaret wonderingly.

"The Honourable Chief Justice himself," said John sarcastically.

Chapter Nineteen

January 28th. Everything has been very dull here since we have been down, owing to the death of the Governor's sister in November; however we have had one ball given by Captain Palliser (the famous explorer), Capt. Haig & myself, in the hall of the Hudson's Bay fort at Victoria . . . I had the floor well waxed to make it slippery, the effect of which was two tremendous tumbles during the course of the evening. Everything went off with great éclat and everybody enjoyed themselves immensely keeping it up till about 4 in the morning.
—Lieutenant Charles William Wilson, RE

In mid-January at Hillside, Lieutenant Wilson announced a ball. "A ball!" squealed Kate, eyes shining like a starved person beholding a banquet. "But who is giving it?"

"Captain Palliser, Captain Haig and myself," he answered.

"Captain Palliser—the Irish explorer who has just arrived?" asked David eagerly.

"The same. His party shares with ours a great desire for dancing, as you can imagine, after having spent such a time in the woods! Captain Haig and I could not possibly disappoint him, so we agreed to assist. I am taking care of the room arrangements, and Captain Palliser and Haig the supper and music."

"Where are you holding it?"

"In the hall of the fort, by kind permission of your father."

"Papa! You knew all along!" chastised Kate.

Mr. Work beamed at the surprised expressions turned toward him.

"He thought you would enjoy hearing it from Charles," smiled Mrs. Work.

"And that Charles would enjoy telling it," laughed Wilson.

"You will be hard put to outdo your ball of last spring," said Margaret. "What plans have you for the fort hall?"

"That, you will have to wait to see," said Wilson mischievously.

The date of the ball was set for the following week, and two days before its arrival Mr. Grahame arrived at Hillside from Fort Vancouver. There was no avoiding it; Mr. Grahame would accompany the young ladies to the ball.

"We haven't had anything close to a ball since Mrs. Cameron died—nearly two months!—which of course is only proper, but after having waited so long, to have to be escorted to the ball by Mr. Grahame! It just isn't fair," lamented Margaret to Mary when they were alone that evening.

"It's been much longer than two months, for you," replied Mary softly. "Before that, you confined yourself here during my—convalescence. It's been very hard on you, I know."

"Mary," said Margaret, shaking her head and laughing, "you always know just what to say to make me thoroughly ashamed of myself!"

"But I did not mean—"

"Yes, yes, I know. That is precisely why you have such a good effect on me!"

"Well, never mind about Mr. Grahame. I will endeavour to occupy him a little at the ball. He will not be fixed at your side."

"You do not have to do that, Mary. It would make me more unhappy to see you miserable than myself."

"I will be far from miserable! I should be very glad to have something to occupy myself with, especially if *he*—if Dr. Tuzo is there."

She pronounced his name quietly and gingerly, as if tasting a strange, bitter dish.

"Besides," she continued after a pause, "I do not think Mr. Grahame so very awful. On the contrary, he would seem to have many a worthy quality."

"You are right, of course," conceded Margaret. "He is not awful at all. He is just so deliberate, and practical, and—well, practical."

"He did lose his wife three years ago. That surely would have some effect on his temperament."

"You are very just," sighed Margaret. "I suppose I have the impression that his loss has merely increased his seriousness, not produced it. It does seem deeply engrained in his nature."

"Well, from wherever it arose, you will not be overly burdened with it at the ball," said Mary firmly.

On their way to the ball, Mr. Grahame, mindful of the shortage of partners, asked his companions for the first six dances, two each in order of their seniority. The anticipation of the first two dances did not make the journey go any more quickly for Margaret.

As with the previous ball arranged by Lieutenant Wilson, the fort hall, when they saw it, was rigged out from floor to ceiling with flags, so that it was hardly recognizable as the room that had so many other associations for Margaret. In her school days at Fort Victoria, during Mr. Work's last few years at Fort Simpson, the girls had boarded in the upper storey of this very building. Bachelor's Hall, they had called it then. It had housed the unmarried company officers on the main floor. Often in the evenings, the girls would pry a loose floorboard up to peer down at the antics of the young officers in their efforts to amuse themselves.

On one memorable occasion, Captain Grant, late of the Scots Greys and the colony's first bona fide independent settler, after displaying his expertise with his sword by slicing candles, declared that Her Majesty needed a cavalry escort to Windsor Castle. Following the gallant captain, the officers hopped about the room, neighing, snorting and pawing at the floor, until their parade was rained on by one of Margaret's fellow students, who poured a jug of water through the opening in the upper floorboards onto the heads of the unsuspecting cavalry below. The girls rolled about the floor laughing; the officers confined their retaliation to taking up a rousing song.

What a different scene greeted them now! Mr. Wilson had the floor, which long ago echoed with the hooves of a distant cavalry, so well waxed it caught the candlelight and positively gleamed. The lieutenant welcomed them warmly, and Mr. Grahame too, but the latter, although civil, did not relax his stiff countenance, and took in the colourful display with a fixed smile and resigned eyes. The ladies all admired the transformation of the room, although it was not as much of a wonder to behold the lieutenant's second miracle; indeed they would not expect anything less from him.

More guests arrived and, as one of the ball's hosts, Wilson, after securing places on the Works' dance cards, excused himself to greet them. Declaring she must say hello to the newly arrived as well, Kate took the opportunity of escaping Mr. Grahame and departed on Wilson's arm.

As she forlornly watched them go, Margaret became aware of being watched, and she turned slightly to meet the eyes of Mr. Jackson. He was close enough that she risked a smile, in hopes of his coming over, but Mr. Grahame had the poor timing to address her just then. With consternation she attended to what he said, and when Mary finally could draw him into conversation it brought Margaret little release, as looking back over to Mr. Jackson she found he had turned away. Her dance card filled with a rapidity that usually would have pleased her, and still Mr. Jackson did not approach. Margaret began to give up hope that she would write his name among the others there when the band began to play and Mr. Grahame offered her his arm.

The first dance was of course the quadrille. Although its slow pace afforded plenty of room for conversation, her partner did not speak, except once to compliment her dancing. The tediousness of the dance was little relieved by the conversation of the three other couples who made up their set. Miss Emma Langford and her betrothed, Mr. Bull, were one. Their conversation was light and frivolous, but even more irksome was the demeanour of Emma, something that declared success, even triumph, rather than happiness, as she looked serenely about herself. Kate and Mr. Wilson were paired in the adjacent set, and Margaret caught a wink from the lieutenant as they walked by. Margaret noticed Mr. Jackson did not dance, but stood off to the side. The quadrille stretched on in the way that only one with a disagreeable partner could, but finally the band struck the final strains.

The second dance with Mr. Grahame she looked forward to with even greater reluctance than the first. It was a galop, and how Mr. Grahame would apply his staid character to the exuberance of the dance Margaret dreaded to find out. His steady earnestness, however, proved to be so entertaining she was glad that, in his diligence, he did not notice her amusement.

The galop sped up as it went along, and Mr. Grahame, instead of being carried along by the music, seemed rather to wish to pin it down. They raced along as if the galop were something to be conquered and they must at any cost stay on top of it. Margaret began to get dizzy; her feet hardly touched the floor as she endeavoured to keep up with Mr. Grahame. Then, for an instant, she realized her feet indeed did *not* touch the floor and down they went with a terrific crash, taking two other couples with them. Margaret found herself on the floor, her skirt billowed out around her like a mushroom.

She scarcely had time to feel how ridiculous she must look; Lieutenant

Wilson was by her side and, with Kate on the other, they quickly lifted her to her feet. The lieutenant gallantly asked her how she was, but the mischievous glint in his eye showed that he did not fear the worst.

"Oh my, oh my, good heavens!" Margaret heard Mr. Grahame say. Either she or her partner had evidently slid quite a distance across the floor before coming to a rest, as he was some way from her, helping one of the other young ladies up. Margaret saw with more cheer that it was Emma Langford, and she felt that seeing the other lady's hot and bothered expression under the flustered attentions of Mr. Grahame might well be worth any bruises she incurred herself.

Apparently no one was hurt any more than Miss Emma's pride, and everyone had a good laugh, Margaret included. The galop was rendered finished by the interruption, and after Mr. Grahame had bowed stiffly to her and apologized solemnly, Margaret eagerly surrendered him to Mary. Lieutenant Wilson, being right at hand, whisked her away for the next dance. "Since you are unhurt, and are blessed with good humour, as well as hardiness, Miss Work, may I say that there is nothing like a well-waxed floor to add to the jollification of a ball!"

Margaret could not completely begrudge him his zeal with the floor wax, and they shared a laugh over Mr. Grahame's serious expression as he thanked her for the honour of the dance. There could hardly have been a more engaging partner, in contrast with her former grey one, than the scarlet and gold effigy before her. And yet she was not so captivated by him not to note that Mr. Jackson again stood out the dance. The room seemed strangely oriented toward him, as if he was magnetic north to a compass within her; she was always aware of his position in the room. Despite her efforts otherwise, her eyes were drawn to him.

Lieutenant Wilson caught her distracted look and tried to follow the direction of her gaze. Trapped for a moment, Margaret made a narrow escape by spying Mr. Bushby standing near Mr. Jackson.

"Is it just a fanciful imagination," she said hesitantly, "or does Mr. Bushby appear rather subdued of late?"

"Homesickness," pronounced Wilson at once, surveying him.

"Do you think so?" asked Margaret, with surprise.

"Quite sure," he replied. "I see it often enough."

"Yes, I suppose you do. Although," she ventured, "you seem to suffer little from it yourself."

"I have the advantage of having a more fixed date of going home. And a group of men whose morale depends on my shining example and brother officers to shore me up when I find myself drooping! Not to mention being welcomed into the neighbourhood homes as one of the family," he smiled warmly at her.

This brought as much pain as it did pleasure. *A fixed date of going home* echoed in her head. Yet more goodbyes! Someone was always leaving the colony; the Boundary Commission, when it finished its tour of duty, would join the list of naval ships she had seen come and go. She repressed a sigh. Wilson's spoken words had a finality to them, that thoughts, however much avoided, did not.

During the next partner shuffle between dances, Margaret's hopes of keeping a few dances open were stymied by Dr. Tuzo, of all people, when he inquired into the possibility that she might have a dance free. Margaret was so surprised she replied, fairly honestly, that she had a "couple of openings." She had, in fact, three.

"Might I then have the honour?"

She was so lost for a reply that she accepted. Even if she had known how, there was no time to retract what she had said; another gentleman, upon overhearing of her openings, jumped in to fill one of them. Having admitted to possessing them, she could hardly refuse.

During the following waltz, her mind, behind a mask of calm, performed its own dance of confusion, leaping from Dr. Tuzo and his unfathomable request to the last free line on her dance card. Fortunately, her feet performed their task like perfect automatons and the end of the dance, when it came, rather surprised her. Her partner thanked her gallantly enough and left for his next partner. She looked down at her card, but could not remember the number of the next dance—the empty line was the one that stared rudely back at her. She looked up to discern Mr. Jackson standing not too far off, and behind him, across the hall, Mr. Grahame approaching. The latter caught her eye, and Margaret was instantly struck with the uneasy conviction that he somehow knew of her last free dance and meant to have it for himself. This was intolerable; Margaret pushed herself into the path of Mr. Jackson.

"Miss Work," he nodded.

There was no time for delicacy. "Mr. Jackson," she replied, "you do not dance."

"No, I am afraid I am not quick enough," he smiled.

Over his shoulder, Margaret could see Mr. Grahame drawing closer.

"Your card, I am certain," continued Mr. Jackson, "must be full."

She glanced down at her card and then up, brightly. "It is not! I have one left. Number eight, a waltz."

"I must not miss the opportunity, then, of—"

"Miss Work!" interjected Mr. Grahame at her elbow.

"Mr. Grahame!" answered Margaret, with barely contained dismay.

"I am so sorry, but Miss Mary has been taken unwell—"

"Mary! Where? Show me, quickly."

Mr. Grahame led her away, weaving through the assembly with Mr. Jackson following, to one of the small dusty rooms adjoining the hall. There sat Mary, slumped in a chair. Margaret was kneeling at her side in an instant, peering up in the dim light into her wan face.

"Shall I fetch a doctor?" asked Mr. Jackson.

"Yes, yes, at once!" said Mr. Grahame. "Dr. Tuzo is here."

Mary started violently and looked up with alarm, her hand clutching Margaret's arm.

"No, wait!" said Margaret. Mr. Jackson stood with his hand on the doorknob, looking sceptically from Mary to Margaret and back again.

"It was so hot in the hall, I only felt a little faint," murmured Mary.

"I really think a doctor—" urged Mr. Grahame.

Mary struggled into a more upright position. "If you would be so good, sir," she implored Mr. Grahame, "to see me home, I could see Dr. Tolmie at the Finlaysons' home, on our way, and no fuss would be made *here*, which is the very last thing I want and quite unnecessary!"

Her agitation had returned a little colour to her face, but Mr. Grahame looked at her doubtfully, and then at Mr. Jackson where he still stood at the door. Margaret saw that the decision would be the latter's to make.

"You will see, sir, that once out of this stuffy atmosphere, the fresh air and the walk home will quite restore Mary," added Margaret to Mr. Grahame, but once she had ceased speaking, her eyes were directed at Mr. Jackson, silently pleading with him for his support.

"It *is* quite warm in there," said Mr. Jackson at length, glancing at the door, but his lips were compressed firmly in disapproval.

"But you *will* see Dr. Tolmie, before we arrive at Hillside?" Mr. Grahame asked Mary.

"Yes, certainly, if it will put your mind at rest."

Margaret breathed a sigh of relief; the moment of suspense was over.

"A glass of Madeira, perhaps, before she leaves?" asked Mr. Jackson of Margaret, who nodded gratefully, and he left at once to procure it.

Mary had so far returned to herself as to quietly suggest, the very moment Mr. Jackson returned, that if Margaret could make other arrangements for someone to see Kate and herself home, they would not have to leave the ball so regrettably early.

Staring at her sister, Margaret floundered for a reply.

"I am not otherwise engaged," Mr. Jackson offered, handing the wine to Mary. It was soon settled; Mary silenced all of Margaret's suggestions that she accompany her sister home. She drank her Madeira, and quietly left the hall through a back door on Mr. Grahame's arm. Her parting smile to Margaret showed how pleased she was with herself, in turning an impending disaster into such advantage. Margaret hoped Mr. Jackson did not see her sister's smile; she could not bring herself to meet his eye. She had got just what she wanted, but oh, how it was done!

"I hope," said Mr. Jackson cordially, "we are not too late for number eight."

"Pardon me?" asked Margaret, looking up baffled.

"Your last free dance, if I remember correctly. If I might have the pleasure?"

"Yes, of course," she smiled hesitantly, and took his offered arm.

Many a raised eyebrow met them when they entered the hall together alone. Margaret blushed, merely from imagining what they thought, which only served to increase the attention they received. Mr. Jackson appeared not to notice. He looked down at his dance card.

"A quadrille—number seven. We are just in time."

The only person Margaret cared to inform of her whereabouts for the last three dances was Kate, and since she, of course, was dancing, Margaret remained at Mr. Jackson's side. She was relieved not to see her seventh partner; not finding her, he had probably gone out for a cigar.

"I must tell you," said Margaret, once her agitation had subsided a little, "how grateful I am for your assistance to Mary."

"Not at all," he replied. "On the contrary, I fear I did not do enough. It was against my better judgment that we did not summon a doctor. I am not accustomed to worrying over young ladies fainting, especially in a crowded, overheated room, but your sister has been ill and does not seem to have recovered—at least, she does not seem to be quite what she was, when I first met her last spring."

"No," said Margaret softly, with an aching heart.

"It was only because the idea seemed so provoking to her, and indeed to you as well, that I desisted. You are better acquainted than I with the state of her health, and I am certain you would not take any risks with it. And, of course, knowing Dr. Tolmie resides near your home is a reassurance."

"She did so want to avoid a fuss," Margaret said, as much to convince herself as Mr. Jackson.

"A modest nature is a fine quality, within reason. I have said something to upset you!"

"No, no," said Margaret, blinking away tears, but she was so far from success that further denial seemed pointless.

"Forgive me," he said quietly. "I have been quite thoughtless. Of course you are worried about her, regardless of your faith in her powers of recuperation."

Eventually, Margaret felt she must explain herself and said, "Since her illness, Mary has regained her health, but not her spirits. Dr. Tuzo has paid no small part in the change you have seen in her. I—I thought she would be worse off for seeing Tuzo, than for not seeing him."

"Ah," he said, "I thought that might be the case."

Margaret began to worry that she had imparted more than necessary, when Mr. Jackson said, "Let me assure you that your confidence is safe with me. How much better that your sister be attended by a family member than by one who has been the means of distressing her. You were right to stop us."

"Thank you," said Margaret. As the strains of the eighth dance began, she counted it her good fortune that it was a waltz. The relief of having shared the burden on her mind, and Mr. Jackson's attendant approval, made the dance even more intimate than usual.

After the succeeding break, during which Margaret informed Kate of Mary's situation and calmed her younger sister's consequent fears, Margaret was startled, upon consulting her dance card, to find that Dr. Tuzo was her very next partner. In all the excitement, she had forgotten her promised dance. She dimly thought of attempting an escape, but it was too late.

"I have not seen much of you or your family in the last few months," was his opening comment as they began their dance. Margaret did not think it worth replying to, except, in the interest of civility, to give a faint nod.

"I am pleased to see your sister looking so much better," said Tuzo.

Margaret looked at him with astonishment. Mary, who had grown so thin and pale since Tuzo's return, looking better!

"If you had but seen her a moment ago you would not think so, sir! She has gone home, unwell."

"Unwell?" Surprise and concern passed fleetingly over his face. Evidently he had not yet noticed Mary's absence.

"She felt faint," said Margaret uneasily, thinking her sister might not approve of her admission.

"Ah," said Tuzo, with some relief. "It is too hot and stuffy in here, especially for young ladies."

He appeared so easily satisfied with this explanation that Margaret fumed in silent indignation, forcing herself not to disillusion him. They danced in silence for a moment and then Tuzo addressed her thus, "I have some concern in anticipating my future wife's arrival. She will be acquainted with no one here, excepting myself, of course, and my sister and her husband, who are but lately arrived in the colony themselves and are limited to a fairly small circle of acquaintance."

Margaret stared at him vacantly; she could not comprehend why Tuzo should possibly wish to relate this to *her*.

"It would greatly ease my mind," said Tuzo, looking at her with the spaniel-eyed expression that Mary used to receive, "if you and your sisters could welcome her and assist in bringing her into society."

"Me and my sisters!" Margaret almost laughed incredulously at the audacity of the notion.

"You are a member of one of the founding families of this colony and with your sisters hold the universal respect and esteem of your acquaintances," pronounced Dr. Tuzo, as if his suggestion made the most perfect and irrefutable sense.

Margaret looked away in confusion. Never had she been so torn between feeling and decorum. Her feeling urged instant refusal, but decorum demanded otherwise. Tuzo had broken no rules of society, only those of the heart, and he could not possibly be aware of the devastating effect on Mary, whose own modesty and sense of duty had tried to hide it from him. *Oh, had he but eyes to see with,* Margaret thought, *he would not ask such a thing of me, of Mary!*

"Your silence, Miss Work, concerns me—"

"I will certainly do what I can," said Margaret quickly, and to herself, *and shield Mary however I can!* But Margaret saw she had planted a seed of doubt within him.

Chapter Twenty

[Prior to the gold rush] whenever a wedding took place we all went to it and joined in the celebration.

—Dr. John Sebastian Helmcken

In the following weeks Margaret mulled over the events of the ball with a keen mixture of happiness and embarrassment. She allotted Mr. Jackson more of the former than the latter, by a narrow margin. Kate's presence on the journey home had put an end to any further meaningful discourse between them, but all the little attentions he had paid her as they struggled through the mud were added to her treasure trove of memories. Never would she forget his assistance to Mary, his concern for doing the right thing by her, nor the grace, and even the pleasure, with which he had accepted her clumsy request for a dance and Mary's equally obvious solicitation that he should see Margaret home. He had seemed flattered, despite their contrivances. And when they had returned to the hall together, his self-assured expression had seemed to protect her, while at the same time quietening the questioning looks around them: this she remembered with particular delight.

The charm of reliving such memories was eventually encroached on by a circumstance in early February. No invitation to Emma Langford's wedding was received at Hillside. Each day during the latter weeks of January Margaret awaited her father's return from town—each day he was empty-handed. The snub, though unsurprising in itself, startled her with how painful it was. She tried to reason it away, and reminded herself that Mr. Langford's relationship with the Hudson's Bay Company had deteriorated even further since the New Year's hoax had been played upon him. Yet at one time everyone had attended marriages in the colony, political differences aside. Unity had enclosed the wedding day like a blanket; ill feeling was shut out, an unwelcome guest. In their small community, weddings had been a rarity, so they were treated like a holiday and made the most of. But now that their society was enlarged, to have it thus reduced! She told herself she would not enjoy the wedding; to watch someone else attain a position out of reach for herself would be a cruelty. Yet reason fell before jealousy.

On the first Tuesday of the month Margaret awoke in a foul mood, which did not lessen by half past eleven.

"And now the ceremony will be taking place, with the bishop himself officiating," sighed Kate. "I wonder how she looks? I have heard so much of her dress, I really ought to have been able to see it!"

And an hour later, while Margaret picked over her dinner, Kate treated the family to this update, "And now they will be having the marriage breakfast! Captain Richards is to make a toast. All the *Plumper* officers will be there, of course."

Visions of officers toasting the health of the newly married Mr. and Mrs. Bull made Margaret feel ill, and she excused herself from the table.

The exclusion added to her other woes, and if there was to be some recompense for, or even alleviation of, Margaret's silent suffering, she could see no sign of it in the near future. Mr. Jackson was apparently content to admire her from afar, if indeed it was admiration with which he watched her. All the effort of meeting with him was hers and she grew weary of his lack of reciprocation. It went against her nature to be continually putting herself forward.

Three days after the Bulls' wedding, HMS *Plumper* left for San Francisco for repairs, and to make matters infinitely worse, the chief source of her amusement, and distraction from her troubles, was also leaving town. Lieutenant Wilson was going to the Fraser River and, although it was only a short trip, it was but a foreshadow of what was to come, for that spring the Boundary Commission planned to depart for the Columbia River and from there to the interior. That would be a journey not of mere days or weeks, but likely much more than a year.

On the eve of his departure to the Fraser, Wilson accompanied the Works to the Finlaysons'. He was as much at home with the family there as at Hillside. Old Mr. Tod had joined them with his fiddle and supplied endless Scottish reels and Irish jigs, setting a jovial tone far from the tenor of Margaret's feelings. While partaking in the dance as much as anyone else and forcing a smile on her reluctant face, she could not banish the thought that it seemed as if her friends were deserting her when she needed them the most.

How her spirits would support her without Wilson's irrepressible good cheer was the heavy question weighing on her when he took his leave. He had walked them home to Hillside. Kate had run on ahead, saying she had something to give him for his trip, and Mary was busy answering Mrs. Work's inquiries as to how the evening went. For a moment he and Margaret were alone.

"It is only for a week," he said with mock seriousness, as he took her offered hand. "I'm honoured my impending absence could cause such a doleful expression."

His eyes sparkled in their customary merry way and Margaret blushed faintly and smiled. A brief pressure of his hand showed his pleasure at brightening her face, and then Kate rushed in upon them.

"Some toffee for the cold you may very likely get camping out in the woods at this time of year," she said cheerfully, pressing a bundle into his hands. She did not let go right away, but gave him a very earnest look, and it was then that Margaret noticed there was a card attached, revealed as she drew away her hand. He hardly had time to thank her when Mrs. Work came over to thank him for seeing the girls home and to wish him a safe journey.

Upstairs, Margaret inquired into the nature of Kate's card.

"A remembrance of tomorrow—that's a good riddle!" she laughed.

"Tomorrow?"

"You haven't forgotten what day it is? The 14th!"

It took a moment before this shed any light. "You gave him a valentine!"

Kate looked away with a secret smile, which annoyed Margaret still more.

"Kate, of all the forward things to do! What will he think?"

As the younger sister's smile deepened, so did the annoyance of the elder, who, rather than say something rash, left the room.

The following Sunday she bore the sight of Mr. and Mrs. Bull with feelings far from benevolent. Mrs. Bull looked positively exultant. Her new identity seemed as palpable as the new attire she wore to celebrate it, and was duly noticed by all. Margaret was one of the more reluctant witnesses of her exit from the church on the arm of her husband. She looked serenely around as if surveying her own domain, basking in a triumphant glow. *Damn her*! thought Margaret, the curse stealing over her with a suddenness that surprised her.

Bitterness left an unpalatable aftertaste. Having pervaded her thoughts, resentment plagued her for two days straight. She wished to rid herself of it, but could not. Failing that, her object became instead to maintain some outward show of normalcy. With this in mind she went, with her mother and sisters, to join the Douglas ladies for tea one afternoon early in the week. Finding her own company intolerable, she hardly thought she could be worse off with others, but immediately after entering the governor's house, she doubted this. Mrs. Young was one of the party and, with an uncanny knack of going where she was not wanted, sat down next to Margaret.

"My uncle," she said, with grandeur enough to rival the very man, "met a particular friend of your family in New Westminster."

She waited with such greedy expectation for Margaret's guess that Margaret, out of perversity, did not give it.

"Lieutenant Wilson," said Mrs. Young at last, "of the Royal Engineers, Secretary to the Boundary Commission."

Margaret smiled. There being no other Lieutenant Wilson in the colony, it was quite unnecessary, but how like Mrs. Young to throw in a few embellishments! Perhaps the afternoon was not to be a complete loss for diversion after all.

"In good health, I trust?"

"Yes, quite."

"Kate will be relieved to hear it. She thought he might catch cold," said Margaret idly, for lack of any other reply.

After a brief pause while Mrs. Young stirred her tea with very measured strokes, she said, "He has some attachment for the colony. I believe he will be sorry to go."

Keenly aware of Mrs. Young's watchfulness, Margaret endeavoured to keep her face perfectly neutral.

"So sorry," the young matron continued, "that perhaps he may be induced to stay, following in the footsteps of my own dear husband."

At this reference to Mr. Young a slight smile crept across Margaret's face. It was her distinct impression that Mr. Young was not well-liked by his fellow officers, and Margaret could think of no one whom Wilson would be less likely to follow.

Mrs. Young, however, took the smile for encouragement and soldiered on. "Perhaps it will be no surprise to you then that Mr. Wilson has pre-empted land at Sumas."

To the contrary, Margaret's surprise was very great.

"Ah, you did not know," smiled Mrs. Young smugly, like a cat having cornered its prey. "Your sister, possibly, is more acquainted with his plans. They seem on an intimate footing."

Cecilia Helmcken, demonstrating a knack just the opposite of her cousin's, joined them when she was most wanted, at least by Margaret, who was saved the bother of a reply. After 10 minutes of catching up with her friend, Margaret left the two cousins, to consider in privacy the extraordinary news Mrs. Young had supplied. She crossed the room and sat down by Kate, Agnes and her sister Jane Dallas. Three more animated talkers would be difficult to find in one drawing-room. One scarcely closed her mouth before another opened hers, creating such a constant and sometimes overlapping stream of chatter that they were too busy to notice Margaret did not contribute anything at all. Consequently Margaret felt no qualms in pretending to listen while giving all her attention to her own thoughts.

That Charles Wilson should consider settling in the colony was nearly beyond her comprehension. Past disappointment had not allowed her to consider this possibility with any seriousness. It was some minutes before she accepted the fact itself and went on to look at the ensuing possibilities. The reason she had known nothing of it until it was a *fait accompli* was quickly settled upon: he meant to surprise them. But to what end? She thought of their most recent meetings and searched for signs of intent that she might have missed. His leave-taking of her was conjured up again and again: the pressure of his hand, his countenance and above all, his words. *I'm honoured my absence could cause such a doleful expression.* Was there less jest in them than she originally had assumed? Or, more to the point, more seriousness?

His name broke into her thoughts. Jane Dallas had apparently made some inquiry into the gentleman's movements, and Kate answered happily, "He returns to us tomorrow, and then we will be lively, won't we Margaret?"

Margaret was unnerved to find herself the centre of attention in a pause of sudden quiet. "Yes." Evidently this was all that was required of her.

Her flustered state, if observed, did not hinder the flow of their conversation, which resumed unabated until it was time to leave.

Wilson's return was eagerly anticipated, but since arrival times in the colony were inexact, Margaret began to fear that the suspense of one week would turn into two. Her consolation was that they could be sure of receiving a visit from him on the very day of his return, as had so often been his custom. The waiting was made a little more bearable by the arrival of the *Princess Royal*, the company's supply ship, and Margaret had the pleasure of knowing she would be in a new London gown on the day of Wilson's homecoming.

Halfway into the second week Wilson ended the expectation by appearing in Hillside's drawing-room shortly before supper. With him was Dr. Hector, one of Captain Palliser's exploring party, who had accompanied Wilson on this last trip up the Fraser. They had evidently stopped at the fort before coming to Hillside, as they were both dressed in the latest English fashions via the *Princess Royal*. The colonists customarily refrained from enthusing over their neighbours' new clothes in public, as they all partook in the transformation together, renewing themselves at the same time each year.

In the company of Dr. Hector, a new acquaintance, the ladies would have been content with a simple compliment, leaving further admiration to the eyes alone. But Mr. Wilson, after the preliminary handshakes and good will, announced happily, "We have just been peacocking about Victoria in our new rig-out. I could not help laughing at the scene: two very dirty, ruffianly looking fellows walking into the store, and half an hour later, two young swells coming out!"

The laughter generated did not quite equal his own. Uncomfortable to have their transformation acknowledged before Dr. Hector, Margaret felt slightly ashamed of her new gown.

"And when did you get in?" asked Mr. Work.

"Two evenings ago, on the *Eliza Anderson*. We had a magnificent crossing, perfectly clear with a splendid view of Mount Rainier. Very lucky for Hector—I've never managed to see it before."

He went on to describe what was left of the American encampment after the short-lived Pig War on San Juan Island, where they had stopped en route, but Margaret could little attend to it. She was still digesting his first piece of news—they had arrived two evenings ago! A few minutes later he supplied her, unprompted, with a justification for his tardiness in paying them a visit; he was up to his neck in work and was to return to the Fraser in three days for the last time, to pay off his men and wrap things up on this side of the Cascade Mountains. But Margaret was not completely reassured and observed him quietly throughout the evening. There was a slight change other than his new clothes. At first she thought it was merely seeing him in the latest English fashions, but as she watched him she realized the change was rather in seeing him with Dr. Hector. The two men had been friendly before, but this trip had evidently strengthened the bond; they were like brothers. The Works no longer had Wilson to themselves.

No mention was made of pre-empting land at Sumas, at least not to her. There was one moment when Kate and Wilson were alone by the fire; Margaret could not tear her eyes from an exchange that was now of the keenest interest to her. Kate, standing in the glow of the fire, looked positively radiant. Wilson's back was to Margaret, and as he leaned in close to her sister, Margaret began to think she was witnessing her sister achieving what she had longed for herself for so many years, when Hector abruptly broke up the tête-à-tête by the hearth. The moment dissolved instantly, with no trace of it left except for Kate's flushed face and, for her, a rather subdued expression. Wilson's face, as before, was hidden from Margaret's view.

Chapter Twenty-One

June 16th, (Headquarters Camp, Chilukweyuk
Prairie) . . . I think [Sumas] is the most beautiful
place I was ever in, the prairie though small . . . is
most lovely, covered with flowers & strawberries
& even in this early period of the year the grass is
nearly up to the waist.
 —Lieutenant Charles William Wilson, RE

The city began to fill out again as winter abated, but despite the
reassurance that Victoria indeed had become a place on the
map, a more negative trend grew harder to ignore. This year's crop of
newcomers injected a decided air of snobbery into the atmosphere, and
those from the previous two years, and even some who predated the gold
rush, caught the feeling anew. If wintering over in Victoria had softened
the newcomers' pretence of superiority over the fur-trading families,
the latest arrivals each spring typically had the effect of reinforcing their
views. Margaret was conscious of being looked down upon for her native
blood; there was no escaping the scrutiny, nor the knowledge that it happened with increasing frequency each passing year.

The loss of the *Plumper*'s society then, was felt all the more keenly,
and even more, that of Lieutenant Wilson. How much more tolerable
were the cold stares and whispers of strangers when one was on the
arm of a military officer, especially one who had singled the family out
for his home away from home! Although he estimated he would be
gone no more than a week this time, Margaret felt it would drag on

interminably. Having expected that her suspense over his future plans would be relieved by now, the tenterhooks she hung on dug in deeper with each day.

The week was not yet up when Wilson made his entrance at Hillside on Sunday evening. Within a few minutes of his entering the room they learned that he had arrived in Victoria in the early hours of that very morning. Margaret's satisfaction that Hillside was the first place he visited did not last long, as his next remark was less encouraging: "Darrah and Anderson came down with me and we all bid a final adieu to the Fraser River—and not sorry for it!"

This surely was an unlikely comment for one who meant to settle near there. The rest of the evening was no more promising in this regard. He was looking forward "with great pleasure" to the journey to "the real interior," as he put it so enthusiastically, with its "immense plains and bracing climate and almost cloudless skies."

"Oh aye, a bracing climate," said Mr. Work, and Mrs. Work chuckled. Mr. Work dryly acknowledged the snowy winters of Colville to be superior to the heavy rain of Fort Simpson. But Wilson was not to be put off by a little cold.

Although he had inquired into their experiences of the area before, he now entreated Mr. and Mrs. Work with even more curiosity for any information they could give him. This was a great deal, as the couple had spent the first 10 years of their marriage travelling between Fort George, at the Columbia's mouth, Fort Vancouver, Spokane House and Fort Colville, where they had met. Wilson's enthusiasm pleased Mrs. Work very much, especially regarding Colville, the home of her youth.

Margaret knew she ought not to be surprised by his avid interest; he was easily taken up by the moment and the next adventure around the corner. Sumas evidently was quite forgotten, lost in the immediacy of his upcoming journey. As she listened to his earnest inquiries, it occurred to her that pre-empting land at Sumas might have meant nothing more to him than land speculation. Perhaps he had never even considered settling there. As she digested this uncomfortable idea she became slightly ashamed of her preoccupation with his plans.

Kate revealed how tedious the topic was to her; the longer the subject of the interior held sway over Wilson, the deeper her pout grew.

"Do not forget your mosquito nets, Charles," said Mrs. Work. "You will need them on the Columbia."

"Indeed, ma'am, I shall not. I will be the envy of all I meet when they see the ones your daughters have made!"

Kate's face brightened momentarily. "I shall make you some extras!" But Wilson, after uttering a quick "Splendid," was soon caught up again in the conversation.

Margaret's disappointment, being more of the mind than the heart, responded quickly to reason. That she had been taken up with an idea planted by someone else, especially the likes of Mrs. Young, was perhaps more galling than her unrealized hopes of a serious attachment. When the idea was uprooted without much struggle, she recognized what she had lost sight of: Wilson was a dear friend, but did not evoke any deeper affection. He was too focussed on the adventure of the moment to capture her imagination for long; that she had considered him in any other light disturbed her.

The next time she saw Wilson, at a dance at Mr. Anderson's a few days later, she had the comfort of being sure of her feelings toward him. They were just as she had previously supposed them, nothing more, and her brief deviation from them, she reluctantly admitted to herself, had been influenced by envy of Emma Langford.

Margaret was less certain of her sister's attitude regarding the young gentleman. Since the night Kate had given him a valentine, Margaret had suspected there was something more than the earnest, but short, audience Kate generally gave to her admirers. It was not the valentine in itself—being forward was not a novelty with her sister—but rather the extra attention Kate subsequently gave him. Like the light atop Beacon Hill, Kate shone out in all directions, but her rays shone more brilliantly whenever they fell upon Wilson. There were now even brief moments when, unattended, her light flickered and burned low as if it might go out altogether.

At the end of a short break early in the evening, while Margaret waited for her next dance partner to traverse the room to join her, a Mr. Wallace approached her. He was one of the newcomers of the previous fall and had joined the large business of Dickson, Campbell & Company. Margaret knew very little of him, except that his air claimed he thought highly of himself.

"Begging your pardon, Miss Work, but I cannot find your sister, Miss Kate. She has promised me the next dance, you know, and it would be so disappointing to miss it." He smiled with such insinuating familiarity, as if they were the oldest of friends, that Margaret balked at encouraging him. Although she had seen Kate but a few minutes before, she replied that she did not know where she was.

"I will look out for her," she added, suggesting he try the refreshment room. When he had gone, Margaret found Kate where she had last seen her, with Alice Douglas, in a window seat around the corner from the dance room. She was now alone, staring pensively into her lemonade and then out the window and back again.

"Kate! What are you doing? Your next partner is looking for you."

"Oh! Do I have one?"

"Of course you do. You always do. It's Mr. Wallace. You don't want to miss the beginning, do you? It's a waltz."

"I would much rather dance it with Charles," she said, putting her glass down. "I've only had a galop with him yet, and they go by so fast! It was over before it started. Still a waltz—it's not to be missed, I suppose."

They entered the dance room together. Within Margaret's growing unease, there was one reassurance: the change in Kate, being subtle, went undetected. Even Wilson himself seemed not to notice; she was very much herself with him, and when they were apart, he was occupied by whoever else was in his company. This was frequently Dr. Hector, and the two struck such a common chord of geniality as to be unaware of much else.

Quite a large proportion of arrivistes made up the assembly, many unknown to Margaret even by sight. Upon introductions, some received her with decided coolness, and even worse in a few cases, with blatant curiosity. She was taken aback when one young lady leaned close and whispered, "I would never have known, except for your colouring, that you had Indian blood. You wear your dress just like you were born to it!"

"Indeed, I was," murmured Margaret and excused herself.

Later she had the misfortune to overhear a group's comments as Kate and Wilson repaired to the dance floor for Kate's long-awaited waltz.

"The redcoat had better be careful whose clutches he falls into. Dancing with half-breeds. What's next!" said one fashionably dressed young lady, watching Kate beaming into Wilson's face.

"A quarter-breed, I'm informed," said a gentleman by her side. "And he is a regular visitor to their home."

"Quarter, half, it amounts to the same thing," she laughed. "Imagine her in London for the season! And do you know she was born—"

At this point she was elbowed by one of her companions, who directed her eye to where Margaret stood a little way off. Their eyes met for a fraction of a second, before the lady looked away and gave a small uneasy laugh. Margaret turned blindly away with no direction in mind other than to be somewhere else, but found an obstacle in her path—Mr. Jackson. How long he had been near and what he had heard, she knew not, but he did not stop her as she passed.

Toward the end of the evening Margaret had a strange and discomfiting experience; she was obliged to sit out a dance. Although there were men unoccupied, they were evidently among the number who would rather not make her acquaintance, even for the sake of a dance. Except for this, Margaret would have cared little. She was weary, but could not enjoy the rest while it drew attention to her. She was the only unmarried lady not dancing.

She listened half-heartedly to the chatter of Mrs. Dallas, with whom she sat, until Mr. Jackson again appeared before her. It took her a moment before she could comprehend what he was asking. She heard "have the pleasure" and saw his expectant look, but it was only when he offered her his hand that she was sure of his meaning and was induced to stand up.

As they joined the other dancers, they saw the fashionably dressed young lady with the barbed tongue eye them as she swept by. Margaret blushed and felt acutely that Mr. Jackson must have overheard what she had said earlier.

"One of the disadvantages I have found with the colony," said Mr. Jackson carefully, "is that despite the many useful, true pioneers it attracts, there are as many bad sorts who aim to be more than they were at home. Without any inner rule, however, they will soon go wild and sink to the bottom where they belong."

Though she appreciated the sentiment, the recognition was too much; Margaret's colour intensified and the evening's stings and slights brimmed within until her eyes welled up, threatening to overflow. Mr. Jackson, seeing the emotion summoned by his comments, spoke no more.

By the early hours of the morning when the last dance drew to a close, Margaret was quite exhausted, less from dancing than from the rigours of excitement mixed with suspicions and hopes. She had never been quite so ready to leave a party and was thankfully pulling on her boots when Mrs. Young cornered her in the hallway.

"I could not let you leave without congratulating you. The only lady Mr. Jackson has danced with! It has been *noted*. I was not terribly surprised, however. I saw him watching you earlier. Not everyone is gifted with my powers of observation. You might have seen it yourself if you weren't so busy watching someone else! Oh, you needn't look so surprised, I think you know whom I speak of. You and your sister both! At least one of you is sure to be disappointed. But you—"

Here Mary cut her off, arriving at Margaret's elbow to assist her as she struggled into her outer coat.

"We will talk later," said Mrs. Young, patting Margaret lightly on the arm. "Lovely to see you back in health, Mary. Although you are too thin. You really ought to see she eats more, Margaret. Good night."

Early the next week Wilson brought Dr. Hector round to Hillside for his farewell visit, as Captain Palliser's party was to leave by the steamer on the morrow. Kate was in high form, though it was unlike her to prefer a small party to a large one. Margaret continued to note her manner with Wilson, but her only new observance was that Hector had developed the habit of interrupting them; they never had more than a few moments alone. These occasions irked only Kate. Wilson looked as happy to be in Hector's company as ever, although he showed no relief in escaping privacy with Kate. Margaret's belief that he was unaware of Kate's growing attachment was confirmed.

After the third interruption by Hector, Kate declared a dance was just the thing they needed. All turned to Hector, the guest of honour, to see if he was in acquiescence. He made no objection, but suggested a reel, for "Auld Lang Syne" sake.

"As another year, God granting, will see me dancing in Old Scotland again," he said, "but we must not forget the present company when we are safely home again!"

This short speech produced a brief silence from the party and a pained smile from Wilson. The "we" was not lost on Margaret and she wondered over Wilson's expression. Was it Hector's departure that pained him so, or possibly his own impending one, or his long absence from home? Or perhaps all of them combined.

The reel itself banished the thoughtful mood and returned an atmosphere of levity to the party in all, it seemed, but Margaret herself. Although her acquaintance with Hector was short, his departure was leaving its mark on her. So many leave-takings, his being only one in a long line, with still more to come. She was embarrassed by the feeling that stole over her throughout the evening, especially when it came time for Hector and Wilson to leave Hillside.

She saw her father's tired eyes moisten as he shook the young doctor's hand and the slight quiver in his voice when he uttered the words, "Soon your feet will be standing on the soil of the Old Country! God speed."

"Thank you, sir. Although I long for home, I leave this place with regret." Hector appeared touched.

Mr. Work made no reply, but pumped his hand up and down several more times before letting go. Margaret felt if her father could keep his composure, so ought she, and she managed to get out "a safe journey" when her turn came.

It was only later, when she lay in bed in the privacy of her own room, to which she had returned after Mary's recovery, that she allowed the tears to flow and knew not whom she cried for most: her father, who would never again set foot on the soil of his homeland; or Kate, who was recklessly following a path that in all likelihood would lead to disappointment and sorrow; or Wilson and Hector and all the others, who might never again see their friends from the colony once they left it; or finally herself, whose own longings she despaired of ever finding a home.

Chapter Twenty-Two

Indians in some number sat and watched the proceedings [of Governor Douglas laying the cornerstone of St. John's Church] near the edge of the forest . . . thus following close upon the axe with the gospel.

—Bishop George Hills

*T*he following morning Kate hummed a little ditty in such a cheerfully annoying fashion that by eleven o'clock Margaret could no longer avoid inquiring into what prompted it.

"Oh, nothing in particular!" But after another repeat of the tune, Kate added, "Dr. Hector, although agreeable in his own way, was rather a hanger-on, don't you think? Poor Charles had never a moment alone!"

"I rather thought his society would be missed," replied Margaret.

"Oh, well, to be sure!" laughed Kate, dry-eyed.

Kate's good humour with Dr. Hector's departure and consequent hope of Wilson's undistracted attention lasted until the lieutenant's next visit. He came to Hillside at the end of the week, to spend his free Saturday riding with the Works. The weather was fine, but it had rained the previous two days, and his boots and coat were spattered with mud. Nothing, however, could be as downtrodden as his countenance. Gone was the sparkle in his eyes that proclaimed readiness to be amused; their flat expression took little interest in his surroundings. He was as immune to the freshness of early spring as if it were the greyest day of November.

Kate was not easily put off. She wheedled, teased and coaxed smiles out of him at every opportunity, but seeing his efforts to respond in his normal fashion made Margaret sympathize with him all the more.

"I suppose the steamer carrying Captain Palliser's party will be nearing San Francisco now," she said when they had all drawn their horses up on the crest of a hill with a splendid view of the mountains to the south.

"Yes," he said with relief, as if grateful to acknowledge the subject closest to his heart. Behind him, Kate shot her sister a reproving look. Margaret ignored her.

"Perhaps they have passed the *Plumper* on their way. She was due to leave San Francisco this past week, I believe."

"Hector should like to see the *Plumper* again," he said, "although how much better if they could meet familiar faces in the city. Bad luck to have missed them! They could have had a final farewell."

"Not so very unlucky," said Kate. "All this drawing out of good-byes! It only makes matters worse. How much better to enjoy present company! And to look ahead to reunions," she added wistfully when Wilson did not respond.

"I wonder when I might see Hector again," said Wilson quietly, staring out into the distance as if he might find the answer hidden somewhere on the horizon.

Two more Saturdays were spent riding with Wilson, and Margaret was glad to see that his mood, much like the weather, showed fairly steady improvement. A few final squalls and winter died inevitably away. In marked contrast, as the sun climbed higher in the sky, a slight shadow crept over Kate. The weeks before Wilson's departure to the interior were dwindling. Margaret thought his enthusiasm for the trip ought to be message enough for Kate, and did not want to bring up an obviously painful subject with her. Convinced of her sister's resilience, she decided to let the matter rest. There would be time enough for talking after he had left.

Mr. Grahame arrived at Hillside late one afternoon in March with Mr. Work, lodging his long face once again in the drawing-room. To Margaret's surprise and discomfort, she learned that he meant to stay a month. Fort Vancouver was closing down its operations, a task with which he had evidently entrusted his second-in-command, the Works' cousin.

"Papa's hospitality knows no bounds," said Margaret wearily as she collected Kate from her room for their second dinner in the gentleman's company. Mary was already downstairs.

"Margaret! How wicked!" laughed Kate with delight.

"I hope cousin John McAdoo appreciates Papa's efforts on his behalf," said Margaret, glad to have produced a laugh from her sister. "Imagine—a whole month! And without the least warning."

"Oh, Papa expected him. He had a letter a fortnight ago."

"What! But why did you not say?"

"I only found out myself yesterday. How like Papa to keep a surprise from us! And what a surprise it is."

"Indeed," mused Margaret.

The evening confirmed her suspicions of the night before. Before, during and after dinner Mr. Grahame's attentions to Mary were so deliberate that no one could escape noticing it. Disregarding Margaret's right of seniority, he escorted Mary into dinner and sat down beside her. The ladies excused themselves after the meal, leaving the men to their port, but when they were all back in the drawing-room Mr. Grahame again took up his station by Mary. Since there was no seat available, he stood near the fire. After the first evening in his company, the family had dropped some of the formalities, so that the ladies were now free to pursue their needlepoint while the conversation lagged. Margaret and Mary were both thus employed. Mr. Grahame, after watching them for a moment, murmured that the light was insufficient and picked up the oil lamp, holding it aloft, more over Mary than her sister. Margaret glanced up; the light, held so closely to his face, made him look sallow and older still than his 36 years.

"Thank you, sir, but it is unnecessary," demurred Mary. "We could see well enough before."

"But you may get eye strain," he said, holding his post.

There was a heavy silence, broken finally by David. "Perhaps you could stand at the harbour, sir, to light the way for the new arrivals." Cecilia giggled explosively. Mrs. Work sent David to fetch some more leather for the moccasins she was stitching.

Kate at last got up, saying, "Please sir, take my seat, before you tire yourself with your efforts."

Mr. Grahame remained hovering, glancing disconcertedly at Kate's vacant seat, which was a little farther away from Mary than where he stood.

"I will take that seat, if you don't mind," said Margaret, inwardly priding herself on her graciousness and drawing the seat closer to the fire. "I'm feeling a little cold."

Unsurprisingly, Mr. Grahame, on the fifth day of his visit, sought an audience with Mary alone. Many of the family were making the most of a sunny break and had gone riding, but Mary had declined. So had Mr. Grahame. Margaret dreaded leaving them almost alone, with the exception of her parents and Suzette. But remembering her promise not to meddle in Mary's affairs, and aware that Mary encouraged his attentions, albeit in a quiet way, she left Hillside with the others; her thoughts remained, however, with those left behind.

When she returned the drawing-room was empty, and she hurried up to Mary's room. Mary sat within, slightly flushed, but calm. She held her bible closed in her lap. It was upside-down. Seeing Margaret she stiffened almost imperceptibly and shifted in her seat. *She's defensive,* thought Margaret, and was struck with foreboding. She didn't know how to begin. Mary saved her the trouble.

"Mr. Grahame has proposed marriage—"

"And you have accepted him." Despite her best intentions, a hint of disappointment crept into Margaret's voice and settled thickly in the room. Although only a few feet from her, Mary might have already been in the far north, so great did the distance between them suddenly seem.

"Mary," she said tentatively, "marriage leaves little room for a change of heart. Are you quite certain?"

"Mr. Grahame is a very worthy gentleman. He is—eminently dependable. I am unlikely to receive another offer from his equal."

"His worthiness, of course, cannot be denied, but your heart—"

"My heart ought to be governed by my head, and since my reasoning is in perfect agreement with the wishes of my father, my heart must soon follow suit."

Margaret looked at her with incomprehension.

"I don't want to live out my days as a spinster, Margaret. I want the comfort of children. *My* children." Her tone beseeched, her look implored, and Margaret found it difficult to meet her eye until she continued. "You know what I cannot mention to any other—that part of my heart is, and always will be, with Henry Tuzo, but he is lost to me. He is to marry another and I must accept it. Would you have me suffer alone for the rest of my life, or take what comfort is offered me? I can love Mr. Grahame in the same capacity he will love me. We will respect and support one another. You would not deny me this, would you?"

"Of course not," whispered Margaret. "But if you were to meet another, for whom you felt as you did with Tuzo—"

"There will not be another. There could not." Mary shook her head emphatically.

Margaret felt a vague chill pass over her and repressed the urge to shiver. "Then, I have only to offer my hopes and prayers for your happiness."

"That is enough," smiled Mary.

Hillside experienced a domestic eruption, as households will do with talk of an impending marriage reverberating through its walls. Mary's trousseau had to be chosen, and anything lacking ordered from San Francisco. The wedding date was planned for early September, leaving Mr. Grahame enough time to finish his business at Fort Vancouver over the summer. Mr. Grahame reiterated his plan, now happily amended to include Mary, to go to England immediately afterwards, on furlough. The pervading excitement of the new plans reached every nook and cranny, but Margaret felt disconnected from it.

She took on the role of supporting her mother throughout the hubbub. Mrs. Work practised quiet forbearance in the midst of the excitement, but when she was alone with Margaret sometimes a sigh escaped her. In sympathy together they looked beyond the wedding trip to Mr. Grahame's as yet unknown posting. Mrs. Work faced the inevitable with resignation. "I have gained Jane back, only to part with Mary," she would say. "Perhaps I may see Letitia home before I must part with you."

"Do not look for either in the near future, Mama," answered Margaret with a pang in her heart. "But as to Mary, perhaps Mr. Grahame will not be posted terribly far. Perhaps he will be in New Caledonia, and we will see Mary every year."

"Hmm."

Margaret's wavering hope that Mary would remain close to them received little encouragement in these exchanges, but it was a relief nonetheless to have an understanding ear and to share at least a few of her misgivings.

———

Plans for a second Anglican church in Victoria had moved slowly ahead over the winter. It was to be built of prefabricated iron, sent from England, and grounds had been cleared at the northern outskirts of town, near the edge of the forest which hid the Hillside estate from view. In mid-April the Works and Mr. Grahame all went to see the laying of the cornerstone of the newly named St John's Church. The event held special interest for the Works, as the new church would be their place of worship. Many more than its future congregation had come to witness the foundation of the new edifice; such tangible signs of progress always drew a large crowd. Numerous visiting northern Indians who were encamped near the Finlayson home came the short distance to watch. A few of these ensconced themselves on tree stumps, and others sat on the ground. Everyone else stood. The rain held off; the cornerstone was duly laid by Governor Douglas, and blessed by Bishop Hills. The bishop said a few words; the governor, more.

Margaret was glad to give her attention to something other than Mary's upcoming marriage. She wondered how many of the spectators, like her family, would be worshipping there when the church was completed—certainly not the governor's family, who lived closer to the Victoria District Church. *How strange it will be not to see them on Sundays,* mused Margaret. She felt as she had when her family received no invitation to Emma Langford's wedding: she had the peculiar sense that their society, while growing, was actually shrinking.

"Mr. Jackson is looking this way," whispered Mary, on a rare occasion when she was not on Mr. Grahame's arm. Margaret did not look. "Perhaps he will be among the new congregation," added Mary.

"I doubt it. He lives in town. He is probably here merely to support the bishop in his new works," replied Margaret.

A few moments later Margaret dared to look in his direction. Even though surrounded by people, he seemed to stand a little apart from the crowd. Just as she suspected, he stood close to the bishop; his very presence seemed to lend weight to the ecclesiastic's authority. *Not likely to waste time with us when the bishop is around*, she thought. Somehow Mary's teasing was far less agreeable now that she was engaged; it had charitable undertones. Mr. Grahame joined them, and presently Margaret excused herself and walked over to the opposite end of the gathering where Mrs. Finlayson stood.

"Father has told you the news?" asked Sarah in a low voice, keeping her eyes on her children, who were playing on the vacant stumps.

"What news?" asked Margaret, following Sarah's gaze.

"A ship came in yesterday from San Francisco with the mails."

"Yes, I know that," said Margaret impatiently.

"You noticed Dr. Tuzo's absence this morning?"

"Not in particular," replied Margaret, facing her sister.

"He received a telegram yesterday."

Margaret pulled her shawl more tightly around herself. Telegrams nearly always brought bad news.

"From Quebec. His fiancée died. Miss Louisa Gowan. Very sudden. Consumption, they say." For the first time she looked directly at Margaret. "Mary does not know then?"

"Dead?" stammered Margaret. "But—are you quite sure?"

"Difficult to mistake death. Even with the telegram, the news was at least three days old by the time he got it. She's probably buried by now. God rest her soul."

"Aunt Margaret, look at me!" called Annie Finlayson. She twirled about on a stump, laughing, her dress swinging out around her. They both watched in silence; Margaret smiled woodenly when her niece stopped for applause.

A reprieve, she thought. *Mary has been given a reprieve! And God forgive me for thinking it.*

"Will you tell Mary, or shall I?" asked Sarah.

"I will," said Margaret, without any idea of how she would accomplish such a thing.

The walk home was too brief to formulate a plan. She had hardly had time to digest the news herself. How could circumstances have changed so suddenly? It seemed to her the pendulum of fate had swung violently, but where did it leave Mary? Betrothed to someone else.

They were home sooner than Margaret cared to be, and when Mary went to her room, Margaret could not allow the opportunity to go by; she followed her. With no grace, but much feeling, she blurted out the news. Mary looked so bewildered that Margaret had to repeat herself.

This time her sister's expression showed dawning shock. "Henry is—"

Free! Margaret wanted to shout.

"—I mean Dr. Tuzo, he is—he must be suffering greatly," Mary said at last, looking disbelievingly at Margaret, then at the patch of sky to be seen out the window, then back at her sister.

Margaret could not find anything else to say at that moment, so after expressing her willingness to listen whenever Mary wished, she withdrew. Now was not the time to speak of what lay half-formed in her imagination. Death, even that of a stranger, was entitled to respect, and she would pay her dues, or at least, give the outward showing of them.

There seemed, however, no stopping the inner tumult of ideas that sprang from Miss Gowan's premature demise. Even while, over the next several days, Margaret went through the motions of listening to the travelling plans of Mr. Grahame, who remained oblivious to the import of the news, at the back of her mind hovered possibilities of a very different sort for Mary.

In the next few days Margaret saw that Mary's behaviour, unlike her own thoughts, was irreproachable. Although distracted, Mary voiced no advantage, if she saw any, in another's misfortune. On the next Sabbath, the Works gave Tuzo their condolences. He received them with the same drawn expression with which he met everyone, but it seemed to Margaret that he held her sister's hand for a moment longer than the others, and that his eyes brimmed fuller of emotion, though he did not weep. It was his sister, Mrs. Alston, who wept, standing between her brother and husband outside the church, as people filed by the black-clad trio.

The grim truth of seeing Tuzo clothed in the garb of mourning, receiving condolences as if it were Miss Gowan's funeral itself, brought suddenly back to Margaret an earlier scene that had taken place at that site. Had she not damned him on that same sacred soil but six months before? Her expectation, even hope, that he would suffer some vague, unknown punishment for giving up on Mary loomed before her, demanding recognition. And against all rational thought, the sickening fear that she herself, in wishing Tuzo to suffer, had somehow contributed to the young lady's demise, slowly gripped her imagination.

Ridiculous, ridiculous, she chided herself, but the fear would not subside. That night Margaret prayed earnestly for the soul of a young lady she had never met, and whose name she had previously heard only with vexation. At the end she asked for forgiveness in presuming to judge Tuzo, and assured the Almighty that of course Judgment lay solely within His realm.

In the fresh light of a new morning, she felt relieved of complicity in Miss Gowan's untimely end. The shock of seeing Tuzo's stricken face had dulled, and rationality reasserted itself. Louisa Gowan's death lay once more wrapped in Divine Will. But hardly did Margaret usher out guilt when alternative futures presented themselves. She tried to shut them out, by way of imagining Miss Gowan's grieving family, but as she could put no faces in the picture, her thoughts inevitably turned back to Tuzo, and from there to Mary. As she tried to make sense of this death, *what could this mean* was followed so closely by *what comes next* that they may as well have walked hand in hand; one could not demand an audience without the other.

Chapter Twenty-Three

May 1st. At 4 in the morning we reached Fort Vancouver, about 90 miles up the river & were received with true English hospitality at the Hudson's Bay Company's fort, one of the gentlemen in charge being a nephew of Mr. Work of Victoria.

—Lieutenant Charles William Wilson, RE

*S*hortly after his proposal, Mr. Grahame announced his intention of staying on at Hillside only to the end of the week. Now that the business of procuring a wife had been concluded, the pleasure of Mary's society and that of her family could induce him to stay no longer; he must return to Fort Vancouver if he wished to close its operations by September. Time pressed Margaret to speak her thoughts to her sister, awkward though they were. Neither respect for the dead, nor her sworn promise not to meddle, deterred her any more. If she was to remain true to Mary and herself, she must speak.

How to broach the subject without causing offence was difficult; in vain she rehearsed, searching for the most delicate way to put the matter.

"Mary," she said gently when the opportunity presented itself, "there is a matter of great importance, which I feel compelled to speak to you of, out of deep concern for your future happiness. You must forgive me, considering my previous promise not to meddle, but—it's regarding the—the change in circumstance of a certain gentleman—"

She broke off in surprise. Mary was smiling.

"I only wonder at your taking so long to speak to me about it. It shows great forbearance on your part," she said, her smile broadening with amusement.

"You can smile," asked Margaret doubtfully, "when standing at the crossroads of your very life, and knowing that, having once embarked upon your path, there is no turning back?"

"Only because I am at ease, having already chosen my path," Mary replied reassuringly.

"It is not too late! You have not yet married!"

"But I have announced my intentions to the world. I have already taken the first step."

"You are not yet bound by God to follow that course. Only by society. And Mr. Grahame would not be vindictive—he would not press for legal damages—"

"Mr. Grahame," said Mary firmly, "does not deserve to be jilted."

"Oh, Mary," said Margaret hopelessly, "won't you think about it? Reconsider—"

"I already have, Margaret, at great length. Even if I did not feel bound by my promise to Mr. Grahame, I am by no means assured that I would receive a second proposal from Dr. Tuzo."

"Nonsense," said Margaret, but Mary shook her head.

"My hesitation cost me dearly, Margaret. I lost his trust. What can return it?"

"Time. Time will. He must know that you suffered. Your illness, regret—"

"And he knows that I recovered enough to accept Mr. Grahame. If I change colours now, he wouldn't want to risk another disappointment. And neither do I."

"And so the two of you, for fear of risk, will not take the opportunity delivered to your very doorstep, and instead, sacrifice your every future happiness to certainty!" said Margaret in exasperation.

"Are you in a position to be weighing the risks of my situation?"

Margaret could make no reply.

"I am truly touched by your concern, Margaret, but you mustn't worry yourself so. I am at peace with my decision. I wish you would be also."

"Promise me you will not yet close the door on the idea, and I will."

"If it will ease your mind."

But Margaret, when she left her sister, was far from easy. It was too much to expect that Mary, who was universally just to others, could be just to herself as well. The few days remaining of Mr. Grahame's visit taxed Margaret's fortitude to the limit. The matter-of-fact way in which the planning was conducted left her feeling empty, as did Mary's seeming acceptance of this state of affairs. *A lifetime of this,* Margaret thought with dread, but kept her mouth shut. When the time came for the lovers to be parted, she was unmoved. It was an almost palpable relief to her that the courting must now be conducted from a distance: the couple would not be reunited until their nuptials. *If at all*, Margaret added to herself, with faint but persistent hope.

Before another week passed the Boundary Commission was also to depart, but, unlike Mr. Grahame, without any promise of a quick return. Miss Gowan's demise, and Mary's reaction to it, had preoccupied Margaret so completely that Lieutenant Wilson's leave-taking almost caught her by surprise. He paid a farewell visit to Hillside a few days before his departure, but the actual goodbyes were delayed until the steamer sailed at the end of April.

The Works had agreed to come and see him off, and at five o'clock in the evening they went to Esquimalt Harbour. Margaret found it distasteful. A crowd had gathered and she felt almost anonymous, having to wait her turn to shake his hand. Once Wilson spotted the Works he made his way through the multitude to bid them all farewell, and had a warm expression for each of them as he took their hands, but the moment passed too quickly. Words were entirely inadequate; Margaret's eyes glistened and she could only hope he caught the meaning there. Many others were eagerly waiting and he was soon lost to them among the other well-wishers.

By six o'clock, the commission were all on board. With the corps of Royal Engineers lining the upper deck and their officers on the bridge deck, the flags fluttering around them in the spring breeze, the steamer *Otter* pulled slowly away from the dock. Margaret kept her eyes fixed on Wilson. The three men-of-war at anchor in the harbour, HMS *Satellite*, *Ganges* and *Topaze,* had manned their rigging and gave three rousing cheers as the steamer passed, their bands taking up the air of "Auld Lang Syne," each in turn. The cheers were returned from the *Otter*, carried over the water with great distinctness, although the figures on deck had grown small. Margaret could no longer make out Wilson's face. He waved his cap, along with all the others of the commission; the men on shore waved theirs, the ladies their handkerchiefs. And then the steamer took on speed, rounded the corner of the harbour and was out of sight.

"Now that was a send-off!" said David as they got into their own small boat to make their way back to Rock Bay. Suzette cried in her mother's arms and was not comforted when David assured her they would be back again in a year or two. Kate had got into the bow and faced forward, but Margaret noticed she still clutched her handkerchief and occasionally brought it up to her face. She did not turn around once all the way to the Finlaysons' landing up Victoria Harbour.

All of Margaret's gentle efforts, in the ensuing weeks, to elicit Kate's confidences, were rebuffed in an unvarying manner of forced cheerfulness. Kate seemed determined to deny she was troubled by Wilson's absence, and busied herself with all her usual activities, but it had a desperate sense, as if her continual occupation could shut out her feelings. A flash of eagerness passed over her face whenever her father announced a piece of mail, her disappointment in its author quickly disguised. She took a growing interest in the goings-on in British Columbia, and was quick to ask for news, although Margaret was doubtful how much of it she actually took in. Of news there was plenty. As the gold ran out to a trickle, "Fraser fever" was abating at last, but the infection had spread to the Cariboo. The miners penetrated ever farther inland, and the locals watched with renewed interest to see how this new twist would play itself out.

"Fewer Americans coming through town this year," said Mr. Work with satisfaction. "It's the British and Canadians who are pressing on into the Cariboo. May God see their safe return!" He shook his head, as if doubting the probability of his last words.

Wilson had, to all appearances, slipped out of their lives as easily as he had slipped in, and the weeks rolled by with a vague sense of loss, glossed over by the latest developments of the gold rush. It was late May, nearly a month after his departure, before the Works received a letter from Wilson. Mr. Work announced it offhandedly, while carving the roast during supper.

It was David and Cecilia who most loudly queried the letter's contents, but their older siblings waited with perhaps greater anticipation.

"My eyes trouble me today," he answered. "Margaret may read it after supper."

Kate did not plead playfully for more information, as hitherto her habit would have been, but endured the wait in silence. The feverish pitch of her colouring, and the keen expression, almost of avarice, in her eye, although directed downward, distressed Margaret far more than if her sister had wheedled and begged. Margaret thought Kate would much rather have devoured the letter than the supper before her. The suspense lasted until Mr. Work and John joined them in the drawing-room. The wait was brief; Mr. Work brought his pipe in with him, rather than finishing it in the dining room with John. This was a liberty he allowed himself in the summer months, on the occasions when they had no visitors. Mary went silently to the window and cracked it ajar. Mr. Work handed the letter to Margaret. With a full heart, but an even voice, she read.

It was not as difficult a task as she had anticipated. The letter perfectly captured Wilson himself—completely taken up with everything that was currently before him. After thanking them for all their kindnesses, he gave them a lengthy and colourful description of the highlights of his voyage. He devoted an entire paragraph to the tobacco-spitting pilot who had guided the *Otter* into the mouth of the Columbia, and who had evidently, with his Yankee twang, supplied her passengers with much amusement. Wilson conceded, however, that "he was a capital pilot and took us safely over the much dreaded bar of the Columbia." He retold scenes that were already familiar to everyone but the youngest family members, yet the Works all listened intently as a fresh picture of their memories was painted before them. Pacific City he dismissed as a "Yankee city consisting of a sawmill and a grog shop." He was taken with Astoria, although more for its history than its present condition, as "hardly anything of its former state remains, the Yankees having started a city there; the immense tree, so celebrated, has fallen, having been chopped down for a wager by two of these 'go ahead' people."

Margaret paused here, as Mrs. Work, although she already had heard of its fate, breathed a heavy sigh for this renowned tree, whose base diameter had been more than 15 feet. It had grown in an area known as the Valley of the Gods.

"They provoke God's wrath by destroying His monuments," said Mr. Work, puffing angrily on his pipe.

Wilson made much of their arrival at Fort Vancouver, where they "were received with true English hospitality" by Mr. Work's nephew, John McAdoo Wark. At this description being given to an Irishman in the wilds of North America, a smile passed over the faces of several of the family members. Mr. Work grunted, but no doubt forgave the slight, understanding that the compliment was the greatest Wilson could offer. The letters Mr. Work had sent were much appreciated by his nephew. Wilson's description of the fort, "now sadly shorn of its glories," gave little to amuse, but was only a confirmation of what Mr. Grahame had already told them: more land was being taken from the company by General Harney, in violation of the Treaty of 1846, and there was hardly an Indian to be seen, "nearly all having died off from small pox, measles, whisky, and intermittent fever and ague." Unlike Mr. Grahame's matter-of-fact statements, Wilson added to the picture the romanticism of past times, and harkened back to the stories Mr. Work had told him of the place: "What a place it must have been in the olden time! When the parties came in from the upper country with their wild crews of Canadian voyageurs, and what stories must have been told round the fire in the evenings! The Indians coming in bands of two or three hundred and camping in the court yard to trade and then the wonderful scenes that used to follow, horse racing, hockey, and now and then a fight between two hostile tribes on the plains outside."

Here Kate let out an audible sigh, and Margaret looked up to see her sister staring wistfully at the fire. Kate usually had little interest in the past, but evidently pined for Wilson's typical enthusiasm for colour and action.

Many of the American officers, Wilson conceded, were "very gentle-manly pleasant fellows and well educated, especially their Artillery and Engineer officers." And after a few more lines relating their dealings with the Americans, he closed the letter with repeated thanks to the Works for all their kindness.

Although she dreaded to see her expression, Margaret looked instinctively at Kate, whose brows were knit together as she stared vacantly at the floor. Mary exchanged a worried glance with Margaret, but was then drawn into conversation with her parents, who conjectured that Mr. Grahame had missed the Boundary Commission on his return to Fort Vancouver, as he had stopped at Nisqually en route. Kate left the room. After a few minutes, Margaret followed her.

Kate had gone to the back porch and was leaning against the railing, which she gripped with both hands.

"You did not," hesitated Kate, as she ran a finger idly across the railing, "leave out anything from the letter?"

"Nothing," replied Margaret. "You may read it yourself, if you wish."

Kate winced. "It is rather surprising, that is all, that no mention was made of—of anyone by name. Of none of us."

"Except our cousin, of course."

"Except our cousin," repeated Kate dryly.

"Kate, it is very much in keeping with his character to be full of his experiences of the moment, all new to him. There is much to occupy him."

"I suppose he must be very busy. Soon he will be in the wilds, and then—" she brightened a little "—well, then he will have plenty of time to write at greater length. Let's do go in, it's getting cold!"

The warning against high hopes that Margaret had intended to give her sister was left unsaid. This small disappointment perhaps would do the job just as well, given time for reflection.

Chapter Twenty-Four

...the Company's officers in those days were
looked on with a sort of mysterious respect and
wonder, and generally supposed to be enjoying
tremendous incomes!!!
—Dr. John Sebastian Helmcken

The only letter the next two weeks brought was from Mr.
Grahame, in which he settled the wedding day for September
the 5th. This would leave him plenty of time to close down the operations of Fort Vancouver. His letter was not read before the family, as it
was addressed to Mary. Margaret could not suppress the pang of envy
she felt when Mr. Work handed it to her. *A personal letter!* Margaret's
were confined to the rare occasions Letitia found time to write from
Nisqually. She tried to remind herself of the circumstances of Mary's
favour. Still, that evening she approached Mary with hopes that the
letter would be shared. Kate had reached Mary first.

Kate was eagerly poring over the letter when Margaret entered
their bedroom.

"What! He scarcely mentions missing the Boundary Commission!
No more than one short line he allots them!" She handed the letter
over to Margaret in exasperation.

Margaret looked inquiringly at Mary; Mary nodded her assent that
she might read it.

"Shutting down operations requires much of Mr. Grahame's attention, Kate," said Mary placatingly.

"But how often does he receive such visitors? With Victoria handling nearly everything, he won't see so much as a trading brigade!"

"Other visitors pass through. Many an explorer—"

"Oh! An explorer! But that is nothing to a Boundary Commission." She looked at Mary as if this surely was self-evident.

Margaret skimmed the letter, which was only one page. After filling it horizontally, Mr. Grahame had turned the page at a right angle and written over it transversely as well, and the criss-crossed writing made it difficult to read. *So business-like with his fiancée*, she thought, but instead said, "September 5th! Less than three months now. It scarcely seems possible."

"It will soon pass," replied Mary. "We will have to make the most of it."

"Yes," said Margaret, a little wistfully.

"It's a bit early for goodbyes yet!" said Kate. She snatched the letter back from Margaret and reread it. "He doesn't stray from the point, does he?"

"What do you mean?"

"Well! Charles' letter shows more feeling for the shutting down of the old fort, after only passing through, than Mr. Grahame, who has been there how many years? Nearly forever, I'm sure."

"Mr. Wilson has not had to run the fort's day-to-day affairs for the past 16 years. No doubt Mr. Grahame sees it from a different perspective."

"Mr. Grahame, indeed! I hope you won't be quite so formal on your wedding night."

"Kate!" interrupted Margaret with a surprised laugh, which she soon cut short.

Kate had provoked a blush from her sister, and as if to belie the warmth in her face, Mary replied coolly, "*You* ought not to use Christian names so freely, Kate. It is one thing in the family to refer to

Mr. Wilson as Charles, but others might be led to make assumptions about your expectations."

"And what if I did have expectations?" laughed Kate, but avoided her sister's eyes.

"Then a public disappointment, I believe, would be even harder to bear than a private one," said Mary with restrained feeling.

Kate's smile reduced itself by several degrees. "Let people suppose what they will. I shan't let them bother me. But if it offends *you*, Mary dearest, his name shall not pass my lips in public." She put her arms playfully around Mary. "I can still be your bridesmaid, can't I?"

Mary laughed and the tension dissipated. Margaret took in the exchange with much relief; Mary had deftly issued Kate a warning in such a way as to avoid any offence, assisted by Kate's feelings of sympathy for her.

As the weather warmed, more northern Indians than ever before followed the path they had taken en masse for the last two years and converged on Victoria. Many took up their favourite campsite near the Finlayson home, and the frequent visits that Sarah Finlayson customarily received from her sisters dwindled to those few times when they could procure an escort.

Coming from Cloverdale, Dr. Tolmie, after dropping off a tincture for Mr. Work early one June morning, agreed to take Margaret to the Finlayson household on his way into town, and at his brisk pace they were there in 10 minutes. Coming around the corner to the back porch at Rock Bay, they saw several young Indian boys walking away with a loaf of bread. They found Sarah in the kitchen feeding her infant. Margaret suppressed a sigh when she saw her sister; Sarah's lips were firmly compressed in ill temper.

Dr. Tolmie's hearty "Good morning" was met with, "Oh, would that it be! Every morning for the last fortnight they come, wanting milk, wanting bread—my pantry is bare, my own children not fed until nearly eight o'clock—"

"Send them to the dairy, to the bakery," the doctor replied.

"They have no money, only fish, and much good would it do them there. What are they to do until they sell their fish? So I have more fish than I need and an empty pantry. I send many more on to Hillside," she said, handing Margaret the child's spoon in an almost accusing manner.

Margaret took the spoon. The little boy gave her a gruel-smeared smile.

"Cantal gives them only vegetables," said Margaret.

"Just so, must be firm," said Dr. Tolmie and, declining tea and giving his nephew a careful pat on the head, he took his leave.

"I think Mama gives them milk sometimes as well," said Margaret in an effort at conciliation.

"Fine for you, living on a farm. Ah, here is Lizzie at last." Taking off her apron, Sarah went out on to the porch to give the Songhees Indian girl instructions for the morning. When she came back her petulant tone had climbed a notch higher. "Now she says her family doesn't want her to come anymore while the Haidas are camped nearby! After all the time I spent teaching her! Mr. Finlayson says we ought to hire a Chinaman, and then I will have to start over—"

Here there were rushed footsteps down the hall and Sarah's daughters, Mary and Annie, slid to a walk in the doorway.

"Morning, Aunt Margaret! Mama, we are going on a botany expedition," exclaimed Mary as they headed for the door, brandishing a net and a basket.

"Stay within sight of the house!" said Sarah. The door banged after them. "*Mon Dieu!* When will my prayers for a proper school be answered? A lot of nonsense Dr. Tolmie fills their heads with. What good is studying plants you cannot eat?"

Margaret scraped food from her nephew's chin with the spoon as if she were shaving him. The boy blew his tongue at her, spraying her with a fine mist of porridge.

"Papa told you of Mary's letter?" asked Margaret, wiping her sleeve and hoping for respite with a change in conversation.

"Something's not right there," said Sarah, lowering her voice suddenly. Margaret looked up, surprised.

"Mrs. Anderson paid a visit yesterday."

"Mrs. Anderson?"

"Of course I told her Mary's news—the day of matrimony being set—and when I spoke the words 'September the 5th' she went quite white, the palest I've ever seen her at any rate! 'There's some mistake, there must be a mistake,' she kept saying, but I assured her I had heard Papa quite clearly and showed her where I'd written it down in my diary. And of course Papa never makes those sorts of mistakes, but she wouldn't believe it at first. She went on about 'poor Susan turning in her grave'—it took some time before I could get any sense out of her."

Sarah stared down at Margaret with the keenness of a hawk about to make its kill. Margaret resisted the urge to squirm in her seat. "And?" she prompted.

"It seems September the 5th will be 13 years to *the very day* that Mr. Grahame married Mrs. Anderson's sister."

"The very day?" echoed Margaret in disbelief.

"The very day."

"How very strange," murmured Margaret, for a few moments dumbfounded.

"Strange indeed. Unnatural! He provokes bad luck," said Sarah vehemently. "It bodes ill—it bodes ill for Mary."

"Perhaps," groped Margaret, "it is merely a—a means of better remembering his anniversary. So that he will not get the two dates mixed up." But she could hardly accept such a limp premise herself, and was unsurprised when Sarah did not.

"What our cousin's wife, Amelia MacAdoo Wark, feels about this I dare not think! Such disrespect to her departed sister. She will be even more distressed than Mrs. Anderson—they were closer you know."

"Such disrespect to *our* sister," replied Margaret forlornly.

"Mary will be better off not knowing. I trust you to keep sealed lips for her benefit. I had to tell someone though. Fit to burst I've been. You and I, and Jane of course; it will go no further. Mrs. Anderson will not speak of it—couldn't bear the shame."

Throughout her long day in the Finlayson household, this latest twist in the winding path to Mary's matrimony distracted Margaret. *Odd!* How peculiarly morbid that Mr. Grahame should wish to remember his first wife in this way on the occasion of his marriage to his second—and exactly *13* years to the day. Margaret refused to entertain the superstitious fears that arose from that number, and focussed instead on the implications of the heart. Was Mary merely a replacement for Grahame's first wife, Susan; did he have no separate feelings for her?

Margaret longed to ask this question of Jane, the only person available to her and the one she most longed to discuss it with, besides Mary herself. She waited impatiently for a visit from the Tolmies, but in vain. Dr. Tolmie was the only member of the family to cross the threshold in the next four days, and he had the audacity to pay this short visit while Margaret was out; she could not even ask to accompany him home to see his wife. John, unprovided with any pressing reason for going, put his sister off to some undisclosed later date. Her own father was in town much of the time and looked so tired upon returning home that she could not in good conscience request of him a visit. Margaret was annoyed that the half-hour walk to Cloverdale should be enough to separate the two sisters.

Struggling alone with the new information, and despite Sarah's command otherwise, Margaret was soon riddled with the quandary of whether or not to tell Mary. For while Sarah considered Mary's marriage a *fait accompli*, Margaret viewed this information as Mary's last chance to reverse her fate. Although remote, there was a possibility that given this latest insight into her intended's mind, or rather his heart, she might change her decision. And yet her conscience pricked her with guilty reminders of her promise not to meddle and the suffering she had already contributed to Mary's lot. She feared that Mary would think that her motives for imparting the knowledge were self-serving—to keep her in Victoria. And still there was a worse consequence: if Mary were to dutifully stick with her decision, what would this knowledge do to her over a lifetime with this man?

In the end, the compulsion to tell won Margaret over, based on what seemed an inexorable truth: Mary ought to be given the chance to make a choice, however faint the likelihood that she would take it. As Margaret wound her way slowly up the staircase to Mary's room, events from two years earlier, when she had advised delaying Tuzo, overcame her thoughts. Then, the consequences had seemed assuredly bright, and Margaret had felt herself to be doing right, with what little forethought she shuddered to remember. Now, she had never undertaken a persuasion more reluctantly.

Mary's face, as Margaret divulged the news to her, showed such a mix of feelings—disbelief, dismay, anger—that Margaret could not tell which held dominance over her. Margaret used her sister's silence to relate all her own reasons for giving the news, in hopes that Mary would be less inclined to shoot the messenger.

After a full minute's pause, Mary said slowly, "I am very sorry, indeed grieved, for Mr. Grahame's choice of wedding date, yet he does not deserve what you suggest."

"He will recover. He cannot have escaped talk of Tuzo and yourself. He chose to ignore it. He has engaged a broken heart. Part of you is missing. He cannot fail to recognize it."

"If he does see it, and I am not convinced he has, it troubles him little."

"Then *his* heart is not engaged, Mary! Forgive me, but you meet his requirements, the same general requirements he saw in me. This is the basis of his attachment."

"You are too hard, Margaret. I think I am better acquainted with the gentleman's feelings than you," said Mary, her voice quavering. "I cannot and shall not repeat Dr. Tuzo's inconstancy."

"But Mary, how can you compare situations of such different natures? Tuzo's inconstancy was to his own heart, and he has paid dearly for it, as much from the loss of you as of his childhood friend. Uncertain of you, he made a safe choice with Miss Louisa Gowan—someone he has known for almost the whole of his life and beloved, it seems, by his own family. Thinking he was lost, you also have made a safe choice—recommended by your father, your cousin, even Sarah, your own sister. As for *your* inconstancy, it would be to a promise spoken from your head, on matters where it holds no governance. Mary, we all deserve a second chance, especially where it concerns the heart. If yours speaks to you, I beg of you, listen to it."

Here Margaret's own heart became firmly lodged in her throat, and she could not continue with all the other points she had intended to make. Mary's eyes threatened to overflow; there was such a yearning expressed there, as if they were indeed speaking what lay in the depths of her heart, that Margaret felt she was looking into a mirror of her own soul. Just then they heard footsteps in the hall. Margaret quickly squeezed her sister's shoulder and went over to the window so that they might each regain their composure before being interrupted. The steps, however, passed on, and the moment was gone. Mary asked to be left in solitude with her thoughts, and Margaret, with great reluctance, complied.

Chapter Twenty-Five

... sometimes however the sailors after leaving
here forgot their engagements.
—Dr. John Sebastian Helmcken

*K*ate enjoyed an early summer vacation from Miss Phillips'
Colwood School in June. In the Indian village across the harbour from Victoria, the murder of a Tlingit chief on the command of
Captain John, a Haida chief, had stirred the latent hostilities between
the two tribes into war. They entrenched themselves around a cove on
the west side of the harbour, firing randomly at one another from their
makeshift forts. While the east side of Victoria Harbour was generally
considered safe, Mr. Work did not want to risk his daughters' safety,
and kept them from school.

By the month's end, Mr. Work felt his precaution well vindicated,
when a schooner leaving harbour was fired upon as it passed the Haida
camp at Deadman's Point. The governor, who had previously made do
with warnings of hanging murderers in accordance with white man's
law, was propelled into action. He dispatched HMS *Ganges* with 100
marines, who threatened to level the encampment if the guilty party
refused to come forward. After a few tense moments, they were surrendered to the police. The Haida were then disarmed, their whiskey
destroyed and the principal perpetrator of this latest outrage given 36
lashes from the cat-o'-nine-tails in front of his tribe.

In July, Captain John and his brother were arrested for the murder
of the Tlingit chief. Captain John had once been a respected figure in

Victoria. Rumoured to have Russian blood, he had a moustache, spoke English well, and was fond of cloaking his stately figure with a military overcoat and cap. He was also known for sobriety, until this summer when he succumbed to the allure of "tangle foot" whiskey, decried in the press as the "vilest stuff that the ingenuity of wicked-minded and avaricious white men ever concocted." The Tlingit chief's defensive knifing of one of Captain John's aggressive dogs had provoked the murder, a circumstance leading to questions of the Haida chief's sanity. Evidently preferring a warrior's death, John and his brother, once they were at the police station, attacked their jailers with knives and were shot in the ensuing skirmish.

The next day the tribal war was essentially over, and while the press stirred up the Indian question anew, Mr. Work considered the harbour safe enough to send Kate and Cecilia back to school at Colwood. On their first day, they came home with the extraordinary news that the sheriff had arrived at Colwood with an execution against Mr. Langford's personal possessions and had begun removing furniture from the house. Miss Mary Langford had urgently called Miss Phillips out of the classroom, as Mr. Langford was out. Through the windows open to the summer air, the students overheard with rapt attention much of the heated conversation that followed. Indignant cries from Mrs. Langford were mixed with a man's apologetic tones, soon recognized as the sheriff's. "Just doing my job, ma'am. Orders from the Crown," was heard repeatedly. His cart being small, not much was taken. Miss Phillips stood on the doorstep and steadfastly told him he would have all the trouble of bringing the furniture back again.

Over dinner, John wanted to talk about the Indian question, but his voice was lost among his family's reaction to the Langfords' furniture removal.

"Mr. Langford refused to pay for his non-suit against the printer," said Mr. Work, shaking his head. "Doubtful if he has the money to pay. A foolish business indeed, pressing libel charges against the printer for the election placard, when its contents, at least, were far from inaccurate. And then he refused to answer questions regarding his accounts! Chief Justice Cameron showed much patience."

"Poor Mrs. Langford," murmured Mrs. Work. Her horrified expression spoke volumes more to Margaret. Although Mrs. Langford had never welcomed a friendship with her mother, they shared a common maternal bond, and to imagine the Law intruding on the sanctity of Home in such a manner surpassed spurned feelings. While Margaret had wished the Langfords' pride taken down a peg or two, this humiliation went far beyond.

Mr. Work's and Kate's return at supper the next day was awaited with anticipation. From Mr. Work they learned that Mr. Cary, who had represented the printer, had intervened in the legal proceedings. Much of the £87 bill that Langford refused to pay was Cary's legal fee for defending King, the printer; apparently Cary, in a moment of graciousness, had deferred payment, possibly expecting financial assistance to Mr. Langford.

From Kate they learned that Langford's friends were indeed rallying round. Sophie Langford had informed the other girls that Captain Richards had paid a visit the night before; he "and many others" could not allow the family to suffer such ill-treatment.

"It will cost them a pretty penny to dig Langford out of his remaining debts," said Mr. Work. "His unsuccessful suit only scratches the surface. Lack of prudence has brought this sorry state of affairs down on his family."

A week proved Sophie right: A committee of the gentleman's friends duly paid his bill. But the whisperings took longer to disperse. The fate of the family was much speculated on, and there were suggestions that the Langfords would not remain long in Victoria. Miss Mary Langford took most of Margaret's sympathy. Mrs. Langford had been unwell for much of the year, leaving Miss Langford to run the household with her aunt. She bore this latest upheaval as she had all the others, with quiet dignity. She had not been linked romantically with anyone since her father had refused to allow her to marry George Lewis, first officer of the company's steamship *Otter*. Rumour had it that he still had a place in her affections. And now she was faced with possible removal to England; duty would require her to follow her father's will, or caprice, for a second time around the globe. Margaret wished fervently that something unexpected might happen, that somewhere, somehow, there was a pleasant surprise in store for Miss Langford.

More certain departures were at hand. At the end of July Victoria had a repeat of the Boundary Commission's departure; after four years stationed on the Pacific Coast, HMS *Satellite* was setting sail for home. The Works, along with most of the town's inhabitants, dutifully went out to see them off. While there was no one on board whom Margaret thought of as a particular friend, the event still had the power to provoke a heavy heart. All of the officers, at one time or another, had visited their home, and had attended many of the same social functions elsewhere in town. Now those familiar faces were to be lost; most they would never see again, at least not in this life.

The family went out to Duntze Head this time, at the mouth of Esquimalt Harbour, instead of to the docks in the harbour itself. There was always a gathering here at such times, as the place afforded the chance for a final, if somewhat impersonal, farewell, before the ship headed out to open water. With ceremonial reliability, the stirring strains of "Auld Lang Syne" floated over to them from the other ships' bands inside the harbour, followed by distant cheers. In a few moments more, the *Satellite* was abreast of their vantage point. The crew returned the waves of the party on shore. It relieved Margaret to engage only in this pantomime of goodbye, to not have to form any words. A feeling of foreboding settled slowly on her. If Mary persisted on her present course, soon she too would be taking a place on a ship and sailing off toward the horizon. As she slowly waved her handkerchief over her head, Margaret glanced at her father. She could see his suffering in the resignation etched into his face and the moisture gathered in his squinting eyes. Between his obligations here, and his uncertain health, what chance was there that he would ever take passage aboard a ship bound for the Old Country?

A flash of white caught her eye. Kate's handkerchief fluttered down toward the shore. David leapt into action and bounded over the rocks to its rescue. He retrieved it just at the water's edge, to the claps and cheers of Cecilia and Suzette, who welcomed a lighter entertainment than a man-of-war's departure. When he handed it back to Kate with the added flourish of a bow, Kate looked vaguely puzzled, as if unaware she had dropped it. But she did not question it, and turned back to the steam corvette moving slowly away from them. Even more than her detachment from her surroundings, it was Kate's expression that dismayed Margaret. Kate was prone to brief bursts of passion at goodbyes, but her natural cheerfulness usually soon reasserted itself. Today, however, there was a pensiveness about her, a faraway look revealing a deeper ache.

Disappointed with Kate's lack of appreciation for her rescued handkerchief, the younger children wandered off in pursuit of other adventures in the tidal pools. Margaret stepped carefully over the rocks to where her sister stood apart from the others, and Kate looked at her as though she had just seen her for the first time.

"Do you think I should wait for Charles?" she asked suddenly.

"Waiting is not an enviable pastime," said Margaret softly.

Kate gave her a probing look. "Have you been so very unhappy?"

The directness of the question hit its mark, and Margaret could not answer for fear her feelings would spill over the narrow confines of her control. She tried to focus her distorted vision on the retreating *Satellite*.

"You never said, and I wanted so much to know, for you to break your silence," said Kate with gentle reproach. "And all my jokes. I've been very cruel, haven't I?"

Margaret shook her head faintly, but Kate didn't wait for further reply.

"When Mary goes, we must stick together. Help each other out. It's silly for us to be lonely when we have each other."

"There was a time when I would have laughed to hear you describe yourself as lonely," replied Margaret. "You, with all your admirers, never wanting for attention."

"The attention loses its thrill when it's wanted most from one who is unavailable to give it. And you have not reached that age, Margaret, when you fail to spark any interest—what of Mr. Jackson?"

"Mr. Jackson!"

"Don't be coy with me," smiled Kate. "Do you think I receive so much attention I do not notice when it's being paid elsewhere?"

"He speaks to me very little."

"He follows you around with his eyes."

David picked this inopportune moment to call them, on behalf of their parents, to walk with the rest of the family back to their boat. Kate offered Margaret her arm and, with a brief look back at the diminishing naval vessel, the two returned arm in arm. The suddenness of this uncertain friendship rather astonished Margaret. The obstacles of eight years' difference in age, opposing temperaments and a history of strife were struck down by the great leveller of common suffering.

Shortly before the *Satellite* left Victoria, Jane Tolmie had moved back to Hillside to deliver her seventh child. She found the disruption of the ongoing building at Cloverdale too much in her condition, and wanted her family close around her. At Hillside, her mother could attend to her during the birth and her confinement, while her sisters could look after her youngest boys. As the eldest daughter at home, Margaret would assist with the delivery. She had faith in the abilities of her mother, who had plenty of experience at midwifery, yet she still wavered between excitement and apprehension. Jane, although large and cumbersome, was moving in her own rhythm, preoccupied and dreamy in an otherworldly way, largely unaffected by Hillside's day-to-day bustle. Margaret realized that part of her was envious in a way she hadn't been with Sarah, who was also expecting again. With Jane, the creation of new life evoked in her a deep sense of wonder.

After a week at Hillside, Jane's absorption shifted subtly to pensiveness. The afternoon after the *Satellite*'s departure, while she and Margaret shared a quiet moment sewing baby clothes on the back porch, Jane, sighing deeply, said, "This one's different. I think it's a girl."

"How do you know?"

"It's just different. I can feel it somehow."

Margaret knew that her sister, after six boys, longed for a girl, but didn't wish to encourage her in case of disappointment. "Well, it's a 50 percent chance."

"Margaret, ever the optimist," Jane smiled. "When will you learn to put faith in your heart, as well as your head?" After an uncomfortable pause, in which Margaret was keenly aware of her sister observing her, Jane asked, "Is it really such a difficult question?"

"How can I put faith in my heart when it troubles me so?" Margaret had no intention of burdening her sister with her own trials, with such a momentous event expected any day, but the words tumbled out anyway. While evasiveness may have been in her nature, deception was not.

"Perhaps God means your troubles to give you faith. Faith cannot grow when rewards are in sight. You must trust without seeing. Do not rely too heavily on your reason, Margaret. Reason can be blind. But faith must be."

"I doubt my strength. My patience fails me—"

"God does not doubt you. He will not test you beyond your endurance."

This was a truth Margaret had already dwelt on at some length but, despite her efforts, she could not see why God had singled her out to test her patience in matrimonial affairs far beyond the majority of her peers.

———

Less than a week after the *Satellite* steamed away, another event came to test her, having as its advantage the element of surprise. A young gentleman arrived on the steamer *Pacific* after an absence from Victoria of nearly two years. Mr. Doughty had been a midshipman on HMS *Ganges,* the admiral's flagship. He had left the service, since he was to be the master of an English manor when he came of age and was at liberty to be particular about his profession. While stationed in Victoria he had formed an attachment to young Edith Cameron. Such attachments were not uncommon, but the ending to this one proved different from others. Often after a return to the home country, attachments waned on one side of the Atlantic or the other and distance eventually put an end to any serious inclinations.

Edith's sister and cousins apprised Margaret of the affair's continuation. They paid a visit shortly after the young gentleman's arrival, ostensibly to give their regards to Jane, who had begun her confinement. Their accounts differed slightly, with varying embellishments of pride and romance. While serving on the *Ganges,* Doughty had proposed to

Edith. Mrs. Cameron, with whom Doughty was a favourite ("a great favourite," simpered Mrs. Young), had reasoned with him over the youth of both ("how like my father was my aunt," sighed Agnes). But Doughty, while conceding that they were too young at the time, was not easily discouraged and went home with an eye to the future. More recently, after the death of Mrs. Cameron, Edith had written to England to release him from an engagement made when both were so young. ("From no diminishment of her feeling, but rather duty to her father," said Mrs. Young, looking pointedly at Agnes.) His response was to take passage on the *Pacific* and renew in person his proposal to Edith. Chief Justice Cameron encouraged further delay, but to no avail. The date was set for less than two weeks away.

The romance of the young lovers' reunion was painfully bittersweet to Margaret. Here was a fairy-tale ending! It had all the right ingredients: a tragic death, Edith's sacrifice to duty, her lover's long voyage and their restoration to happiness. And, at the tender age of 17, Edith was to become the mistress of an English manor. Theberton Hall was a name Margaret could not escape hearing dropped frequently among the Douglas clan. Edith, while barely a woman, had achieved what Margaret had cherished for years as little more than a dream.

Weddings were in the very air; avoiding the preparations was futile. Doughty and Edith, like Mr. Grahame and Mary, booked passage on a steamer leaving for England shortly after their nuptials. Comparisons were inevitably drawn. Bishop Hills was to marry both. Edith's wedding ceremony was to be at the church, Mary's at Hillside by special request. The reason for this was given as difficult roads and conveyance, and the bishop had reluctantly agreed. But Margaret suspected a deeper reason from Mary—that of avoiding the sight of Tuzo on her wedding day. Tuzo was in the midst of supervising the building of the company's new wharf and store, and his name came up occasionally when Mr. Work described its progress over dinner. Margaret watched Mary's placid expression during these moments, and wondered what stirred beneath her calm exterior. Her eyes, usually downcast toward her dinner plate whenever the subject arose, suggested they had something to hide. Margaret felt with growing inevitability that Mary's course was set. As the date grew closer, turning back became more impossible.

Margaret could not help drawing her own comparisons, but between Doughty and Tuzo. Doughty, who was now only 19, had weathered nearly two years' separation, and discouragement from both Edith's parents and Edith herself. Here was constancy! He had made the long journey from England on faith. And yet Tuzo, who was nine years Doughty's senior, could not keep faith for mere months. She told herself that Tuzo did not deserve her sister, but knowing where Mary's lot was to fall instead made Margaret's regret all the more palpable as the days before the wedding dwindled down.

Chapter Twenty-Six

[Edith Cameron] wrote to England to say they
had been very young when the engagement was
made & that she would release [Mr. Doughty].
He instantly set off & in six weeks was here
pressing his suit. The Chief Justice [Cameron]
would not permit the marriage to be at present,
[but] he persevered, gained his point & his bride
in a fortnight.

—Bishop George Hills

A week after Mr. Doughty's arrival, Jane went into labour. It was
the hardest delivery Margaret had ever witnessed. Jane had
previously assured her mother and sisters that her last few births at Nisqually
had been fairly short and uncomplicated, so as hour followed endless hour
her attendants grew increasingly concerned. They sent for another midwife,
known locally as Ma'am Grace, in the early hours of the morning, as well as
Dr. Tolmie, who did not attend his own family as a physician, but whom
Mrs. Work wanted to consult before sending for Dr. Helmcken.

The baby came before either arrived at Hillside. She was very
small, despite the difficulty of her entrance into the world. Even Jane,
though exhausted, showed some surprise at her size. "So tiny," she
whispered as she took the infant from Margaret into her arms. More
unsettling were the baby's weak cries, so different from the hearty
wails of Sarah's infants, or from Suzette, whom Margaret remembered
as being spirited from the day of her birth.

Margaret's misgivings only increased when Dr. Tolmie and Ma'am' Grace arrived. They were both quiet and reassuring to Jane, but Margaret caught a worried exchange when their eyes met. In the morning Dr. Tolmie sent for Dr. Helmcken. He too encouraged Jane, who grew distraught at the baby's weak attempts at nursing. Dr. Helmcken joined Dr. Tolmie in the library, with the door closed, before departing. Not much could be done, it seemed, but hope and pray for the infant to gain strength from what little nourishment she took in.

Hillside received another blow when, a few days after the baby's birth, Mr. Work was struck by a recurrence of malaria, contracted during his trip with the brigade into California the year before Margaret's own birth. By Thursday he had taken to his bed with the ague, and while Mrs. Work nursed him, Margaret was left to oversee Jane's care. His feverish spells took a turn for the worse on Saturday, and although Margaret tried to stay reassuring with Jane, her worries increased. Even if she had been invited, she did not need to go into the library with Dr. Helmcken and John; she read it all in their faces when they came out. They feared the worst. It was doubtful that Mr. Work could fight off another attack of this old, familiar enemy.

She went into the library after they had gone and sat down at her father's desk, resting her head on clasped hands. "Please God, not now," she whispered. "Not now."

By Sunday it appeared her prayers had been answered; Mr. Work, from some hidden reserve, found the strength to rally and did not succumb. The hot and cold sweats and fits of violent shivering gradually subsided, leaving him weak and even more frail-looking than before, but he had yet again emerged the victor; it was not the final round.

Edith Cameron's wedding came on Tuesday. Margaret begged that she might remain at Hillside with Jane, but as Mrs. Work intended to stay behind, Mr. Work asked Margaret to attend on their behalf. Duty prevailed and she numbly acquiesced.

The other potential distraction from the family's worries was the opening of the female educational institution; it awaited only the arrival of the Anglican mission party, expected any day. Kate, Cecilia and Suzette would attend. Kate offered no complaints about leaving Miss Phillips' tutelage. "I like her better than any of her nieces, but their company is growing rather tiresome," she confided to Margaret, as they put on their dresses for the wedding.

"It's been a difficult year for them," said Margaret.

"You are too generous," smiled Kate.

Margaret hoped the change would do Kate good; her sister had always been partial to novelty. At the church, Kate faced Edith's wedding with an expression of wistful hope that wrenched Margaret's heart. She plainly longed for her turn. On her other side sat Mary, with the secure look of one who has taken the sensible path, her own wedding now only two weeks away. *Will she wear that look so well a few years from now,* wondered Margaret with dread.

Agnes, Alice and little Martha Douglas were Edith's bridesmaids. Agnes was in the full flush of happiness; her eyes sparkled with it as she walked down the church aisle. *She is sure of Bushby,* thought Margaret suddenly. In marked contrast, Mr. Cameron's countenance displayed such a turmoil of pride mixed with sadness in handing his radiant young daughter to Mr. Doughty that Margaret could not refrain from shedding a tear.

At the wedding breakfast at Belmont, the Douglas ladies formed an elegant background while Edith greeted her guests as Mrs. Doughty.

"You look like the cat with the canary in its mouth," said Kate to Agnes as she leaned over to kiss her. "Pleased as punch. Is it all for Edith?"

"Since you ask," beamed Agnes, "I am sharing in Edith's happiness in more ways than one. Her joy will soon be followed by my own! Papa is adamant we wait until at least next year to be married, but soon our engagement will be official! We didn't want to take any of the limelight away from Edith's wedding."

"Wonderful," said Kate with a fixed smile.

"We'll talk about it later," replied Agnes enthusiastically.

Margaret, who had preceded Kate down the receiving line, overheard much of the exchange, and was apprehensive that the conversation might continue. Agnes was blissfully oblivious to Kate's tenuous state of mind and would feel free to gloat and gush at will. Kate had the Work pride; she had not let on to her friends how much she missed Wilson. She would pretend to be as resilient in matters of love as she had ever been, and while she pretended, suffer in silence.

It was not until after the wedding breakfast that Agnes had the opportunity to catch Kate alone. Margaret, who had been keeping a watchful eye nearby, reached them in time to hear the following from Agnes: "Did you know that the name Doughty, in antiquity, means valiant? How romantic! And Edith's name will be added to Burke's *Landed Gentry*. Papa has a copy of course, but he will have to get a new edition now! There are several Douglases in it already, you know—some distant relations. Arthur and I will go eventually and then perhaps I may meet them! Wouldn't it be grand? I should like to see Lanarkshire for myself, to see where my roots are, the place of Papa's forefathers, his birth—"

"His birth?" queried Kate.

Margaret could hear from the tone in her sister's voice that Agnes had gone too far in her boasting. It was well known in trading circles that Governor Douglas had been born in Demerara, West Indies, of an illegitimate connection. To make matters worse, John had been standing behind Agnes with his back to her, and had evidently heard much of her effusion, since he now turned toward her with an amused look of cynical expectation. Margaret felt a pressing need to avert the course of the conversation, but it flowed too quickly.

"In Lanarkshire, Scotland," said Agnes, "although the family is somewhat spread out—"

"I understood he was educated in Lanark," said Kate cuttingly, "but was born in the West Indies, as were your aunt and cousins."

Agnes stood dumbfounded, trapped. Kate's latter statement regarding Edith and her family was irrefutable, making it difficult to answer her former question about Governor Douglas' birthplace. *His* origins were never questioned openly, at least not to his family. Margaret looked on with horrified curiosity.

"I am a Douglas," said Agnes indignantly.

"Perhaps you are related to the Black Douglases in Burke's *Landed Gentry*," said John sardonically, leaning over her shoulder with a sly grin. "It would have a certain irony, wouldn't it, considering your father's dark complexion?"

"That's the pot calling the kettle black indeed!" hissed Agnes. "How dare you! Would *your* origins stand up to scrutiny?"

"No worse than your mother's—"

"Enough, all of you!" said Margaret, putting herself between Agnes and John. "Remember why we are here—"

"And your family ought to remember their place," retorted Agnes hotly and left them; the reference to *both* her parents being of mixed blood was evidently too much for her.

"Thinks herself superior!" said John. "So our parents married *a la facon du pays*, so did hers. And what of it, anyway? A wedding is a wedding—in a church or in the custom of the country."

"John—"

"I expect weddings have changed somewhat in the colony," said a voice at her elbow, and Margaret was mortified to see things were getting worse—it was Mr. Jackson. Margaret had to marvel at his ability to turn up at the most inopportune moments. If her family were to lose face, evidently he was always available to bear witness to it.

"I sometimes wonder if the advances the gold rush has brought to your town are worth all that it has lost. The dreadful snobbery to be found here now is far worse than any I have encountered in the Old Country. Only in America have I seen worse," said Mr. Jackson.

"High praise indeed," said John.

"Perhaps the snobbery may subside over time," suggested Margaret.

"When the gold rush dwindles, I am convinced it will. The possibility of a quick fortune attracts the worst kind of immigrant."

"Be careful, sir, you may do yourself out of your job," laughed John.

"The growth occasioned by the gold rush may have brought me here, but slow, steady development is what the colony needs now, and will no doubt support me."

He said this so firmly that Margaret took the chance of saying, "So you intend to stay, then."

"I believe the colony has much to offer."

"There is a feeling among the earlier settlers that when the gold bars no longer yield, there will be a permanent mass exodus," said John.

"An exaggerated apprehension in my view," countered Mr. Jackson. "There are many inducements to stay. A favourable climate—"

At this point he was interrupted, their circle was broken, and the conversation took a more general turn. The other attractions he found in Victoria were left unsaid. This brief exchange turned out to be the highlight of Edith's wedding for Margaret. Since Letitia's marriage three years before, weddings had gained a vaguely threatening finality, and with Mary's but two weeks away, the overtones of loss were too much to ignore. With each successive wedding she had attended since turning 20, Margaret found it increasingly difficult to join in the celebration of the betrothed, while her own happiness hung ever more uncertainly in the balance. Now, not all the fancy dresses, white linen, silverware, and fine china in the world could dispel her mood.

Chapter Twenty-Seven

At half past ten I rode out to Hillside to per-
form the marriage ceremony for a daughter of
Mr. Work, a member of the Council, Miss Mary
Work to Mr. J.A. Graham. There was a large
assemblage. It took place at the house, by the
express wish of the family for special reasons,
though against my own feelings in some respect.
But in these countries while roads are difficult of
passage & conveyances are scarce, there must be
exceptions made to the rule which would have
marriage in the church & sustain the solemn
character of the ordinance.

— Bishop George Hills

Two days after Edith's wedding, the Anglican mission party
arrived from England aboard HMS *Cortez*. It was comprised
of three clergymen, a Mrs. Pringle and two Misses Penrice, the latter
two included for the purpose of assisting the clergy wives in running
a Ladies' College. On Sunday Bishop Hills announced the opening of
the school on the first Monday in September, only a week away. This
pleased Margaret for Kate's sake, and even slightly for her own, as the
opening would offer a diversion during the week of Mary's wedding.

The Tolmies' baby weakened further that Saturday. Margaret
assisted her mother and the midwife throughout the day, but there
was little for the three of them to do. In the evening the midwife went

home, promising to return the next morning, and by then the little girl, whom Jane had named May, had rallied somewhat. Margaret had taken the extra bed in the room that night and awoke in the early hours of the morning to the sound of Jane's encouraging murmurs and the sight of her relieved smile.

Amidst the family's concern and hopes for little May, the inexorable wedding march soldiered on. Margaret fervently wished that the marriage could be postponed, but although Mary broached the subject with her intended, Mr. Grahame was reluctant—he had booked their passage to England and all their travelling arrangements were made. It was not customary to delay under such circumstances. Margaret was reminded that life does not stand still, and guiltily remembered the silent criticism she had heaped on Jane Dallas for marrying when the Helmckens' daughter, Daisy, lay deathly ill. Now the Works were to have a repeat, in their own family, of celebrating life despite the threat of loss.

After a final interminable week of preparations, September 5th arrived. Margaret could now barely tolerate Mary's company, so overshadowed by her impending departure had it become. She was sadly aware that Mary's life was taking a divergent path from her own. Mary's worries and concerns were now manifold, and parting with her family was only one facet whereas to Margaret, the separation was the chief effect of her sister's marriage and as such an undeniable focus.

September 5th dawned clear. *If only it were Tuzo, I could bear it all so much better,* Margaret thought, leaning heavily on the window casement and blinking out at the soft morning sunshine. She comforted herself by remembering that it would all be over in just a few hours.

Upon arising, Mary could eat little more than bread and tea. She soon returned to her room with Margaret to begin dressing, leaving Mrs. Work to oversee the final touches downstairs. Kate drifted in and out, helping occasionally in a fitful way before wandering back to her own room to assist Cecilia, to whom at age 11 weddings had suddenly taken on a new significance.

After doing Mary's hair and helping her on with her dress, Margaret and the transformed bride both paused to absorb her image in the mirror.

"This is my wedding day, not my funeral," whispered Mary over her shoulder in Margaret's ear, as if she were imparting a secret.

Margaret attempted to brighten her outlook, even if she could not feel it in her heart. Her bravado failed her. "I hope when you return from England you will get a—a favourable posting," she said tentatively, squeezing her sister's hand.

"Fort Simpson was not so very bad, was it? I have fond memories of our time there. Remember ice-skating on the lake? And our fishing trips?"

"The ones when the Haidas informed Papa afterwards that they could have taken us as slaves?" said Margaret through a film of tears.

"But they didn't," smiled Mary.

Margaret waited with her sister while the guests arrived. Finally Mrs. Work came to get them. Their mother looked at Mary for a long time, then embraced her. "It's time," she said. Margaret had the strange image of Mary, Queen of Scots, being led to the executioner's block, and suppressed a nervous laugh. This at least prevented her from crying. Mrs. Work led the way down the stairs. Margaret followed Mary in case her dress should get caught behind her.

All the world's a stage, she thought, when the guests who had crowded into the drawing-room came into view. She steeled herself for the wedding service, keeping herself in frozen outer calm throughout. She knew many eyes were upon her, morbidly searching for some sign of envy or resentment toward Mary. Society upheld seniority, and Margaret was keenly aware that she defied tradition, whether purposely or not, by remaining a spinster at nearly 26 while her younger sister married. Either way, she was the subject of scandal or pity. She preferred the former and held her head high. She betrayed her feelings only once by swallowing to relieve the tightness of her throat, but otherwise played her part, just as circumstances dictated, impeccably.

With the deed done and the weight of sanctimony lifted, the marriage breakfast following did not seem quite so terrible as she had anticipated. Margaret smiled and chatted and did her part in making the guests feel at home, but the inconsistency with her inner feelings grew harder to bear as the morning wore on. The sheer effort drained her. It was not until after the breakfast, and the following toasts, that she could slip away to the back porch for a moment of respite.

At the end of the porch a rambling rose worked itself up a trellis. She bent over to inhale deeply of their heavy scent, but they had lost their ability to intoxicate. Numb to their effects, she shivered, hugging herself. She heard the mincing footsteps of women approaching from inside the house and knew that guests would soon overflow into the garden. Thinking she should not be caught alone, she turned back to go in; her hand was on the doorknob when she heard the footsteps turn into the back sitting room, and she caught the familiar tones of Agnes Douglas' voice through the open window. Suddenly feeling unequal to an encounter, Margaret wavered.

"I wouldn't much care for Alice getting married before me. Imagine giving precedence to a younger sister! Following Alice into all the drawing-rooms of the town. My goodness, it doesn't bear thinking of! It's only natural for an older sister, like yourself, to have precedence, but dear me, a younger!"

"Yes, poor Margaret. Quite a different thing to have a younger sister marry than an older," came the reply, bereft of sympathy, from Jane Dallas.

"How fortunate for her that Mary is leaving town shortly. Margaret will not be troubled with giving her sister precedence for long."

Margaret twisted the doorknob. She took no pains to remain undiscovered, and walked down the hall past the sitting room doorway with eyes directed forward. A barely perceptible "Shhh!" reached her ear. She stopped and turned back to the sitting room.

"Oh," she said, "I thought I heard something."

Agnes had the decency to blush.

Jane was holding her toddler, from whom she rarely allowed herself to be separated since the death of her infant daughter earlier in the year. "Not joining the party?" she smiled. Despite her loss, and even despite the recent threat to little May's new life, for a moment Margaret really hated Jane Dallas—hated her pale skin, her auburn hair and her cupid bow lips pursed into a kiss on her child's fair head.

"In a moment. It's very difficult, you know, to see Mary without being reminded of how soon we will be separated from a most beloved sister."

"Of course," said Jane, fussing with her child and not looking Margaret in the eye.

"Excuse me," said Margaret, "I'll leave you to it."

From the hallway she stepped back into the dining room, thinking that, for lack of another option, she would fortify herself with a cup of tea. Some of the guests mingled there, and one, in passing, complimented her on how "lovely" she looked. After thanking him, she stood stirring her tea distractedly and wondering how this could possibly be, when it contrasted so markedly with how she felt inside. But earlier compliments, whether vocalized or merely approving glances, confirmed it. Strolling through the drawing-room, she calculated that most of the guests would be gone within the hour. Then, after helping to tidy up, perhaps she could escape and give her tension free reign in privacy. *I'll go for a ride,* she thought, feeling marginally better for at least formulating a plan.

It was late afternoon by the time she got away. She accompanied the Tolmies back to Cloverdale, doubling one of the younger boys on horseback. Mr. Jackson had also been invited to Cloverdale and came with them. Margaret avoided him, not having the heart for either sparring or longing. Jane welcomed her to stop when they reached home, but seemed to understand her need for solitude and did not press her to stay. Margaret left Cloverdale before Dr. Tolmie could insist on it.

Instead of turning directly back to Hillside, Margaret headed toward a large meadow on the Tolmies' estate. It had been a dry summer, and some of the deciduous trees were already turning shades of yellow and brown. She didn't see a soul and, reassured of her privacy, she let down the coils of hair Kate had teased into place for the wedding. Shaking her locks free, Margaret set off across the field at full gallop. Whatever relief the exhilaration gave her ended abruptly with the meadow, when she had to rein in her horse where the trees became thicker. Her mount was sweating in the sultry heat and she decided wearily that she should return to Hillside via Spring Ridge to allow her a drink. She loosely repinned her hair.

Not wishing to encounter anyone, she went to a small pool of the spring that was less frequented, where she dismounted to let the horse drink and sat down herself on the rocky gravel bank, peering into the water. Mary's wedding replayed itself in her mind's eye and she began to wonder if perhaps her sister had done the right thing after all, that perhaps they were meant to accept the sensible path. At the moment it seemed immensely preferable to her senseless struggle for real belonging, for a prospective home she could not quite realize, but of which she only caught tantalizing glimpses.

She heard another horse approach and got back on her feet. While she mused, her loyal steed had wandered into the stream. She whistled. The horse, water dripping from her muzzle, merely snorted contentedly in reply. The spring was only ankle-deep, but with someone drawing near she could not be found with her boots off, going in after her mount. Margaret called, clucked and whistled again, but the animal looked back at her with doe-eyed innocence and lazily swished its tail. She waited impatiently for the rider to emerge from the trail, and Mr. Jackson presently appeared through the trees. He perused the situation, smiling somewhat smugly at her predicament, and urged his mount into the stream. Apparently this was enough inducement for her own horse, which meandered obediently back to her. Reluctant to be rescued, Margaret felt her irritation grow.

"What would you have done if I hadn't arrived?"

She was in no mood for delicacies. "Taken my boots off and gone in after her."

"I'm sorry I missed it."

She could not manage a smile.

"Despite the Indian troubles this summer, you still persist in riding alone," he observed in a more serious vein.

"Because of the troubles, the Indians have been subdued once again. Besides, one must be alone sometime," she replied peevishly.

He dismounted and led his horse to the water. "Your brother, Dr. Tolmie, is not as confident of the Natives' peacefulness as you are. He asked me to check that you had reached Hillside safely. You do know he worries what will become of you—"

"Dr. Tolmie," laughed Margaret angrily, "who looks down so gravely at me as if—as if he can see original sin etched into my very face!"

"Yes, Dr. Tolmie," he said gently, "who worries after you as his own sister, as does Mr. Finlayson."

This Margaret seriously doubted, but at the same time it touched her so surprisingly that tears instantly brimmed, threatening to overflow. Unable to reply, she was as mortified as Mr. Jackson appeared bewildered.

"I did not intend to upset you," said Mr. Jackson softly.

"I'm sorry," she mumbled to the ground from behind her hands, trying vainly to wipe the tears away. She felt, rather than saw, him move closer, and then his hand rested gently on her shoulder. This slight touch let the floodgates open and, helpless to retain control, she allowed herself to lean into him. His arms encompassed her. A silent sob caught in her chest, unleashing a paroxysm of sorrow that shuddered through her and into him.

After the violence of her grief had subsided, a slow resurgence of self-restraint gradually reminded her of decorum and she took a reluctant step back. *Well, that's one way to break the ice,* she thought, but dared not look at his face. He pressed a handkerchief into her hand.

"We never quite measure up," she said helplessly, by way of explanation.

"To Dr. Tolmie?"

"To Dr. Tolmie, to Mr. Finlayson, to everyone, even to each other, my sisters and brothers. We are always measuring ourselves against some invisible standard, invisible but insurmountable, and lately, with so many endings, it's too much—"

"You have recently borne more than your fair share of loss, real or threatened. Life is about striving to overcome, in my estimation, and you have endured. But I fear you are like the candle, blown by society's harsh wind of criticism, even if unspoken."

"A candle!" smiled Margaret through her tears, dabbing her eyes with his handkerchief. "No, I think I am much more like a lump of coal."

"Coal?"

"Of the country and inclined to smoulder."

He shared her tenuous smile. "An invaluable and necessary discovery of the country."

Chapter Twenty-Eight

September 13, Thursday. Consecration of St.
John's Victoria.
The day dawned brightly. The service was at
eleven. There were twelve clergy including
myself. A good congregation filled the building.
A voluntary choir of some twenty-five persons
had practised & [sang] admirably... Nothing
went amiss. I never was present at a consecration
which passed off so smoothly. It brought home
old England most vividly.
—Bishop George Hills

*T*he Anglican mission party had opened the Ladies' College
two days before Mary's wedding. The younger girls had been
excused from attending school for the wedding, but went back the
following day. Since Jane had already returned to Cloverdale with May
and her two youngest boys, Hillside was left eerily quiet, with the exception of Letitia and her son Willy, who had come from Nisqually for the
wedding and a long overdue visit. They were a welcome distraction to
Margaret, but their presence was a harbinger of future emptiness. Even
Willy's playful footsteps rang hollowly through the large house.

Mr. Grahame and Mary, who were staying at a hotel for the few
days before they left for England, paid a visit. Now that she was Mrs.
Grahame there was a strange awkwardness between her and Margaret.
Even when Mr. Grahame and Mr. Work left the ladies for a time, the old

familiarity held a subtle, but definite, change. There the four of them sat in the drawing-room together, as they had so many times before, and yet they each knew it was different. Perhaps it was not knowing when they would be reunited, or perhaps it was Mary's change of status. Mrs. Work left the room to get the tea. As Willy wanted to "help" his Grandmama, Letitia followed to minimize the damage.

"Do you feel different?" asked Margaret, feeling her tact was hopelessly failing her.

"In a way," said Mary, and then after a pause, "an odd way."

"An odd way?"

Mary seemed unable to explain.

"But, you are happy?" Margaret persisted.

"As I expected. Do not worry for me, Margaret. Just think of me when I am gone, as I will think of you."

"You cannot doubt the latter, but as to worrying—"

Mrs. Work, with Willy trailing behind, returned with the tea things, and gave a small drawstring purse to Mary. "Ginger root. For the morning sickness, when it comes."

Mary blushed. Letitia looked on knowingly. Mrs. Work continued undaunted, although her voice caught audibly. "Make it into a tea. Grating is better than slicing. Some wives find lemonade helps as well."

"Thank you, Mama." Mary looked down at the small purse on her lap. When she lifted her head, Margaret thought her eyes revealed a flicker of panic. The slight pang of envy Margaret had felt was quickly swept away by sadness. She thought of Jane's last delivery, and wondered where Mary would be when she bore her first child, and whom she would be with. The chances that it could be her own kin seemed remote.

So heavy had her dread of the event been, Margaret was almost glad to get the final goodbye with Mary over with. Letitia and Willy left days later. The strange stillness at Hillside gave her more than enough opportunity for mulling over Mary's chosen lot. She still needed to make some sense of it, as she sifted and recombined the elements, searching for its essence. But each time the crucible, in the end, revealed only fear. To risk her feelings with Tuzo twice was just too costly. The right path, for Mary, was also the safe path.

Although she had railed against Tuzo for the same fear, in retrospect Margaret had to accept Mary as equally culpable. And accepting that weakness in Mary, she had to consider it in herself. Wasn't she always playing a balancing act? If there were a retreat she would match it, if a step forward, she would take one too, but always equal, never more. From fear of tipping the scale heavily against her, she seemed incapable of taking the proverbial leap of faith. Her feelings were revealed only when they suddenly broke from her restraint. She had to admit that the result, although embarrassing, could be worthwhile, such as her out-pouring at Spring Ridge with Mr. Jackson, and she thought she might just get used to the embarrassing part.

St. John's Church was consecrated the following week. Many of the old District Church's congregation came to the service, includ-ing Mr. Jackson who, like Lieutenant Mayne and many others, had lent his support to the bishop's new works. The early autumn sun, in seeming agreement, also blessed the day with its presence as it glinted off the iron structure. Margaret had been pleased to learn Mr. Jackson had joined the new congregation. Inside, his participa-tion on the church committee had given him a pew much closer to the Works than in the District Church; his position behind the Tolmies afforded Margaret a closer, although less surreptitious, view than formerly. She had not seen him since Mary's wedding day and, not knowing when she would next, she was bold enough to look his way several times during the exceedingly long service. The first time gave her the impression he was troubled, the second confirmed it, and by the third it was set in stone. He was drawn and preoccupied. She did not like to see anyone suffer, but thought she could accept it if she were the cause. She then at least would have the chance of taking the trouble away. Unfortunately she had to contend with the possibility that, even if it were caused by her, it might be beyond her influence.

A courtship with her, she was painfully aware, would be a one-way passage for Mr. Jackson. To marry her would also mean marrying the colony. She was born to the country, and to take her back to the Old World would be nearly unthinkable. A visit, such as Mary's, might be considered, but the likelihood of acceptance in the Old Country seemed faint. If Mr. Jackson did respond to her in the way she did to him, what must he sacrifice? It hardly bore contemplating.

Jane Dallas foiled her hopes of getting closer to Mr. Jackson after the service. "How quickly things change, don't they, Margaret? It seems only yesterday we saw St. John's cornerstone laid, and now here it stands." She beamed proudly at the iron edifice, as if it had arisen from her own efforts.

How like her father she grows, thought Margaret, but the effort of response was too much for her.

"Yes, change is in the very air," stated Mrs. Dallas, drawing some of it deeply into her lungs. Then her expression underwent an adjustment to gravity. "Rather a shock receiving news of Governor Simpson's death. Quite a shock."

"Yes," said Margaret, but she suspected Jane had been anticipating his demise. She knew from her father that Mr. Dallas, who held a position of authority in the Western Department, was poised for a move upward. Sir George Simpson, "the Little Emperor" as he had been known, had enjoyed a long reign over the Hudson's Bay Company, but his loss stirred no sympathy or enthusiasm within Margaret. There seemed so much more to grieve for at home than a stranger residing in Quebec.

"There is talk among the gentlemen as to who will fill his shoes," imparted Mrs. Dallas in a confidential tone.

Margaret could not flatter Mrs. Dallas with her interest. "The vultures will circle," she replied honestly, enjoying the momentary freedom of her words.

Mrs. Dallas readjusted her face. "The question must be addressed. Of course, Sir George will be difficult to replace. His responsibility was a momentous one. The future of the company will reside in the hands of his successor, who must appreciate the late governor's tremendous power and the heavy mantle of his duties."

Margaret feared she might have provoked a eulogy from Mrs. Dallas. *Perhaps she is cut out for leading lady of the company, after all.* In her peripheral vision, Margaret saw Mr. Jackson preparing to leave with the Tolmies. His fledgling friendship with the doctor had strengthened through the family's ordeal with May's birth and he was now a frequent guest at Cloverdale. Although glad of it, for everyone's sake including her own, at this particular moment Margaret felt defeated; she had missed her opportunity to speak to him. *And only to listen to Jane Dallas preen!* Margaret kept her focus, however, on the other lady, as it wouldn't do to give her any fodder for conjecture.

Leaving the church, Margaret hung back from her family, in hopes of giving Mr. Jackson a chance to catch her alone. But as she dallied in the September sun, another availed himself of her solitude. It did not seem his initial intent; when Dr. Tuzo strode by, he veered toward her so suddenly his direction appeared to alter in mid step, and he came to an abrupt halt a few paces from her. Margaret didn't know if she managed to hide her surprise.

"Miss Work."

"Dr. Tuzo."

They floundered momentarily, unable to get beyond the civilities.

"Your sister got away safely—with the steamer?"

With Mr. Grahame. "Yes, she's gone now."

Dr. Tuzo nodded, looking up at St. John's iron roofline, squinting against the sun. "It was a dream of hers to see England," he said. "Soon she will realize it."

"It was one of her dreams. One of many."

"A difficult thing, to realize all of one's dreams in a lifetime. Providence has provided her well."

"But perhaps not for those dreams closest to her heart." Mary's loss seemed greater somehow for being unacknowledged; Margaret could not hold her tongue.

Tuzo glanced sharply at her, then back at the iron church. "Still, England—the trip of a lifetime."

It struck Margaret that Tuzo was looking for confirmation that everything was as it should be. He did not want to know otherwise. "As you said, a short time to realize all one's dreams. Sometimes only the lesser ones bear fruit."

"Your sister's lot in life is fortuitous. Indeed the envy of many. A secure position in society, every comfort attainable—"

"Mary was not one to place creature comforts above all other considerations!"

Margaret had his full attention now; his eyes were riveted on her. His response hung half-formed between them; his eyes questioned, but his tongue did not follow suit. He broke eye contact. "She did well for herself, measured by the common yardstick."

"Listen to us," said Margaret wearily, "speaking of her in the past tense. As if she were dead."

"It's only natural for you to miss a sister like her. She will return to you, and with such stories of the civilized world. I hope to see more of it myself someday, at some distant point in the future." His feet squarely on the ground, he eyed St. John's Church optimistically.

He has his work and achievement, thought Margaret resignedly. *Perhaps it is enough.*

Chapter Twenty-Nine

I ministered to the mourner & the family, showing to her how God was pointing out her path.
Nine months ago he seemed to strew it with
flowers, now he appoints a cup of sorrow. See in
all his hand & his love, ordering for the best.
—Bishop George Hills

Two days later, on September 15th, Margaret had another
ordeal to contend with—her birthday. At 26, she felt intoler-
ably close to 30 and inescapable spinsterhood. She shared the birthday
with Suzette, 20 years her junior, and tried her best not to blight her
youngest sister's sixth birthday with her own aversion to the celebration.
To aggravate matters, Mary's birthday was only a week and a half away,
and the group of family birthdays only accentuated her absence. Mary
would be turning 23, and Margaret felt her mid-20s mark slipping into
the horizon with her married sister.

Margaret cast about vainly for some gain to replace her receding
youth. Mr. Jackson, although not quite avoiding her, seemed in no
hurry to build on the intimacy they had experienced at Spring Ridge.
That afternoon took on a dream-like quality in Margaret's memory. She
began to wonder if he shared the feelings evoked by that reminiscence
at all. Yes, he had comforted her, but perhaps it was merely common
decency that had stirred him. She could have sworn she saw something
more in his eyes, when she had drawn back from his embrace, but as
time went on, with no recognition of it, she began to doubt herself.

Might she have seen only what was in her own heart, mirrored in him? What she became more certain of as the autumn passed slowly by was only that she wanted him to return those sentiments, and the longer the question remained unanswered, the more cruelly it nagged her amid her accumulating losses.

Margaret's hope that the new collegiate school would distract Kate from missing Wilson gradually showed signs of materializing over the fall. Letitia's visit for Mary's wedding had helped; Letitia had a temperament similar to Kate's and her presence had bolstered her younger sister. Kate's outlook improved enough to acknowledge, although distantly, another admirer—Mr. Charles Wentworth Wallace, a managing partner of the large firm Dickson, Campbell & Company. His interest in Kate had continued despite, or perhaps because of, her preoccupation elsewhere. He bore a faint similarity to Wilson in looks and disposition, but his simpering manner appeared to Margaret a caricature of Wilson's agreeability. But as Kate returned his attentions with uncharacteristic reserve, Margaret felt relief that her sister suffered less, rather than concern about an impulsive attachment.

Repeating the previous fall's disturbance, November brought another funeral. Emma Langford, after being Mrs. Bull for mere months, suddenly became a widow. In his prime and apparently in good health, Mr. Bull was struck down with no warning. The papers emphasized his good character, but this did not silence the speculation that, as with many sudden naval deaths, drink was the culprit. The family had already endured months of attention in the newspapers since the election placard hoax; only the previous week Mr. Langford's heated claim, this time that Attorney General Cary had obtained money under false pretences, was dismissed in court.

Death had a way of dispelling social barriers, and many more people went to Mr. Bull's funeral than to his wedding. Despite a brilliant naval ceremony, the earth received the departed in gloomy damp under a grey, indifferent sky. With shocked disbelief the gathering watched the casket settle uneasily into its grave, holding a man who had walked among them but days before. Emma Bull's transformation was equally shocking, her victorious serenity completely overturned by incomprehension, horror and fleeting panic.

As the family waited to pay their respects to Emma following the funeral, the whispered murmurs passing through the large gathering held their own morbid fascination. Emma had not been married long enough to receive the military widow's pension, and was left as destitute as her father. Milling in the November drizzle with her family, Margaret waited with uncomfortable remorse, remembering the ill feeling she had borne the young widow. When her turn finally came, Emma's hand felt chilled.

"Be careful what you wish for," she said bleakly, like someone beyond defeat. Her expression was so nakedly honest that Margaret's surprise limited her reply to a choked, "I'm so sorry."

Others, extending their sympathies, broke their timeless exchange of grief, and Margaret turned away. Her eyes locked next on Mr. Jackson, who had joined the Tolmies standing behind her. His look revealed he had heard the widow's warning to her, but Margaret was incapable of speech and could only return his keen gaze momentarily before the crowd shifted and moved her on.

The intensity of Jackson's gaze remained with her in the quiet weeks following Mr. Bull's funeral, even when the shock of the latter's death began to fade. She longed for confirmation of his meaning, whether it was a remembrance of witnessing her own grief or a search for something more. She felt that his penetrating look had wondered what, indeed, she did wish for.

Although Mr. Bull was not a particularly close acquaintance, his unexpected demise affected them all. Margaret noticed the change especially in Kate, who, quite abruptly, stopped moping over Wilson. Faced with a sudden inexplicable death and the grimness of young widowhood, she responded by grabbing hold of life. At first overjoyed to see her younger sister's returning zest, Margaret quickly became appalled to see where Kate attached herself—to Mr. Wallace. The young businessman, equally surprised by his sudden success in courtship, apparently did not have the sense to question her about-face, and recklessly increased his pursuit.

Like Mr. Bushby, Agnes Douglas' fiancé, Wallace had attained a position with a firm shortly after his arrival. But unlike Bushby, who had soon accepted an appointment with the colonial administration, Wallace seemed content to remain in business, his eye on the main chance, however distant in the future. He had already tried his hand with a coal company and the mail steamer agency, and though he had been with Dickson, Campbell & Company for a year, Margaret sensed this would last only until he was taken with another opportunity, which he would probably leave before providing any real security for Kate. This, combined with his impression as a dandy, grated on her.

How to broach the subject with her infatuated sister yet remain faithful to her promise not to meddle left Margaret in a dilemma, but Kate soon shared the acceleration in her attachment without reservation.

"Charles Wentworth Wallace. It is a well-sounding name," said Kate. "Much better than Midshipman Henry Doughty. For all his place in Debrett's Peerage, I would not exchange them. *Mrs. Charles Wentworth Wallace*—it has a certain ring to it, does it not?"

"Kate, I am concerned your courtship with Mr. Wallace may be a little—premature."

"Don't be silly," Kate laughed. "He has been pursuing me for months."

"I meant, receiving his attentions so soon after your attachment to Charles Wilson."

"But Margaret, you advised me not to wait for Charles! And it's been weeks since he left—an entire season!"

"The strongest attachment I have known you to have was to Charles Wilson," said Margaret gently. "A few months do not seem so very long to release it."

Kate's needlework took on a stabbing motion. "Is this about losing precedence to me?"

"Precedence?"

"Yes. Mary wasn't here long enough after her marriage for you to experience giving precedence to her as a married woman. But to me, a sister eight years your junior! Having to follow me into all the drawing-rooms of the town, the parties, the balls—is this the basis of your concern?"

"Your future happiness is my concern, nothing more, and as a much older sister who has some experience with suffering!"

Margaret's tearful anger rose so close to the surface that she hurriedly left the room, and then the house, before it could erupt. Instead, she channelled it into stomping along the muddy road in a driving wind. Rare thunder rolled in the late-November clouds and echoed in her heart. She gained nothing from her trek but a cold, and the regretful realization that she must bite her tongue and Kate must make her own decisions, without interference. That Kate did not see Wallace's shortcomings was only too obvious when, the next week, she accepted his offer of marriage. Mr. Work insisted, however, on postponing the nuptials until the following year.

One of the few events Margaret now had to look forward to was seeing Mr. Jackson on Sundays at the new church. The week in-between stretched on interminably. The fall's boisterous beginning eased in early December, but on one particular Sunday the slight drizzle when they entered St. John's Church turned to rain soon after the service began, increasing until it was drumming down incessantly on the iron roof. To make matters worse, the wind picked up and howled through the eaves.

Reverend Dundas spoke louder and louder, but despite his efforts to compete, in the end he was no match for the elements and was drowned out. Mr. Jackson, in the opposite pew, caught Margaret's eye and they shared an amused, sympathetic smile. Margaret turned her outward attention back to the reverend's gallant efforts, inwardly revelling in sudden happiness. Unless she was very much mistaken, Mr. Jackson *did* admire her.

Her guiltily selfish prayer that Mr. Jackson would join them after the service was answered. Unfortunately, so did Mr. Wallace, his face festooned with a smile. He had evidently met Mr. Jackson before, but not as Kate's fiancé, and Margaret withered to see Mr. Jackson's surprise at the connection and his cool reception of the younger man's obsequious manner. Mr. Jackson accompanied them to Hillside on his way to the Tolmies' farm. Apparently believing this a perfect time to bolster business, Wallace ingratiated himself with the banker on the long, windy, wet walk.

Having just shared witness of man's attempts to overcome nature in the Iron Church, Margaret did not relish Mr. Jackson witnessing her future brother-in-law's equally ridiculous human nature. In addition to his fawning demeanour, Wallace seemed to have adopted the American go-ahead attitude from his time in San Francisco, despite his English roots, and she feared that to a man of Mr. Jackson's forethought, Wallace might be the last speculative straw on top of all the other obstacles of her birth and family connections. Margaret retreated to her own room to escape Mr. Wallace and Kate in the drawing-room. The urge to form a plan, to convince Kate of her fiancé's flaws, picked up force with the horizontal gusts of rain hammering the window. Eventually the impulse abated, however, as she remembered her promise not to meddle. Kate, after all, appeared perfectly happy with her choice.

Chapter Thirty

... vessels had been lost on the coast in the heavy gales which had prevailed since the beginning of November ... On the 23rd of December H.M.S. *Hecate* made her appearance, and it may be fancied how eagerly we all hurried on board to see what our new home was like. We were greatly delighted with the change, for though possessing no external beauty, she was very roomy and comfortable within—my new cabin alone being nearly as large as our mess-room of the *Plumper*.

—Richard Charles Mayne, RN

In her efforts to suppress the urge to influence Kate, Margaret took to walking in the winter's tumultuous weather. With each rain more ground turned into quagmires, making travel by foot preferable to riding. Perfectly reflecting her mood, the storms provided her with a tangible force to fight against. Windy days supplied the fiercest opponent, when she could lean into the gusts, conquering one step at a time. Overcoming the rain proved more futile, and during one downpour she had just decided to accept defeat for the day when another impediment appeared in her path—Mr. Jackson.

His look of utter surprise made her laugh, but the wind snatched any audible sound from her mouth. He took her arm and turned her back to Hillside.

"What on earth were you doing out in this weather?" he demanded once they were inside the house.

"Defying it."

"You'll catch your death!"

"Then I'll be in good company," replied Margaret stubbornly, wringing out her hair, "since you share my penchant for walking in the rain."

"I came to bring you this," he said abruptly, handing her a bedraggled letter from inside his coat. "Your father, being a man of sense, is staying at the fort tonight to avoid the inclement weather, despite wishing to bring you a letter from your sister Mary. Instead he allowed me to deliver it."

"Thank you," said Margaret, meekly taking the letter, the fight draining out of her.

"I'll leave you to read in private," he said turning back to the door.

"No, no, come and warm yourself by the fire first. After coming so far—please."

He pulled a chair closer to the fire for her and then stood by, warming his back and giving her a small measure of privacy. Sitting on the edge of her seat, skirt dripping and steaming, she read.

Although Mary evidently saw much to amaze her in England, what stuck with Margaret was her sister's description of her treatment there. "I'm a curiosity at best," she wrote, "although without the overt snubs to be had in Victoria. Although they never seem to take offence, I have never been at such a loss as to how to behave. I wonder how John survived three years of this . . . My heart longs to be home with you. Even when Mr. Grahame is posted, we will still be connected by the land . . ."

Margaret hoped the water dripping from her hair would help disguise her tears. Mary hardly mentioned Mr. Grahame at all and she sounded painfully alone. At times Margaret had wondered if, eventually, their differences would complement one another, but given Mary's silence about her husband, Margaret feared they would wear each other away over the years.

"It is not bad news, I hope," said Mr. Jackson gently, pulling Margaret out of her thoughts.

"No, it is only that she is homesick, despite all the novelty."

"You wish to be there with her, sharing her experience," he said intently.

"No, I just want her to be home again with me here," she replied brokenly, tears streaming and mixing with the rain on her face. She hung her head, covering her eyes with one hand, and grasping the letter tightly in her lap with the other.

Mr. Jackson knelt down beside her, holding the hand that clutched the letter in his. He tilted her chin up to see her face, but before he could speak, Suzette burst into the room.

"Oh!" she cried, running back out down the hallway. "Mama!"

Jackson was on his feet by the time Mrs. Work appeared in the doorway.

"It is a letter from Mary. Mr. Jackson kindly delivered it," said Margaret to her mother, wiping away her tears. "She is fine, but misses us all so—"

Eager to have Margaret read the letter to her, Mrs. Work came to the fire, and Mr. Jackson respectfully excused himself and departed.

The next news received at Hillside was the marriage of Miss Phillips, Mrs. Langford's sister and Colwood's schoolteacher, to Dr. Benson, a company trader. With the Langfords devastated by their personal war against the company, it seemed a strange twist to have a family member marry into it. But somehow it was also strangely fitting to have the two merge matrimonially, even while the rest of the family was rumoured to be considering a return to England, courtesy of further assistance by their friends.

John lost no time in bringing Margaret's attention to Miss Phillips' age—older than she was. Despite his snide comments encouraging her not to lose hope, she found that she felt little envy. What plagued her were the bittersweet memories of the brief moment when Mr. Jackson had been at her side on bended knee. To be so close, yet so far, from a dream realized, left her in a continual state of pensive anticipation.

Her longing blended into the Yuletide season and Margaret wished for the gift of a future. It tempted fate too much to expect fulfilment for Christmas Day, now only a week away; instead, she prayed for a sign to arrive for Christmas that her hopes might materialize.

She did not see Mr. Jackson before Christmas, nor anything she could construe as a *sign*. She most wanted to commiserate with Mary over the gentleman's absence from Hillside during that week, but her closest sister's absence only intensified the missed opportunities. The one event of notice was the arrival on December 23rd of HMS *Hecate*, to replace the ageing HMS *Plumper*. The officers would remain on the Pacific station with the new ship, but Margaret found she could not rejoice even in that. What a change she had undergone in the past year, but the recognition did not console her. A military marriage seemed a childhood dream, clothed in the brass buttons and gold braid of pomp and circumstance. Now what she longed for was right here at home, yet maddeningly out of reach.

The only consolation to look forward to was a party in the New Year aboard the *Hecate*. The officers were thrilled with the spaciousness of their new ship, and had extended the invitation widely. Margaret could only hope that it included Mr. Jackson, and that he would attend.

She had never felt quite so sick with trepidation on the journey to Esquimalt. The tour of the new vessel, conducted by Lieutenant Mayne, held little interest in comparison to the other groups of arriving guests being shown round. There was no sign yet of Mr. Jackson. Since the Hecate was so much roomier than the *Plumper*, the guest list had grown accordingly but Margaret found only disappointment; the most sought element eluded her.

Trailing behind her party, she looked over the gunwale into the sea's unfathomable glassy surface. She stood on the *Hecate*'s lee side, where the protected water offered a dark reflection of the ship's lanterns and her own dim image. The winter squalls had mostly subsided during the festive season, and the water was disturbed only by occasional ripples. Following the reflected lanterns along the mirrored gunwale, her eyes were arrested by another form leaning over the water. Straightening, she faced Mr. Jackson.

"Do the depths reveal their mysteries to you?" he smiled.

"I can't get past the surface," she replied ruefully.

"Our eyes often hinder our vision," he offered, approaching her.

The ship's band on the upper deck was warming up with "Auld Lang Syne," accompanied by many heartfelt voices carrying over the water.

"The New Year recalls absent friends. Your heart must be full . . . ?"

"With my sister Mary, of course. But I know I am blessed to have many loved ones here at home."

"There is no particular loss, other than your sister, that troubles you now?" he ventured slowly, as if testing the water.

"Only those close at hand, who might as well be an ocean away."

"Miss Work—Margaret—forgive me, but are you not bound elsewhere by ties of the heart? Do you not have an attachment, strained perhaps by absence?"

"Sir, who else might I be bound to? I am bound by birth and breeding to the country—I do not have an attachment stronger than that." She felt she had leaned out precariously far from safety, and gripped the gunwale for support.

"I must be direct. Are you not waiting for Mr. Wilson? Your attachment to him—"

"Is like that of a brother."

Margaret had never seen a non-engagement produce so much happiness in another.

"I had heard of Wilson's pre-emption of land, and thought he might also have claimed your heart, and indeed, your hand."

"I am unclaimed, and indeed, my heart chooses of its own accord, free from governance, including that of my own head!" And to remind her of its independence, her heart caught her voice and blurred her vision.

"There are, however, times when the heart must bend to custom," he said softly, stepping closer.

"To custom?"

"Is it not customary, bringing in the New Year, for gentlemen to bestow a kiss on the ladies of this country?"

"Yes. And there are times," she smiled through her tears, "when the heart welcomes the customs of the country."

And stepping closer yet, she demonstrated the advantages of the country, as one who was born to it.

Epilogue

On February 5, 1861, the Work family had a double wedding: Margaret to Edward Henry Jackson, and Kate to Charles Wentworth Wallace. Mr. Work gave both couples land on the Hillside estate.

The Jacksons had a large home built on a hill facing south toward the Olympic Mountains, near what is now Hillside Avenue and Cook Street. Leaving the Bank of British North America, Jackson devoted himself to agriculture, until he was elected to the legislature for Victoria District (with Dr. Tolmie) in 1863. In 1864 he resigned from the legislature to accept a position with the colonial treasury. He died in 1877 at age 43, "after a lingering illness." Margaret survived until 1900, the "relict" of E.H. Jackson. They had four children.

Mr. Work had a cottage built for the Wallaces, which survives as Point Ellice House, near the Bay Street Bridge. Although successful with the firm Dickson, Campbell & Company, Wallace went to Europe, apparently without his family, when Victoria experienced a depression in 1865. In 1867 he built a telegraph line between Victoria and Esquimalt at his own expense, and by November was bankrupt. The following year he developed a coalfield on northern Vancouver Island. Of the latter venture, retired fur trader John Tod wrote to a mutual friend in 1868, "a son-in-law of your old friend, Widow Work, after dissipating his own and his wife's fortunes in a long course of riotous living, left the ill fated victims of his profligacy the other day for somewhere in the vicinity of that country, recently united, by purchase, to the American Republic."

Later that year Wallace sold Point Ellice House to the O'Reilly family. Business took him to San Francisco in 1869, while his creditors were in a publicized Supreme Court case. Kate died that year at Hillside, only 27 years old, leaving two surviving daughters who were brought up by her mother, Mrs. Josette Work. Three other children predeceased Kate during her eight-year marriage.

Returning from England, James Allan Grahame was promoted to Chief Factor in 1861, serving in the outposts of Quesnelle and Fort St. James. In 1873, he became Chief Commissioner in charge of all the Pacific Coast operations of the Hudson's Bay Company, allowing him and Mary to settle finally in Victoria. He retired in 1885, and died in 1905. Mary lived until 1919. They had three children who survived infancy, the youngest named Margaret.

In October of the year he saw Margaret and Kate married, John Work Sr. was bedridden with another recurrence of the malaria he had been infected with more than 25 years earlier. He died on December 22, 1861, having lived to see six of his eight daughters married. His wife, Josette, survived another 35 years, living on at Hillside Farm until her death in 1896.

Of John Work Jr., John Tod wrote in 1864, "I often visit the large family of our departed friend Work—the girls are all well married and in very comfortable circumstances—the eldest son however, I regret to say, seems to have been cast in a very different mould to that of the others, he has been in a sort of voluntary exile ever since the death of his worthy father, and had they not succeeded in getting him out of the way of his profligate companions, it is thought he would have squandered the whole estate in riot and dissipation." Eventually managing Hillside Farm for his mother, John died at age 46 of "dropsy" (edema).

Of David Work, John Tod wrote in 1868, "the other son, although sufficiently temperate, as regards Drink, is yet in my opinion, a much more despicable character than his brother." David entered the service of the Hudson's Bay Company, but died at 31 of a seizure.

Suzette Work married Edward Gawler Prior, who later served as both premier and lieutenant-governor of British Columbia.

Jane (Work) Tolmie's youngest son, Simon Fraser Tolmie, also became a premier of British Columbia, following his father's interest in politics. Although 10 of the 12 Tolmie children survived to adulthood, Simon was one of only two who had children themselves. Two of the Tolmies' five daughters died in infancy.

In January 1861, the Langford family left the colony to return to England. Langford was unable to pay the £90 legal fee that Chief Justice Cameron had levied for his non-suit against the election placard hoax. In 1870, George Lewis, the Hudson's Bay Company ship's officer who had been denied marriage to Mary, the second daughter, by Mr. Langford, proposed to her again in London, and was accepted. They returned to Victoria, where they lived for more than 30 years.

Although Agnes Douglas had a successful marriage to Arthur Thomas Bushby, whom she waited until 1862 to marry, her sister Alice eloped in 1861 with her father's private secretary, Charles Good, to Washington State. Governor Douglas insisted on a second British ceremony later that year. However, by 1870 they were estranged, and later divorced. Alice eventually moved to California and remarried.

In 1861 Lieutenant Richard C. Mayne received a promotion to commander, left HMS *Hecate* in San Francisco and returned to England. He later published an account of his time on the Pacific coast, *Four Years in British Columbia and Vancouver Island.*

Lieutenant Charles W. Wilson left Victoria to return to England in 1862. Despite his passion for exploration, he was given a field command in the Khartoum campaign in 1885 and became a scapegoat for the British failure in the Sudan. He was partially later exonerated, and received a KCB as a major-general. He never returned to British Columbia.

Henry Atkinson Tuzo left the Hudson's Bay Company in 1870 to become the manager of the Bank of British North America (a post formerly held by E.H. Jackson). Four years later he was transferred to New York to become manager-in-chief. In 1872 he went to England and married his cousin, the daughter of a London merchant. He retired to England in 1876, dying there in 1890.

Bibliography

Published Sources

Bagshaw, Roberta, ed. *No Better Land: The 1860 Diaries of the Anglican Colonial Bishop George Hills.* Victoria, B.C.: Sono Nis Press, 1996.

Belyk, Robert C. *John Tod: Rebel in the Ranks.* Victoria, B.C.: Horsdal & Schubart, 1995.

Dee, Henry Drummond. "An Irishman in the Fur Trade: The Life and Journals of John Work." *British Columbia Historical Quarterly* VII (1943): 229-270.

Gould, Jan. *Women of British Columbia.* Saanichton, B.C.: Hancock House Publishers, 1975.

Green, Valerie. *No Ordinary People—Victoria's Mayors Since 1862.* Victoria, B.C.: Beach Holme Publishers, 1992.

Higgins, D.W. *The Mystic Spring.* Toronto: Wm. Briggs, 1904.

Ireland, Willard E. "Gold-Rush Days in Victoria." *British Columbia Historical Quarterly* XII (1948): 231-246.

Lugrin, Nan de Bertrand. *The Pioneer Women of Vancouver Island.* Victoria, B.C.: Women's Canadian Club of Victoria, 1928.

Macfie, Matthew. *Vancouver Island and British Columbia. Their History, Resources and Prospects.* London: Longman, Roberts & Green, 1865.

Maloney, Alice B. "John Work of the Hudson's Bay Company." *California Historical Society Quarterly* (1943): 97-107.

Mayne, Richard Charles. *Four Years in British Columbia and Vancouver Island.* Toronto: Toronto Public Library, 1969.

Pettit, Sydney G. "The Trials of E. E. Langford." *British Columbia Historical Quarterly* XVII (1953): 5-40.

Pool, Daniel. *What Jane Austen Ate and Charles Dickens Knew: from Fox Hunting to Whist: the Facts of Daily Life in Nineteenth-Century England.* New York: Simon & Schuster, 1993.

Pritchard, Allan, ed. *Vancouver Island Letters of Edmund Hope Verney, 1862–1865.* Vancouver: University of British Columbia Press, 1996.

Reksten, Terry. *More English than the English: A Very Social History of Victoria.* Victoria, B.C.: Orca Book Publishers, 1991.

Smith, Dorothy Blakey, ed. "The Journal of Arthur Thomas Bushby, 1858–1859." *British Columbia Historical Quarterly* XXI (1957–1958): 83-198.

____. *Lady Franklin Visits the Pacific Northwest.* Memoir No. XI. Victoria, B.C.: Provincial Archives of British Columbia, 1974.

____. *The Reminiscences of Doctor John Sebastian Helmcken.* Vancouver: University of British Columbia Press, 1975.

Stanley, George F.G., ed. *Mapping the Frontier between British Columbia & Washington: Charles Wilson's Diary of the Survey of the 49th Parallel, 1858–1862.* Toronto: Macmillan of Canada, 1970.

Tolmie, William Fraser. *William Fraser Tolmie: Physician and Fur Trader.* Vancouver: Mitchell Press Limited, 1963.

Van Kirk, Sylvia. *"Many Tender Ties": Women in Fur-Trade Society, 1670–1870.* Winnipeg: Watson & Dwyer Publishing Ltd., 1980.

Newspapers
British Colonist
Daily British Colonist
Daily Colonist
Times Colonist (Islander)
Victoria Gazette

Unpublished Sources

Provincial Archives of British Columbia, Victoria:
Grahame, James Allan, family. Biographical information.
Jackson, Edward Henry. Vertical file.
Tod, John. Letters to Edward Ermatinger.
Tuzo, Henry Atkinson. Miscellaneous material.
Wallace, Charles Wentworth, Jr. Vertical file.
Wark, John McAdoo, family. Vertical file.
Work, John, family. Vertical file.
Oregon Historical Society:
Huggins, Anne. Letters to Mrs. Eva Emery Dye.
The Huntington Library, San Marino, California:
Wark, John McAdoo. Letter to Edward Huggins.

Acknowledgments

I never imagined this project would be such a lengthy one, with many phases and interruptions. Although writing became an act of faith, I am grateful for the encouragement I received along the way that helped me to persevere with it.

I would like to acknowledge the staff of the British Columbia Archives for their assistance in navigating the research journey and narrowing the seemingly endless possibilities of historical exploration.

Many friends lent their support, often by their reminders of the achievement of completing a novel, let alone publishing one. Special thanks go to James Webb for his interest and readiness to answer naval-history questions, and to Bill Wrathall for reading one of the many drafts. I am thankful for the sympathy of those friends who are also writers, particularly David Gurr and Mollie Kaye who, by sharing their aspirations, frustrations and humour helped to lessen the frequently isolating experience of writing.

I welcomed finding a home for this endeavour with TouchWood Editions, and would like to recognize Marlyn Horsdal's dedication and diligence in giving editorial advice.

I appreciate the continuing support on many levels of my parents, Christine and David Winn. My father has been a constant source of assistance, in particular with nineteenth century word usage and his remarkable memory for examples, backing up my own vague intuitions. I am grateful to my family, especially my daughters Gwen and Caitlyn, for accepting my path, even when I didn't know where it would lead.

Vanessa Winn's non-fiction has appeared in *Monday Magazine* and her poetry has been published in *Quill's Canadian Poetry Magazine* and *Island Writer Magazine*. She has a Bachelor of Arts with a major in English from the University of Victoria. Beyond her love of the written word, Vanessa finds inspiration in music and dance and currently teaches Argentine tango. Born in England, Vanessa now lives in Victoria, BC, with her two daughters. *The Chief Factor's Daughter* is her first novel. Find out more at www.vanessawinn.com.